NEMO'S WORLD

THE SUBSTRATE WARS 2

JEB KINNISON

www.jebkinnison.com
jebkinnison@gmail.com

Library of Congress Control Number: 2015903816

Contents

Part One: Nemo's Planet

Chapter One: The Menace from Earth

BBC Reporter

Amanda Sundaram-Smythe's body clock was still off, so she woke early enough to see two small crescent moons rising in the eastern sky before dawn. She had been surprised when the sky otherwise looked much the same as it did on Earth, but the astronomers had explained that New Earth's atmosphere had near-Earth levels of oxygen and nitrogen, so it was nothing unexpected. She planned to research that point later.

It was an hour before breakfast would start in the mess tent, so she went to work on her laptop, trying to organize the mass of stories she would be able to release once the embargo was off and the New Earth rebels allowed her to communicate with her editors at the BBC. Even the minor stories would have been blockbuster revelations if they were not overshadowed by news of gateways to the stars and an ultimatum to all Earth governments to give up nuclear arms. She felt like the only embedded reporter on Captain Nemo's Nautilus, cruising the seas looking for warships to sink while governments plotted to destroy it.

She filled out the planning document with story ideas. Some of what she had guessed from interviews so far would have to remain unsaid—like the news that all of the world's nuclear arms had already been removed from Earth by the clever Steve Duong, who had stumbled upon the gateway technology while doing research in quantum computing. She knew this was still a secret kept by both the governments and the rebels, and she could not report on it until the rebels were ready to approve the story. So including that news in a working document was unwise.

It was almost time to go to breakfast, so she stopped work on the page:

```
[NOT FOR RELEASE - STORY NOTES]

From: Amanda Sundaram-Smythe, BBC
Working Notes: Grey Tribe and Student Rebellion

Headline Stories

•January explosions at California university now
 explained
•Grey Tribe and student rebels escape pursuit by US
 Homeland Security
•Rebels start first colony on New Earth
•"Gateway" technology: instantaneous travel to
 anywhere
•Viewed as threat by world security forces
•Secret talks between rebels and governments
•World Security Proposal: Nuclear disarmament and
 monitoring

Side Stories:

*US program for mind control by brain implant re-
 vealed, 'Gulags'
•Secret US weapons fabrication program: Project
 Arrow
•Dylan Foster, newly-appointed head of National
 Security Lab and Project Arrow
•Kidnapped family members: Chinese government de-
```

nials

Subject Backgrounders:

- •Nuclear warheads: How many and where
- •Quantum Computing and Gateways
- •Mutual Assured Destruction (MAD) and the Cold War
- •Gateway technology: many other uses
- •Medicine: future uses

People Backgrounders:

Michael McCulloch: International Grey Tribe leader, hacker activist. Homeland Security was out to arrest him for illegal encryption and aiding terrorism (as they defined it) but could not find him hidden in Switzerland. [Many stories to link to.] His role was to aid communication and round up technically-capable rebels willing to risk leaving Earth.

Professor Walter Wilson: [Link to story on his Artificial Life work from 2021.] Friendship with Michael McCulloch, his former star grad student, drew the attention of Homeland Security. Homeland Security made threats to force him to cooperate in finding McCulloch, led to student movement to defend him from Homeland Security. Arrested and held in "velvet Gulag" for months, but knew nothing of the gateway or the rebels until he was rescued. Drugs and an experimental neural implant used to condition him before his escape.

Justin Smith: 25-yo grad student studying simulated biology under Prof. Wilson. Instrumental in rounding up student support and contacting the Grey Tribe for help. Assisted Steve Duong in developing the gateway and planning for the escape to New Earth. Home-schooled [link to background material on the US home-schooling movement] and not an activist before this.

Steve Duong: [link to story of his recruitment by university, straight from self-education in highlands of Vietnam.] 23 yo researcher in advanced quantum computing. Discovered gateway while working on US government-funded research. Worked with Justin Smith to develop software for use. The technical genius. [Link: "What is Asperger's?"]

Dylan Foster: 27-yo grad student in Physics. Son of Silicon Valley venture capitalist Wentworth Foster [links]. Member of Students for Liberty [link] and had been seeing Samantha West. Because she had broken up with him, he shadowed her and accidentally witnessed the gateway in operation. He broke into the Quantum Computing Lab computers and stole their software, which he later offered to the government in return for his appointment as National Security Lab Director [link]. He operated the gateway to steal gold from the US Treasury, but an accident caused an explosion which damaged the lab and caused Homeland Security to seize it.

Professor Ray Bubna: Quantum Lab administrator turned logistics wizard. Helped find and steal other quantum computers to prevent Dylan Foster's stolen software from being used immediately by Project Arrow.

Samantha West: 23-yo daughter of Hollywood producer Elton West [links]. Active in Students for Liberty, and introduced Justin Smith to others on campus who were willing to defend Prof. Wilson. Rebel economics expert and currently attached to Justin Smith.

Ben Ramirez: 25-yo grad student in EE and Law. Led campus chapter of Students for Liberty and had already made contact with the Grey Tribe when approached by Justin Smith for help. [Interview] Admirer of US Constitution and compares rebel Council to US Continental Congress. Member of the Council, which is working on governing documents for rebels.

Need statements from:

- UK Prime Minister Dalal
- US President Stanton
- Chinese President Liu
- EU President Ulrich Beringer
- Usual security experts

Amanda closed the laptop and stopped by the communal lavatory to wash her face again before making her way to breakfast at the mess tent. Justin, one of the unofficial leaders of the rebels, greeted her in the serving line: “Good morning. I’m sorry we haven’t really had a chance to talk yet. Did you get the material you were looking for yesterday?”

She checked to make sure she was recording and replied, “Mostly. Professor Wilson was very interesting, and I have a lot of good footage of him explaining the events that led to a group of students and hackers outwitting the government of the US and starting the first off-world colony. He can be the wise older presence, but I need a lot more first-person accounts from you and Steve and the others.”

They got their food trays and sat at an empty table in the back. Justin said, “We were lucky. First in the brilliance of Steve’s work and his choice to share it with me before anyone else; then in finding the right allies on-campus and off, and joining with the Grey Tribe to get our people off Earth and safe from retaliation. Without friends we would never have succeeded, and we could have failed anyway if one of the primary people in charge of chasing us down hadn’t let me go after I was captured—Jim McDonald. He’s just joined us and you should get his story—he knows what the Unity Party of the US has been doing in the past few years to keep its hold on power, and what they have planned for the rest of the world.”

Amanda checked the recording quality as seen through the head-up display in her glasses; the lighting was good and the camera was doing well at capturing Justin’s face as they talked. She said, “If you have time, today would be a good day to interview you. You seem to have been central to the scheme at every point even though you had not been a political activist before.”

"I just happened to be in the right place at the right time," Justin said, "and Steve trusted me. I grew up reading economic and political theory, as well as history, so I already saw a lot that was wrong. I just had never been put into a position where it made sense to take a stand. And then suddenly I was."

"It's just as lucky that you contacted me to do this story because Michael of the Grey Tribe had worked with me before and persuaded me. At the BBC, I've been shunted away from hard news lately, and I see this as an opportunity to get back to it. That's why I've agreed to your terms and the embargo, which amounts to holding me prisoner until you think the time is right. How many people would have agreed to being incommunicado for who knows how long? But it's the story of the century, and I'll have all the original material even if you fail and are wiped out."

"Being wiped out is not part of our plans. And we hope to have you back in a month or less, when we want publicity. Until then, we've told earth governments we will not disclose our existence until the deadline for their response. If they act responsibly, panic can be avoided. You can do a lot to help by presenting the story straight so they can't use their usual propaganda techniques."

"I won't be used by you, either. I will present the truth—noble motives or not." She gave him her toughest look. "So don't ask me to distort my reporting for you."

Justin laughed. "I wouldn't. You've agreed to let us review your work and remove anything that threatens our security, but otherwise we want people to know the whole truth. Their governments are trying to keep the status quo in place because they have a lot of power to lose if they agree to our terms. When the people know a much better life for everyone is being kept away from them by their corrupt governments, they won't stand for it. The truth is a win for us."

"Then there should be no problems," Amanda said. "One thing I might need your help with is getting Steve Duong to stop working long enough to let me interview him. He hasn't responded to my notes."

"He's been very busy working on refinements to the software for transporting objects and putting them into stasis fields. When he's obsessive, he doesn't check messages. I'll talk to him and make him set up a time."

"So how about you? Can I have an hour of your time today? I'd like to get a clip of you talking to Prof. Wilson, since your relationship was central to the events."

"Sure. I have some time before lunch. Let's head over to catch the Prof before he gets going."

They put their trays in the wash rack and headed out. Before they had left the tent, Samantha arrived to join the serving line and said, "Justin, Amanda. Sorry I missed eating with you."

"Not to worry," Amanda said. "I had a chance to talk to Justin alone, which is high on my agenda." Amanda had noted Samantha's beauty —her hair was auburn, her eyes green, and her lightly-tanned skin a shade lighter than Amanda's inherited darker tone.

"He's too modest," Samantha said. "Be sure to use what I told you, not what he tells you!"

Amanda laughed. "I will use everyone's contributions, and I'm sure the importance of Justin's efforts will shine through despite his efforts at modesty."

Justin gave Samantha a kiss and said, "Sam, I'll be back at the gateway in an hour. Amanda and I are going to visit the Prof before his classes start to get some footage of us talking."

"Okay," Sam said. "Not that it bothers me that you're leaving with a raven-haired beauty with a cultivated English accent."

"She's a reporter," Justin said. "Focused. No time for dalliances."

"Wait—I'm right here, you know!" Amanda said, laughing. "I can certainly dally if I spot a reason to. So far, too busy. Though I did see a gateway tech who looked like he'd be fun to chat up."

"See?" Justin said, "I'm safe. Which you knew." He gave Samantha a squeeze. "Come along with us to see Prof. Wilson. It should only take a minute."

"Let me get some coffee, and I'll follow after," Samantha said.

Justin and Amanda walked along the gravel path toward the Prof's tent. As they reached it, he appeared, dressed for teaching in khaki pants and a soft tan flannel shirt.

"Good morning, Justin. And Amanda. I am headed over to the class building to do some orientation."

"Do you have just a moment to talk with us?" Amanda said. "I need some footage of you two discussing how Justin tried to organize support for you when you were arrested by Homeland Security."

"I have a few minutes. Is this a good spot?" Prof. Wilson said.

"Yes," Amanda said, checking her camera view. "Good lighting."

Samantha joined them, coffee in hand, and said, "Have I missed anything?"

"No, I was just about to start the interview," Amanda said. "First question: Tell us why you you told your student, Justin, about Homeland Security's blackmail attempt—"

A *whuff* in the distance told them something was wrong. Justin looked down the street at a cloud of smoke rising and said, "That was at the gateway. Let's—" *Pop-pop, pop-pop-pop.*

Prof. Wilson's eyes rolled up in his head and he collapsed, moaning.

Samantha caught him as he went down, and held him up. "Professor, what's wrong?" she said.

"The implant. They're here," he said. And then he went limp.

Amanda heard a buzzing sound and looked down the street again. She saw four black things flying together out from where the smoke was rising. "Drones!" she warned, as they split up and flew off in different directions. One was coming straight at them.

"Dammit. Where did we put the guns?" Justin said. "Get back into the tent and hide!" Justin told Samantha and Amanda, and ran down the path toward the gateway tents. Amanda followed, checking to see if the camera was getting good footage. *This dramatic video won't do me any good if I get killed,* she thought. *But that almost never happens.*

The Raid

Justin ran toward the drone, but then crossed over to the next lane through the space between tents, followed by Amanda. He remembered where the guns were and ducked into that storage tent to grab a few. Amanda came up behind him, and he said, "Take these," handing her two rifles.

"I can carry two or use one," she said, "but I'd rather use one," and she put the other back. "I'm not supposed to get involved at all."

"Consider it defensive."

They opened the tent flap cautiously but there was no sign of the drone. Approaching the gateway tents from the other side, the firing had stopped. Justin slowly looked around the corner.

"Two men with guns in front of the tent," he whispered at Amanda. "Don't shoot unless you really have to, because any stray bullets will pass right through the tents. We can't have a firefight here."

"I didn't realize you had experience at this," Amanda said. "I've only shot at firing ranges."

"Same here, but I've logged thousands of hours in games just like this," Justin replied.

Justin edged around the corner again with the rifle aimed. Neither of the two men looked his way. *I have the shot,* he thought, *and I can probably take them both out.* The bulk of their black tactical outfits suggested bulletproof vests, so he aimed for the head. *This cannot be happening,* he thought, squeezing the trigger slowly.

The rifle kicked back and he aimed for the other soldier. But the first shot pinged off a mirror-bright statue the soldier had become. Both soldiers were now frozen statues.

Justin and Amanda cautiously moved around the corner. When they reached the gateway tent door, they could see one of the techs on the ground, bleeding. Monitors were shattered all around, and the big industrial-sized gateway was closed. Another tech still sitting at the console looked dazed. Eight mirrored statues stood in various poses in front of the gateway, several still holding mirrored military rifles. There were other automatic weapons and boxes of equipment scattered on the ground nearby.

Steve Duong came around the corner from the next gateway bay. "Looks like they found our warehouse in Sweden and planted troops there to invade. I heard the noise and saw they were holding our people hostage at the gateway to let more troops in. The operator closed it when he realized what was happening. They pistol-whipped him and demanded he reopen the gateway. Maybe they don't know we have several gateways—anyway, I was able to get to the other console and use the new software option I developed to put anyone not wearing a talisman into stasis. It did what it was supposed to do."

"What's the damage?" Justin said.

“The machine is fine. The monitors can be replaced. Gunther has a wound to the leg, and we'd better get him to Medical.”

Others had rushed in and Justin said, “You two, get Gunther into a chair and carry the chair to Medical. With his leg elevated.”

After some fumbling, two strong techs left carrying Gunther, who was moaning but conscious.

“So back to what happened. There were quite a few shots,” Justin said, looking over at Amanda, who was obviously recording every second.

“I didn't see it, but I think they jumped through on the conveyer belt and set off the flash-bang. Then they started shooting to establish control. Gunther was probably shot by accident.”

“And then you froze them.” Justin walked up to the nearest and tapped on the mirrored surface. “I assume they're okay in there for now. We should talk to Ben about how to deal with them, but I'm inclined to send them to a maximum-security prison cell in Sweden with a note explaining that they're US troops violating Swedish sovereignty.”

“That,” Ben said, coming out of the crowd that was gathering, “sounds like an excellent way to handle them. Record what happens on their arrival and we'll use it later when the denials start. And Marco was hit out on the street—he's been taken to Medical, but it looks like he's dead. One murder to start. So you can attach the evidence to that note.”

“Just collateral damage for these people,” Justin said. “One more person they didn't know or care about, dead.”

The crowd was silent for a moment.

“There's a bug in my program,” Steve said, pointing at a pink object on the ground. “One of their fingertips. The edge detection mostly worked but got a little confused in the trigger area. Complex topology, I need to check those cases."

"And what's this?" Justin said, poking at a steel box with his toe. "Dials and switches. A controller for something. Maybe the Professor's implant control box. He was in bad shape when I left him." Justin picked up the box and turned all the dials to zero.

"Maybe. I think we should rush on getting that thing out of his head. When I get the bugs out of the edge detector—"

Samantha made her way through the crowd, helping Prof. Wilson along, and said, "Good thing you shut them down. The drone was tracking the Prof here and came right up to us inside the mess tent. Then it just hovered there while we left."

"The operator stopped paying attention," Justin said, gesturing at one of the frozen soldiers holding what looked like a tablet computer.

Samantha went on, frowning at Steve. "And I don't think you should be removing things from anyone's brain until you're sure of your edge detector. A fingertip missing is a minor punishment for someone who attacks us, but a missing piece of brain is—"

"Don't worry," Steve said, making calming motions with his hands. "Nothing with living subjects until I've succeeded with watermelons and animals."

Prof. Wilson raised his head and whispered something. Samantha repeated for him, "Thanks for shutting it off."

"Are you okay?" Justin said, "Do you need medical attention?"

His voice stronger, Prof. Wilson replied, "No, I'm much better now. But I agree getting rid of the implant would be a good idea. And the implant itself will make good evidence to prove they did it; we should release scans of it to the public for analysis. They won't be able to stop armchair analysts from talking about it online."

“That is a good idea. But I wonder why they didn’t just toss in a bunker-buster and call it a day?” Justin shivered a bit thinking about it. “Then they’d have stopped us and our leaks without taking any risks.”

“I think they wanted something,” Steve said. “The technology. And probably me.”

“Let me know if anyone else was hurt,” Justin said, “or if there’s anything critical that was damaged. Our supplies will hold us for a few weeks. But we have to strike back, and hit them hard. They broke the agreement. And that means war.”

Part Two: Before the Raid

Chapter Two: Four Months Earlier

Justin and Sam

Four months earlier, Justin had just escaped from Homeland Security custody and returned to the camp on New Earth, where his fellow rebels were putting together a tent city. With his last energy, he rounded up people to help him remove the gateway they had left in the warehouse on Earth. When they had finished, he let Samantha take him "home."

Samantha held open the tent flap and ushered Justin in. "Voilà!" she said. "I took the liberty of taking one of the double tents for us. I know we didn't discuss it—"

"You did good," Justin said. "I'm hoping we get more prefab units soon, so this is just temporary. But having a separate bedroom—or at least a nook with a curtain—is great. We can live out of our suitcases for now."

"I just mean we haven't really talked about where this is going," she said, turning red.

"Yes, we have. Just not directly. You know where we're going."

"I didn't want to presume," she said.

Justin held her close. "Being with someone is good because you can presume a lot. You can count on me and predict what I think and feel. I can count on you and rely on you to understand me. And together we can do a lot more because we support each other."

"I should trust my instincts?"

"You should trust your instincts. We've had a hard few weeks and there's lots more trouble on the way, but you know how I feel about you. We'll do something about it when things calm down."

"Is that a hint of a promise of a proposal?"

"Yes," he sighed. "I think if I were going to run, I would have run some time ago. You're where I want to be, and I feel lucky that you feel the same." He kissed her and said, "I'm mighty tired. I walked ten miles to get back to the warehouse gateway after escaping detention. I barely slept last night and I'm crashing now that I can."

"Sit down," she said, and when he did, she took off his shoes and began to rub his feet through his socks. "How's that?"

"Heaven," he sighed, closing his eyes. "I may just sleep here."

"We'll get you to bed soon and I'll leave you be. I was only a little worried when you took so long to get back, but it's a good thing I didn't know you had been arrested."

"Well, now we know it's not safe for any of us who are being tracked by Homeland Security to even walk down the streets in the city. The cameras will recognize our faces and bring them down on us. So we can't go back even for short visits."

"Now you have me worrying about our families."

"Me, too. But so far they've just questioned them and left. So we have to hope the government doesn't try to use them as bargaining chips."

"We'll think about that tomorrow. Stop worrying and get to sleep." She led him over to the bed and undressed him. "Tucking you in is fun." She kissed some of his tender parts. "My, you *are* tired...."

New Features

A month after they left Earth, Steve Duong gave a chalk talk before the Council to report on his recent work.

"The first gateway relied on the simplest possible algorithm," Steve said, drawing a doorway and an arrow crossing through it. "It disconnected a particle that crossed the plane of the gateway from particles on the side it had been on, and added connections to any particles it wasn't already connected to on the new side. That way an object in motion across the plane kept all of its internal connections, so changed location with minimal disruption." He paused and was glad no one brought up the mouse he had killed the first time they tested the gateway on a living creature, when the parameters he had programmed in had been too loose to preserve the mouse's neural activity.

"This simple planar gateway was easy to program and understand," he went on, "but there are lots of things we can do if we have more computing capacity and more sophisticated programs. I've worked out a way to transfer programs into storage in the substrate itself and run them there—which eliminates the need for a local quantum computer to run the computation. Which also means there is almost unlimited space and program power available. Which removes the limitations of using Vortex-style quantum computers to do substrate-based manipulation of the real world."

"I've never understood where this substrate is," Samantha said. "You might try to explain that again."

"The substrate—"Steve paused, thinking. "For humans, you can think of it as a vast computer that is calculating every particle's response to the particles it's connected to, continuously. It doesn't work like a computer and it doesn't have spatial memory location—there's no mapping from cells of the substrate to locations in space. It isn't anywhere, it's the framework the universe is built on. But you can use a mental model of it as a computer to talk about it."

"So if it's doing all these calculations to make the universe run," Ben asked, "where do our calculations run? Won't our programs interfere with particle calculations?"

"Our programs are stored and run in cells that aren't doing much," Steve answered, drawing a scattering of dots on the whiteboard. "Finding out how to find those was a big part of the problem. Picking substrate cells—processors—that aren't associated with particles at the moment allows computation that minimally degrades performance. Like using the sidebands or the subcarrier of a radio station to send data, our computations get done without degrading the main particle computations which determine future location and interactions."

"And what about other civilizations that may be out there?" Justin asked. "How do we not interfere with their programs, if they're there?"

"We take care never to erase anything," Steve said. "If they are using a cell, it probably won't be picked for our use. I'm not seeing any real evidence of major activity out there, but I'm not looking for it. And the substrate is as vast as the universe; there's almost infinite room. One of these days I'll write some sniffer programs and go see what's out there. But for now we have more important needs. And it would be wise not to draw attention to ourselves, if there are other civilizations out there."

That stopped questions. "Okay, moving on," Steve said. "I've still got a lot of work to do on the OS which will live in the substrate and run apps as we ask it to. The boot loader could in theory accept programs by reading bar codes, or etched plates, or printed programs—but I kept it simple by working with the Grey Tribe guys," he said, nodding to Michael McCulloch. "They are setting up the universal Net. One of its key parts is direct sensing of signals like wifi and radio as well as light; so I installed a module for the loader that lets it 'listen' as if it was a wifi router. When presented with the correct ID and in the presence of an authorized person, programs can be uploaded into the substrate at high speed. What I need to do is write the OS that handles all the apps in use and knows about all the locations where they're being used. Not to multitask, because the substrate is inherently parallel, but to allow apps to be started, stopped, and killed, and to provide communication between apps and a kind of 'runtime library' of functions all apps can use."

"Whew," Samantha said. "Apps? Like on a phone?"

"Kind of," Justin said. "You will certainly be able to control a substrate app using a phone app via wifi. Or a voice control system, which is planned. But let's keep this moving—we just want you to have an overview since we're all too busy to check in with each other enough." He nodded to Steve to continue.

"The first thing I worked on after getting a program loader to work was object boundaries," Steve said. "I want to be able to move an entire object at once to a new location. The first problem is figuring out what a contiguous object consists of—exactly what particles are members of this object. That means finding a volume in space where all particles are connected, but where there is an edge where the next particles are of a different character—say, atoms in molecules of a gas instead of a solid. This is harder than you might think, since we have to adjust parameters to include what we want and exclude what we don't want, but those parameters depend on the object. It's analogous to drawing programs where you'd like to isolate the image of a vase in a background field to move it."

"So you have a program that works?" Samantha said.

"Yes, mostly. It has no trouble with easy cases like a metal object on a wooden table; it can determine that the metal is very different from the tabletop and the gases surrounding them, and determine its outline with precision. But imagine a person standing on normal ground: The person's feet are encased in shoes, so it can decide to draw the boundary between the shoes and air. But what about the boundary between the soles of the shoes and the soil? That requires the program to find that there is no nearby boundary that limits the soil, and so no place to draw a boundary which would include the soil; at that point the algorithm decides I must mean leave the soil behind and take the shoes along."

"It sounds like you have solved the problem," Justin observed.

"Not to my satisfaction," Steve said. "I have the system set up to draw an outline onscreen of what it's thinking of as being the intended object, and I have caught it in errors. Complex topologies—loops—and gradual boundaries cause problems. But it can be used now, with care."

"So what does the user interface look like?"

"In the prototype," Steve said, "you point and click on screen. I open the viewing window to a warehouse on Earth, say, and point and click on something I see there. The system draws a visual boundary around what it thinks I want moved. If that looks good, I hit the right mouse button and the object is transferred all at once to the target location, with the air it would otherwise displace from the new location moved to where it had been, so there's no 'pop' of a vacuum being filled."

Justin said, "I know the answer, but for others present: how do you avoid moving something into already-occupied space?"

"The program makes sure there's only uniform gas or liquid in the target volume, and it moves that out of the way at the same time. So nothing gets moved into a block of cement. Or at least that's the plan."

"Tell them about the shrink ray," Justin suggested.

"Oh, right," Steve said. "I've added a geometric refinement to the object move—you can move the particles into a more compact volume, compressing the original as desired. Which will come in handy, but I don't want to reveal that trick until later."

"Next on the list," Justin said, "is stasis fields."

"Not literally," Steve said, "but we're adopting the science-fiction terminology everyone knows. Once I had the object volume, I thought about what you might get the particles inside to do. One command I've added is to tell them all to hold position relative to each other despite their momentum and other forces acting on them. And so whatever is inside the volume is frozen at absolute zero, essentially—all action is suspended. It's not a 'stasis field' because time continues inside as it does everywhere—time is the one thing that can't be modified. But it might as well be. And when the command is reversed, it's as if no time passed inside."

"What would happen if you did that to the entire Earth?" Justin said. "Just theoretically. Would it keep orbiting the sun, or stop moving, or fly off in a straight line?"

"I discovered while experimenting with it," Steve replied, "that you had to let the particles respond to forces and particles outside the object volume or bad things would happen—the first object I put into stasis became weightless. And it could penetrate other objects. Allowing particles to respond to external forces means the whole object acts as a single unit under gravity and pushes back against other objects. I added a complete reflection of photons from its surface to prevent electromagnetic radiation from crossing, which protects everything inside. So the answer to your question is that Earth would sail serenely through its orbit as usual, while protected under a mirrored skin."

"I have thought of a number of uses for that feature already," Justin said. "For one thing, you could store your food in a stasis box instead of a fridge. Fresh bread would stay fresh until you opened it. But that's not exactly important to our cause…."

"How is the talisman work going?" Ben asked.

"Well," Justin replied. "We've got the 3D printers set up and produced some prototypes. A talisman is a plastic cube a few millimeters on a side with a 3D rectilinear pattern of carbon filaments that is unique in the universe—which is surprisingly easy because the numbers of possible patterns increases so quickly with complexity. Plug the pattern into substrate pattern matching and it locates the talisman."

"So we'll have to carry a talisman with us at all times?" Samantha asked.

"For now, yes," Justin said. "Or they can be made small enough to be surgically implanted, like chipping a dog. Steve's thinking we'll have direct DNA detection next year, though, which would remove the need for carrying one."

"Probably my turn to talk," said Michael McCulloch; Michael was Prof. Wilson's grad student of a decade ago who had become leader of the rebel Grey Tribe, a band of geeks, wizards, and rights activists that tried to resist their governments and provide encrypted communication. "As Steve said, we've been working on a universal network, which we're naming 'the Net' for simplicity, since there will be no other net. A background program running on the substrate will listen for conventional wifi or fiber-optic signals at a list of locations, then transfer the data into the all-encompassing substrate network, which is based on IPv6. We don't see any need for more than IPv6's 2-to-the-128th addresses, which should be enough for millennia of human expansion, even if every object has one. The routing algorithm and packet handling will be similarly fault-tolerant, which should address concerns about noise and alien boojums interfering."

"So," Samantha asked, "every person and device on every planet can be hooked into this super-network?"

"That is the idea," Michael answered. "Close to zero delay whether across the hall or a galaxy away."

"And so we are birthing Skynet," Justin said. "Let's hope it works out better in this timeline. I think that's enough unless there are more questions. All of this is why we're starting a research institute, or university, which will be run by Prof. Wilson here for awhile." He nodded to where the professor was sitting. "There's more to be explored than we can possibly handle with just our group. So when there is peace with Earth, we'll open up a place to do research using the powers of the substrate. Where we can keep an eye on it, since it will be a long time before we trust many people with using it directly. That's all, thanks for coming."

People started leaving the room. Prof. Wilson stopped Justin and said, "I'd like to start some classes now on what I see upcoming in new research. Get people started thinking about it."

"I don't see why not," Justin said. "Talk to Bubna about setting up a spiffy new portable building when they're done extending the septic fields. We need a community hall anyway, something more formal than the mess tent. Get Amy to coordinate the use schedule when it's ready—she's turning into town secretary. And then put a notice on the mess tent bulletin board. You'll get a good crowd in the evening since people are tired of old movies."

Steve and Rasna

Samantha stopped by the gateway tents to pick up Justin for their planned lunch. She found Justin deep in conversation with Steve, so waited politely for a lull before breaking in: "Lunchtime. Can you guys take a break now?"

"Sure," Justin said. "We were just discussing how the large number of surveillance points we've established has overwhelmed our ability to actually listen and watch them. Steve wants to try uploading some of the same software the NSA uses to search for keywords and do semantic analysis."

"It's not especially smart," Steve said, "but it will flag interesting segments for human analysis and cut way down on the total time human operators need to spend listening to dull conversations."

"So where do you get this software?" Samantha asked.

"The open-source movement leapfrogged them on basic data analytics a long time ago," Steve replied. "There are open-source packages that can do deep semantic analysis and string together meaningful segments. The NSA builds their own systems on them now."

"And we can find them online in repositories in the neutral countries," Justin said. "Some of the Grey Tribe people were miffed because they participated in writing the software, then the NSA tried to have it restricted."

"I can understand how they feel," Samantha said. "In economics we use a lot of big data analysis packages, and the open-source ones started to be better than the expensive commercial ones years ago. Then the expensive providers tried to tie use of their datasets to their proprietary software. That didn't work, but it got messy."

"Now that we have infinite computation space available," Steve said, "I want to upload a lot of the big packages and hook them together in modular ways. Even the limited AIs we have now will be more powerful when combined with bigger databases and instant search. Like the brain has an executive level that coordinates a lot of specialized hardware analyzers, the most commonly cited example being the facial recognition hardware—which is why you can't recognize even a familiar face upside-down. Because it's hard-wired."

Justin and Sam looked at each other. "Well, with that it's time for us to go to lunch," Justin said. "Coming, Steve?"

"You guys go ahead. I am expecting Rasna to come by."

Again Justin and Sam exchanged glances. As they walked toward the mess tent, Samantha said, "So what's up with them?"

"Rasna's taken over Steve's tent and is spending nights there. I guess they're an item."

"But last I heard, they had tried going out last year and it went nowhere."

"Don't ask me. Steve is a good guy, but so focused on work that I can't see wanting to be his partner. Like I don't think Newton ever married. As I recall, Einstein was married, but still negligent. But it's none of my business. Maybe Rasna realizes he's likely to be one of the most famous people in history."

"She doesn't seem the type to go after fame. But who knows, maybe there's a hot-blooded Steve we've never seen."

Justin laughed. "He can be passionate—about physics." They reached the mess tent and waited in the serving line.

* * * * *

They were nearly done eating when Rasna and Steve joined them with their trays. Rasna said, "Justin, Samantha. How are you guys doing?"

"Well enough," Justin said. "Too much to do and no time. We know they're hard at work trying to duplicate our work down there."

"And plotting to take us out of the game entirely if they can," Samantha added. "Steve's work is so dangerous they'd rather eliminate us than work with us and chance some other power getting it. Which makes sense in game theory."

"Minimax[1], least-loss optimization," Steve said. "Each player picks the strategy that guarantees the least loss, even though another strategy might result in a much greater reward. So we have to narrow their choices to only the ones good for humanity, or else we all lose."

Rasna put her arm around Steve and said, "This man's brain is wanted on two planets. So far. How can we protect him? And the rest of us?"

"We're working on that," Justin said. "By making ourselves worth more to them alive than dead. And if that fails, removing their capacity to attack us. Something Steve and I have been planning."

"One thing they probably don't realize yet," Steve said, "is how good the parallel search capability is. If they build a gallium arsenide plate as large as the ones used in the Vortex machines, we can locate it and steal it. Or destroy it, since we won't even need them soon—they're just backups in case something goes wrong and we need to upload the boot loader again."

Rasna looked at Justin and said, "I wonder if we'll ever get a chance to run Prof. Wilson's ALife simulator in the substrate? Didn't you finish the quantum-computation version of that?"

"Mostly," Justin said. "Another research area we will look at when we are secure and there's time. Right now we have a real life that's in danger."

"So, changing topics back to real life," Samantha said. "How are you two doing? I've been dying to ask but Justin here tells me to mind my own business."

Rasna laughed. "Steve has work to do. I try to support him and contribute where I can. While he's obsessing, I work at the intelligence tent going over intercepted conversations. By the time we're both home, we're both tired. But getting away from campus and all the superficial people there has focused me on more important things."

"She is good for me and doesn't demand I stop what I'm doing to pay attention to her," Steve said. "And she listens. She follows what I'm saying and can sometimes help. The only other time I tried to live with someone, she made it all about her, everything was me-me-me. So the 'us' is good, and I can do more with her support." He put his arm around Rasna.

"And Steve is there for me when I need him, Rasna said. "Which isn't often, because I've always been independent. But he's always willing to stop if I ask. I just don't ask unless it's important."

Samantha squeezed Justin's hand under the table and said, "I'm glad. We felt bad that Steve was alone."

"I was fine alone," Steve said, "but now I'm better." And he smiled.

Wendy and Sam

Samantha made her way to the third gateway tent where a machine was usually available for making "calls" to Earth. One of the Grey Tribe people was there speaking to what she guessed was a loved one —probably his mother. They were speaking Italian, but she could still sense the affection in their voices as they wrapped up the conversation; the old woman waved and he waved back, then he gestured to the operator to end the window.

As he left, he grinned at Samantha. She didn't know him so she guessed that was intended to be flirting. She smiled back and shrugged. Turning to the operator, she said, "I need a window to Wendy's apartment—it's 11 AM there now, right?"

The operator pulled down a menu on the screen and read the data. "Yes, just a little after," she said. "I'll open it one-way first so we can check for problems." The window opened, showing a leather couch and a flower arrangement on the coffee table in front of it. No sign of Wendy, but then she usually was in earshot.

"Open it both ways now," Samantha said. The operator clicked a mouse button. "Wendy? Are you there? Wendy?"

"Right here," Wendy said. "Just getting some tea." She came into view, then sat on the couch with the mug of tea in her hands.

"How's the week gone?" Samantha said. "And your hair is—striking." Wendy's hair had a streak of white down either side against today's black color, making her look like an X-Men heroine.

"Thanks, just a little something I fixed up. I'm in black-and-white mode this week. And the week has gone well, mostly routine. The big news down here is that your old boyfriend Dylan has got himself appointed as head of the new National Security Lab."

"We saw that in the news feeds. So we know the Feds went for his deal, and he's got their backing to try to duplicate the gateway. Using the software he stole from Steve's lab."

"You know how to pick'em, sister," Wendy said. "Nobody batted an eye at his age, and they made up stuff about his brilliant career as a researcher, hope for breakthroughs, that kind of thing. Disgusting."

"How's the campus?"

"Quiet. But underneath full of disquiet. Since you guys left, the administration has clamped down on everything. No meetings, no explanations for what happened, just silence. Rumors, of course, mostly wildly off. Did you know you seduced Prof. Bubna to get him to join the rebels?"

Samantha laughed. "Steve and Justin did the seducing. With words. But I'll have to remember my reputation as a femme fatale in case I need to use it."

"Otherwise things are on autopilot," Wendy said. "I never have to call Quinn since you guys give him the orders over gateway-phone. It's about time for me to deliver another large bundle of bills to him, though. Your supplies aren't cheap. And I'll need more gold bars soon to top off the accounts."

"Okay, I'll let Justin know," Samantha said. "We had a chalk talk from Steve about new features he's been working on, and one of those makes it a lot safer to pick and grab things from monitored vaults. So getting you more gold should be no problem. But—" Samantha's face turned serious. "I've been working on the plan for introducing new technology without crashing the world's markets or economy. It turns out we have to withhold information about almost everything it can do until later, when we can make it available. So mum's the word—trust no one, say nothing. We pay Quinn for silence, but he mustn't guess we can do more than open chat windows."

"Got it, Sam," Wendy said. "I know not to talk about anything not required—I've read spy novels. I've been tempted to wear a red trench coat to meet Quinn, but so far I've controlled my flair for the dramatic."

"Okay," Samantha said. "I'll check with you next week this time and we'll try to have the gold ready. Steve's also got the first batch of talismans ready, so we can give you yours—then you can call us by voice command. If he gets the software ready in time, anyway."

"That would be useful," Wendy said. "I'm also looking forward to knowing I have a bugout strategy."

"'Bugout strategy'?"

"Plan for a quick exit if everything goes to hell. I've been waiting for the men in black for weeks—I'd like to be able to escape to join you guys if anything goes wrong."

"Anything else?" Samantha asked.

"One more thing. My father's asked me to come home this weekend to help him out with a problem he's having with his trucking business."

"That sounds serious. How could you help?"

"I don't know yet," Wendy said. "He didn't want to talk on the phone or text me, so I think my lectures on secure communication got through to him. My stepmother might have been hanging around, too."

Samantha considered whether she should tell Wendy to warn her father to sell the business, since trucking would be one of the first businesses to disappear in the new world that was coming. *That's years away,* she told herself, and said, "Let us know if we can help. You can certainly help him with any money problems he has."

"Right," Wendy said, "but he's never asked for help before; usually he gives me money! I should be back by Monday, though, so I can tell you next time."

They said goodbyes, and Samantha signalled the operator to close the window.

In Council: Samantha

The members of the Interim Council (which went by that name pending some work on how they might govern themselves, expected from Ben Ramirez) met in the quiet mess tent after dinner, after shooing out some people playing esoteric board games.

Justin came to the front and said, "Secretary," he nodded to Amy, "let the record show Justin Smith, Steve Duong, Samantha West, Prof. Wilson, Prof. Bubna, Michael McCulloch, and Ben Ramirez are present. That being all the members of the Council, we can begin. Tonight's meeting is mostly for Samantha to present her report on the future economy and the plan for introduction of the new technologies." Justin sat down.

Samantha stood up and rolled a dish cart into place, then stood behind it, using it to hold her stack of notes. “This might be better as an online presentation, but rather than spend a day putting it together, I thought just presenting it would be faster. You can see the background documents in my public directory folder.”

Justin stage-whispered: “Louder!”

“How’s that?” she said, speaking more firmly. People nodded.

“Okay. I did some research on past technological revolutions and their effect on economies and employment. While we know security agencies are after us for the military use of the technology, that’s only one of the interests we threaten. And because knowledge of the additional technologies we are developing could be so destructive and dangerous, none of what I am about to say should ever be spoken of with anyone not on the council. Steve,” she said, looking into his eyes. “This means you can’t go telling every visitor what you’re doing. I know you like to explain what you’re thinking, but for the time being save your info dumps for us only.”

Steve nodded and said, “Yes, I can see the need, so I will be more careful.”

She went on. “If Steve is successful at cheap replication and design software, free energy, and free commodities, more than half the world’s industries and jobs will go away. Industries that will be wholly or mostly unnecessary when all the technologies are available to everyone: energy production: oil, coal, gas, solar panels, generators, turbines, all unnecessary in the long run. Mining: every material can be provided by the gateway, so no more mining. Transportation: Most needs go away with instant transport to anywhere, on demand. That means much less need for trucking, railroads, airplanes, airports, ships, and pipelines. Real estate values will be drastically changed when commuters can live anywhere in the settled universe and be at work in seconds, if they even need a meeting place to work. Shortages of pure water will be a thing of the past, one of the good things we can do.

"Almost a billion people work in agriculture—and you'll be able to get all the food you want from a replicator, for free. So those people have to be among the first to get replicators—so they won't starve when no one needs to buy their production. Manufacturing will also shrink as replicators can create most any desired product. About three billion people work in manufacturing or related services, and most of their current jobs will go away.

"The saving grace is that if we get replicators rolled out before anyone loses their jobs, no one will go hungry or unsupplied. The trick is giving the economic system time to adjust and allow people to find new kinds of work."

"What does that leave?" Prof. Wilson asked. "We can't all be academics, artists, or poets."

"When your basic needs are satisfied," Samantha said, "you can be an artist if you want. While some people without strong community or cultural ties may decide to do nothing, research into societies in very rich environments, where basic needs take only a few minutes a day to meet, shows that most humans will work creatively, to build and display, even in the absence of need. Much human striving is for social position and status, which in our society comes from wealth and professional status. People will continue to work to win the admiration of others, and they will develop new arts and leisure activities which will give them a respected place in society. Progress will continue as people work to serve others by designing and creating new experiences others are willing to pay for. Scientists can research to their heart's content to get that paper out that will establish their reputation—they just won't need to spend half their time looking for funding, or bending their research to satisfy the funders.

"One of our plans is to set up a limited copyright and patent system, to continue to recognize and encourage creative development of arts and technologies. This would recognize the right of a holder to receive a small royalty when replicating a covered design or device. The designs would be kept in a substrate repository, and become free for use after the patent or copyright expired. Since we control the replicators, we can make sure they will only replicate covered designs with payment.

"So creativity in the world will continue to be rewarded, and creators will be recognized for their contribution by payments—which will allow them to buy designed goods above baseline subsistence. And there will still be lots of personal service jobs in teaching, counseling, medicine, and the like. One major job will be teaching people how to use their replicators."

"That's a terrifying amount of change for nearly everyone," Justin said. "Which, as you said, will threaten all the vested interests there are, just about. So how do we get from here to there without disaster?"

"We already have the military and security forces after us. What we want to avoid is having all of the other power centers that would be threatened discover that they are in danger and form a united front to oppose us. We do that by staying absolutely silent about the new technologies—and give away no more information on the gateway itself than we already have. In fact, we need to start putting out some *dis*-information—false limitations and costs to the gateway, to make it seem costly and impractical for use in daily life.

"One of the worst things that can happen when a new technology appears is the abrupt fall in investment in the old technologies between the time the technology is known to be coming and when it actually arrives. Buggy-whip makers stopped building new factories when only a few cars were available. Digging of new canals stopped almost as soon as railroads appeared. Announcing all of the things we have planned would crash the economy and leave billions without work or food.

"So to slow down the disruption caused by reduced investment, each technology has to be quietly introduced in non-threatening form. Transport gateways will at first be rare and congested, so they will only save some time, not eliminate the need for transport entirely. Personal replicators will at first be limited and the food will taste different. And manufacturing, which provides so many jobs, will have to be gradually reduced by making replicators only gradually more capable of replacing all those products."

"What are the implications for our universal Net?" Michael McCulloch said. "How long until everyone gets to use it?"

"We're going to offer substrate Net by wifi to any location where there's a talisman, and to other locations where we hook into the global Internet. But like the other technologies, mass usage should be rolled out in stages. And for a long time people will still need electronic devices as interfaces. Though Steve foresees a time when substrate AIs directly write to screens or even the optic nerve and get their inputs the same way, meaning computer hardware will be largely unnecessary. Science-fiction 'augments' without implanting any physical device. But that's a generation or two of development away."

"How long do you think it will take, this transition period?" Prof. Wilson asked.

"Ten years for much of it," Samantha said. "If we go forward with the plan for starting hundreds of colonies, we want to avoid having those colonists striving for years to set up an agricultural economy like where they came from, only to have it wiped out by replicators. So the colonies should get those replicators quickly. Otherwise we can add new technologies in stages and look at the results before loading more change onto the system. If there's chaos, we can hold off any more changes until that's calmed down.

"And the hazards include misuse of the technology. Someone getting hold of it who shouldn't, and using it to keep change from happening. A major part of our current politics and society is aimed at preventing other people from doing anything that might imperil the status of the wealthy and powerful. They will not go along with giving everyone the freedom to say 'fuck you' when ordered to serve them."

Wendy's Dad

Wendy packed her car for the weekend trip to LA. She tried not to worry about the "problem" he had mentioned, and the drive was uneventful. Traffic was not as heavy as it had been when the economy was stronger, and many people had given up unnecessary driving after higher taxes and road metering were put in place to reduce emissions. But the roads were in bad shape, and she hit a ridge in the freeway pavement that almost made her lose control.

She exited the freeway and went east on Florence Avenue in Inglewood. The old neighborhood had not changed much since she had been at school: a McDonalds on the corner had been remodeled into a Greenz Cafe, with an FDA-approved healthy menu and subsidies. But it was still a nice area, and she remembered when they had moved from South Central to get away from the dangers there.

Her dad came to the door, and after hugs and getting her suitcase up to her old room, he sat down on her bed with a serious look on his face.

"I didn't want to talk on the phone," her dad said. "You warned me not to give away anything important."

Wendy nodded and said, "Especially now, after the incident on campus. They might be listening in on my phone."

"Gotcha. And I know you haven't told me everything you know about that, but I know you're smart enough to keep secrets when it matters. So here's the problem. You know my company does trucking all over the West. And I know you know about the side-businesses—"

"The long family tradition of running black-market goods," she said. "Yes."

"Our latest is vaping supplies. When they outlawed vaping without a prescription and they legalized pot but put a huge tax on it, they made it too costly for people to keep their habits going. Enter our business: supplying vaping setups, cartridges, nicotine and cannabis liquids, artisanal and organic varietals. Low prices and big selection. Wholesaling to some of the little stores in our territory. We drop off Twinkies and beef jerky at the local gas station store, the owner gets a package from our driver. The times they've been caught we paid the driver to take the rap, so we look clean."

"Sounds risky," Wendy said, "but nobody gets hurt except the revenuers. So where is the problem?"

"We've always made regular, big contributions to the city councillor in South Central where our dispatch is. The cops have been encouraged to not notice anything we do, and to not put two and two together. Our councillor was just replaced by a Unity woman, and apparently our costs are going way up."

"How exactly did you find that out?"

"One of our drivers was pulled over and searched right after leaving the warehouse, so of course the cops found supplies in the hidden bin. I called the new Councillor—a woman—and she seemed upset to have a business owner calling her directly."

"She has probably never in her life had to talk to anyone grubby who had to make their living by selling." Wendy said. "So what happened?"

"She said she would look into it. And a few minutes later, I got a call from a guy at the Unity local. Could I please come in for a chat? So I went there and he told me how it was going to be from now on: Two hundred thousand a month donation to the Unity local fund. Then my problems would be seen as important enough to help with. It's like they had looked at my accounts and knew exactly how much we really make in profits—that much would wipe us out. I might as well sell out and retire."

"We've been wanting you to do that anyway. You're getting old and Denny and I don't want to do trucking."

"I had hoped to leave you two some inheritance," her dad said. "If I have to sell under the gun and without the 'extra' business, I won't get anything like what the business is worth."

"Just between you and me, Dad, money is not going to be a problem much longer. I do have some secrets—and one is that I can give you enough to keep the payoffs from hurting you. They won't be going on for much longer."

"Child, you scare me sometimes. What have you got yourself mixed up in?"

"If I don't tell you, you can't be forced to talk about it." She got up and rummaged through her bag, pulling out a bundle. "Here's a hundred thousand in unmarked bills. I'll get you more next month. Just hold on for a few months, and I'm pretty sure things will change."

"I don't like this," her dad said, bristling. "I've never had to take money from anyone—"

"Pride is useless when thugs are running the government. Between the ones that want to save you and the ones that want to bleed you, there's no room left for living."

* * * * *

Wendy's stepmother Doreen knocked on her bedroom door the next morning. "William, it's Sunday," she called, "church at 10 o'clock!"

"Okay, okay. I'll be ready." Wendy sat up in her bed and looked around her old room: costume contest and drama trophies, diva posters, a dresser still full of boy's clothes, her first wig stand. She was grateful her family accepted her desire to live as a woman and dress as a fashionista, but one tradition she had never broken was going to church as a boy. When she came for a visit, suddenly she was twelve again, and the old compromises came back. More for Doreen's sake than her dad's—he would just have chuckled thinking of how the church ladies would titter if she sashayed into church in one of her more arresting outfits. While she had mastered the art of subdued dressing and could have easily gone as a prim and proper young lady, she didn't think it was worth the trouble.

So she sighed and started to dress like the dull young man she used to be. At least her old suit was well-tailored.

Chapter Three: Lao-Tzu

Grid Search

"Interesting news," Justin said, walking into the second gateway tent where Steve had set up his lab.

"What's that?" Steve looked up from his screens.

"I talked to Quinn. You remember those gallium arsenide grid plates we ordered from the German fab?"

"Yes? We don't really need them now, I suppose, since I got the boot loader working."

"Well, they were stolen from the fab a few days ago," Justin said. "At least that's the word from Quinn's go-between."

"Hmm. Who would do that?"

"I think we know. Dylan has the source code, and if he can exactly duplicate our machines, he can use it to open his own gateways. And while the company the fab thinks ordered the plates is only a mail drop in Zurich, they can try to work backward from the phone records and mail drop to find out who's behind it. Two layers back, they'll find Quinn, and behind him, us."

"They've had days," Steve said. "Did Quinn say anything about trouble?"

"No, but then he might not know if they were trying to pressure his agents. He says he's quite sure their anonymity can't be penetrated—they've been evading authorities for decades. But when the CIA and NSA are focused on one thing, they can bring a lot of pressure down. So we're laying low and stopped ordering materials to be shipped to the Swedish warehouse while we keep an eye on its surroundings to look for suspicious activity."

"That seems prudent," Steve said, "though we do need that stuff."

"We have enough to last for months. And we can spot-steal now a lot more easily using your point-and-click mover. But for now, let's work on the current issue: where are those plates?"

"We last did the search for gallium arsenide plates large enough to be useful a few weeks ago, and there were none on Earth," Steve said. "Let's try that search again. And by the way, he may not realize how we do searches, since I hadn't added a good UI to make it easy, I just typed in parameters by hand. Now I have saved searches and a whole named parameter store added. So the source code he has doesn't make it obvious what you can do with it."

Steve pulled down a menu and selected a line that said "GaAs plates." Almost immediately a list of locations came up, sorted by distance.

"What about the lines just after Earth's?" Justin said. "2.5 million light years away?"

"I haven't had time to look—that's in Andromeda galaxy. Most likely another civilization exploring quantum computation."

Justin looked at him and said, "Doesn't that strike you as too exciting *not* to go look?"

"It's not a project I want to start, because it will take me away from things we must, *must* do immediately. Or sooner. Like defend ourselves against half the Earth's governments, and get these talismans working, and software refinements for the surveillance points."

"Good point. But—"

Steve clicked on the first line. "These are in New York, at one of the fabs that built our plates. Let's go look." He clicked another button and they were viewing a dark workroom interior. He clicked again and the view brightened. "Infrared night vision. There are the containers holding the plates." He clicked on one container, and an outline appeared. "This is the new point-and-click move software." One more click, and the container vanished from the screen and appeared on the raised platform. "Get that moved off, would you? I haven't got the program knowing how to stack when it encounters something already in the target zone."

Justin pushed the container off the platform. Steve clicked a few more times, and a second container appeared. Justin pushed that one off. Soon, they had four.

"Big order," Steve said. "Now we go look at the second location." He clicked. "Another US fab, in Arizona. Two here." They repeated the procedure.

"Next: Germany. Location coincides with a US air base—I bet that's the one we ordered, being shipped back to the US." The view showed a brightly-lit floor full of stacked crates and a forklift already picking up one. "He'll be back for the one we want. So we grab it first and maybe he won't realize it's gone." Steve pointed and clicked, and an outline showed around the crate. He clicked again, and it appeared on the platform.

"And two more," Steve said, clicking through. "In China. Hmm, searching the geographic database... a military complex near Beijing."

"That's disturbing," Justin said. "We knew Chinese spies were skulking about the campus, but how would they know what to build?"

"The basic design was published last year," Steve said. "And who knows, they may have an agent at the fab we were using for our project who was willing to feed them the exact design docs. The Chinese have technical and academic spies everywhere high tech research is done."

Justin pushed one more crate off the platform, and in a minute they had two more crates. The tent was getting crowded.

"Whee," Steve said. "That was so much easier than lugging them through a gateway was."

"We need to do this every week," Justin said. "Can you set it up to run automatically and warn you when it finds something new?"

Steve typed in a few complicated lines of text. "Done. Cron jobs by Unix command-lines, piped to email. Still handy. And I can write a substrate app to keep watch continuously, when I get a chance."

"This has implications. We know Dylan has the backing of the US government to run a crash program to duplicate our work. But if we can prevent him from ever getting access to a Vortex clone by stealing the grid plates before he gets them, he'll never be able to use the software. What do you think he'll do when he realizes we can grab them faster than they can make them?"

"There are other approaches to generating arrays of braided anyons," Steve said, "and many other approaches to quantum computation generally, though none has ever been as stable and scalable. I would bet a lot of research into quantum computation will ramp up very quickly. He'll have the best brains in the country to help him to rewrite the software to access the substrate from another type of quantum computer."

"Which will take a lot longer, we hope," Justin said. "Send those locations to Rasna for surveillance. We might pick up some information from the reactions when they discover their plates missing. And we need to find and monitor everyone who's anyone in quantum computing, because they'll all be recruited—or forced—to help."

Dylan

Dylan Foster mentally prepared himself for the visit of Christine Immerman, the liaison between the new National Security Lab he now headed and the White House. Sometimes her true role was recognized in the title "Political Officer," or from the old Soviet Union, commissar. She was responsible for directly communicating the White House's desires and orders outside the sometimes less responsive official bureaucracy.

The military had already prepared a secret fab space under a kilometer of Colorado mountain for their own specialized chip production needs, and he had been given free rein to take over as much of it as he needed. But setting up his dream lab had not gone smoothly. There had been a lot of foot-dragging when the Defense Dept., officially in charge, was ordered to give him assistance and as much room as he wanted—equipment had been installed slowly, and contamination issues required a new filtered ventilation and cooling system to replace the inadequate one he had found in place. Everything took more time than it should have, and despite his unlimited budget, there was no way to force work to be done more quickly.

So the grid plates he had ordered at outside corporate fabs were finished long before he was able to start production in his own fab. Which turned out to be a good thing when those plates at outside fabs were stolen in high-security zones. Security cams showed nothing. There one moment, gone the next. Which told him the rebels had some new tricks.

NSA interceptions and visits to a German fab capable of producing the oversized gallium arsenide grid plates revealed two in production, ordered by a mysterious company with no traceable records. Correspondence about the orders revealed nothing, but the design files were the same as those used by the rebel's university lab. He had agents seize the plates, and they were in transit back to the US when they, too, disappeared.

Analysts could not determine how the rebels might have known about the plates stolen in transit. The plates stolen from the US fab were in a facility that had made them before, so it was easy to see how the rebels could have found them. But the plates in transit, stolen at a US Air Force base in Germany while awaiting shipment, should not have been locatable. Unless the rebels had greater eavesdropping and sigint capabilities than had been suspected.

Dylan had drafted a memo to Christine Immerman about his conclusion that the rebels were apparently able to read even encrypted communications, or possibly had the ability to listen in on secure meetings via some gateway variant. She had replied suggesting they discuss the matter during her upcoming site visit, her first to the new lab.

Dylan remembered visiting the lab the first time. The underground space was vast, room after room carved from solid granite, with pillars left to hold up the kilometer of rock above. It had been dug into the mountain much like the NORAD headquarters in Cheyenne Mountain nearby, so a road led up to the entrance and entered a tunnel sloping down that went deep into the mountain as the rock grew thicker above. LED light panels on the ceilings made it seem bright as day in the areas in use, but most of the space was still dark, raw and unused. Blast doors protected the entrance and points along the tunnel. Now he spent most of his time there, living in a small apartment that felt perfectly normal aside from the LCD "windows" which showed whatever scenery he chose.

The receptionist buzzed him to announce Christine Immerman's arrival, and Dylan went to meet her at the reception area for his lab. He bowed slightly as she got out of the electric cart and said, "Ms. Immerman, welcome."

"Dylan." Her smile was cold. "Why does it still smell like wet rock in here?"

"Much of the space is still bare rock, and there is always a bit of water in the cracks, making its way down through the mountain. Inside the labs the air is purified."

"Interesting," Christine said. "Do you think it's safe to talk here?"

"I think so," Dylan said. "Our exact location has been a well-kept secret, even from contractors and employees. It's probably the most secure facility we have."

"Your concerns are reasonable, though. We've kept knowledge of your project restricted and need-to-know."

"Since they can read screens over someone's shoulder," Dylan said, "there is no completely secure communication. If they know where to look. So we need to restrict all communications to the bare minimum, and only from unexpected locations. You are probably more secure talking to me on your personal cellphone while walking down a public street than you are on your secure phone from your office—which they can locate."

"I'll keep that in mind. You have so instructed your people?"

"Yes," Dylan said. "We have a new set of procedures to reduce chatter and leakage."

"At the White House they have tried to tighten up security without discussing why, putting filters on the screens to make it hard to read them from most angles and installing sensors to try to detect any unusual activity. It's done some good in that people are now aware that they might be overheard, but the level of paranoia is high—most of them think we're worried about conventional bugs by the Chinese."

"They might as well not bother. Everything that takes place at known locations is an open book, if the rebels have time to listen. But I suspect they don't have time for much of that."

Christine looked down the road at the looming buildings that held the labs, and said, “Show me what you’ve done so far.”

They toured some of the fab rooms, viewing them from the gallery since entering them would have involved lengthy cleaning procedures. Dylan explained as they walked down the glassed-in hall passing the massive machines that created the tiny circuits on the chips: “Gallium arsenide is more expensive in large die sizes and less flexible than silicon for chips, so it has been used mostly for very high-frequency applications and where heat resistance is critical, which is why the military has begun producing their own—it’s good for missile circuits that might be exposed to very harsh environments. But even small amounts of dust during the deposition and etching processes can ruin fine circuit elements. When the chips are done, they are tiled on a metal backing and connected to each other along the edges to make the large plates.”

“Very interesting,” Christine said. “I understand the processing is entirely automated?”

“Ideally. There’s a robotic handling system that stores the work-in-progress inside a cartridge which is only opened when the cartridge reaches the next processing machine, which might be an oven or an etching bath. The surface of the wafers are never exposed to even the filtered air inside the lab enclosure. Of course when things go wrong, which is frequently, someone has to go in in a bunny suit to fix mechanical issues and get things moving again.”

“How is the work going?”

“We were delayed a long time by bureaucratic issues,” Dylan said. “While I was supposedly given authority over the military’s workers here, I’ve had to hire and bring in new workers from other fabs to get the ball rolling. And a manager to oversee them, a security chief, a hiring consultant, and an HR person—is there anything you can do to give this project higher status that would let me do what needs to be done without endless rules?”

“Possibly, but it would take a secret executive order. I’ll talk with the chief of staff and see if it can be set up quickly."

"It's critical to speed up the timeline. I've got recruiters combing the universities looking for talent in quantum computing that will join us —you wouldn't believe how much money some of them want to leave their academic track, and I've had to threaten their funding to get them to see the light. But we need more brains. And it worries me that the rebels have managed to steal the Vortex grids we were having built, as well as the ones apparently being built for them in Germany. They are probably watching all the fabs known to be capable of the work closely—but this one should be safe from inspection."

"So when can you have a working machine?" Christine crossed her arms and looked at him skeptically.

"We've just started to process materials and work out bugs. They tell me we should start to see chips that pass inspection in a few days. If all goes well, we might have enough for a machine in a week. Then it will take some time to set it up with the software and run tests."

"That sounds like an if-everything-is-perfect timeline," she said. "More realistically, when should we plan to be able to neutralize them?"

"Realistically? I'm pretty sure we'll have a working quantum computer in a month. Getting it set up to open a gateway to the rebel camp may take longer; I'll have to experiment with the locations stored in the software."

"The president is nervous about them and wants something done as soon as possible." Christine pulled out her pad and started a note.

"If the president is nervous, the president should authorize my request for CIA and NSA assistance in tracing the shell company that ordered the plates in Germany. It took so long to get that operation going that we almost missed stealing them from the fab. And give me a direct liaison at NSA with unlimited authority to search for unusual patterns of commerce. If they are stealing their supplies, I want to know where from. If they are ordering them and picking them up somewhere, I want to know where. We may be able to catch them with their gateway open when they make a pickup."

"Those are in process," Christine said, snapping her pad shut, "but I'll have the chief of staff accelerate them. We'll give you contact points and spread the word that what you ask the agencies to do is to be treated as a direct order from the president."

"However we do manage to get at them, should I assume we're going to send them a tactical nuke?"

"The president and National Security Council agree that Steve Duong is to be captured alive if at all possible," she said. "He may be the most important mind of this century, if our experts are to be believed, and a valuable asset. So, no, we try to take the camp and arrest the rebels if possible."

"And if it's not possible?"

"Then we wipe them out."

* * * * *

After showing Immerman out, Dylan went back to his office, calculating the possibilities. He hadn't allowed himself to react in front of her, but the news that the White House favored capturing and using Steve Duong threatened to upend his plan—how could they use Steve as a source of the new science while giving him the credit? Credit for the new technology was supposed to be his—that was the agreement he had made with the government. Recognition and position in return for giving them the source code and helping them use it to get the gateway technology. When they named him head of the lab in a public ceremony, he thought it was safe enough to give them the source code for analysis. But now that they had it, his bargaining position had weakened. *Fuckers.*

He spent some time writing down ideas for getting back some leverage. And the most obvious was finding a way to have Steve Duong end up accidentally dead.

Sam and Justin

It had started to get crowded in the mess tent at dinnertime, so Samantha and Justin took their trays back to their tent to eat. It was a pleasant dusk with a hint of dampness in the air, and the local equivalent of crickets making noise somewhere out in the grassland.

They sat at the folding table—someone had brought in a lot of cheap portable office furniture, which they were using everywhere. The single LED in the tent lit Samantha perfectly, while Justin's face was in darkness—*I have the better view,* he thought. He couldn't get used to how her beauty would sneak up on him—one moment she was a pal, a friend, someone to laugh with. And then he could tell that her mind had gone somewhere else, her face relaxed, and all he could see was how the light glowed in her hair and how the curve of her neck was just the most perfect thing he had ever seen.

"Hey," she said. "Lost in space?"

"Just admiring you. I like to do that. You looked like you were in Deep Thought."

"Just remembering Dylan, the last time I saw him. And wondering what he's up to." She made stabbing motions with her fork.

"Up to no good, no doubt," he said. "Our intercepts don't tell us much. His new lab is run as a top-secret operation, so it's all need-to-know, and even the people in charge of its accounts don't talk about anything useful. We don't know where it is, though we do know from last week's grid theft in Germany that the CIA is working against us."

"He always wanted to be a star physicist," she said. "Apparently it doesn't matter how, if he's willing to help them come after us. I always thought the comic book villains like Lex Luthor weren't realistic. But now I wonder."

"One thing we do know from the appointment ceremony videos," Justin said, "his face still has the burn scars from the explosion when he opened the gateway into the Sun's atmosphere. They're perfect for a supervillain. Scars outside reflecting the ugliness inside."

"A little too cliché," Samantha said. "He's just insecure."

"Hitler was maladjusted," Justin said. "Misunderstood! If only we could have helped him…." He feigned cradling a baby.

"If we had a time machine, maybe we could." She looked thoughtful and continued, "What if we used the gateway to go to a spot about 130 lightyears from Earth. Couldn't we look back and see the young Hitler?"

"In theory, with a very good telescope, you could," he said. "But you couldn't change anything. And if you used the gateway to go to Earth from there, it would still be today, not 1890-whatever. You can't go back in time, only forward."

"Oh. I thought I had a Steve-like idea there."

"Keep thinking. You look beautiful lost in thought."

"Thank you," she said. "You're pretty, too."

"Thanks. So moving on… Ben is supposed to report on his governance committee's work tonight. I've talked to him about my half-baked ideas. Did he come around to talk to you?"

"Yes, last week. I didn't have much to add to the usual liberty-oriented boilerplate: Golden Rule, least interference with personal decisions, what has to be done by government should be modest and limited. Avoiding the mistake the US made, of delegating far too much authority to a permanent bureaucracy."

"Students for Liberty talk, in other words."

"Yes," she said. "Though there are some new possibilities on how we might achieve that, given the universal Net, perfect identification and authentication, and instant transport."

"His committee was supposed to investigate the best new ideas, and the Grey Tribe people are all up on the cybergeek aspects. Something called 'liquid democracy' was mentioned."

"Sounds gooey," she said. "And we're running a little late." They picked up their trays and headed back to the mess tent.

In Council: Ben Ramirez

Council met in the mess tent again, since the portable building being erected as Community Hall was still not ready yet. Ben carried his notes but didn't look at them as he began to speak.

"At the beginning of the United States, the rebels took inspiration from their common law, with its protections for individual life, liberty, and property, and tried to create a system of limited governance that would allow the many diverse societies that made up the early US to get along as one nation. A common framework, with decentralized power and a republican form, which was intended to stay limited and allow maximum freedom for the individual.

"As we have all seen, that eventually broke down, and like all of the democracies in the developed world, the US developed a large permanent bureaucracy that allowed for consistent administration of a much larger state than the designers of its government had intended. This happened because at every step along the way, the voters put in place representatives who saw their role as doing more, identifying and solving more problems, and major wars enabled those who wanted a larger government to obtain emergency powers that stayed with them long after the emergency was over.

"European democracies evolved large bureaucracies even earlier, led by France and Germany, where government had always been seen as more central to daily life. Universal public education to mold the citizenry originated in Prussia in the mid-1800s, and Otto von Bismarck in Germany began the social welfare state as we know it in the 1890s, with government health and pension plans. The French invented the word 'bureaucracy,' of course, and even in the Soviet Union, the administrators ruled as much as the Party did, and the useful word *nomenklatura* was coined to describe them.

"The Communist states collapsed because their micromanagement of daily life and commerce simply could not compete with freer societies with free markets and responsive producers. While they tried to plan ahead, no one can integrate and organize all the required information to provide the myriad goods and services a population requires. But the Western bureaucratic state was able to continue and grow because it left most producers and consumers relatively free to maximize their own welfare in the choices they made."

Michael McCulloch put a hand up, and said, "Until recently!"

"Yes, until recently," Ben continued, "when a kind of virulent perfectionism took hold, a belief that the population's thinking should be molded to reach Utopia—a belief similar to what motivated early Communists. The terrorist threat was used as an excuse to collect data on ordinary citizens, and the rights once protected in most democracies began to erode as a security state took over. Fearful voters put into office seekers of power in alliance with seekers of Goodness, in a classic Bootleggers and Baptists coalition. Of course the power-hungry actually run the show, but use the coalition with the true believers in 'social justice'—the Baptists—to disguise their real motivation.

"We have an opportunity, provided by Steve's work in giving us both the key to human expansion and a weapon to defeat the governments that are the enemies of the future. We can try again to create a government that is strong, and stable, and most of all *small*, and respects its citizen's rights. And this time we have technologies that might help it last longer."

"We've been talking," Justin said, "about a human population which will eventually be scattered on hundreds or thousands of planets, or even uploaded into the substrate some day, while being able to change locations on a whim. So why does it make sense to think of people as citizens of a geographic area?"

"It doesn't," Ben said. "And that's one thing we're looking at. A small community of like-minded people who want to live a certain way should be free to do that, whether they all live in a mountain village, or are scattered across light-years. So where the US Constitution created a Federal state that would handle only national-level functions while leaving states to create their own systems for handling local issues, and so on, we are thinking of how to set up a state that creates a framework for intentional communities—for groups that want to live by their own rules within a larger system."

"What if someone wants to be a member of more than one group?" Samantha asked.

"It's not hard to imagine a case," Ben replied. "Suppose you live on an island on a tropical planet where the island citizens like rules against vehicles and loud parties, and at the same time you are affiliated with a group of ultra-orthodox religious people who insist Friday is the sabbath and work is forbidden. If you can successfully live your life without breaking the rules of either group severely, fine."

"What does that have to do with government?" Justin asked.

"Government is about resolving disputes and enforcing law by use of force, if necessary. We are proposing that only the universal government can use force, while all groups that participate under it must agree to limit punishment of transgressors to social ones like shunning, or at worst expulsion. Every citizen is free to leave any association at any time, and the local rules of a group can only be enforced insofar as they don't violate a citizen's universal rights. If your town wants to put a lien on your house because you haven't paid for town services, they can. If your town wants to flog you because you had sex with an animal, you have the option of taking their punishment or exiting the community. If your crime is so grave that it is recognized by the universal government, like murder or major fraud, your punishment may be to be banished from the protection of civilization, to a planet where it does not operate."

"Coventry," Justin said. "Or Coventries."

"We'll think of a more original name. No 'Botany Bay' or 'Devil's Island,' either. But anyway, we're trying to get away from the view of governments as territorial entities that control all citizens inside geographic boundaries. It won't work when people will be free to move around as much and as often as they like. And while at first justice will have to be policed and administered by people, we have hopes that Steve's prediction of powerful AIs operating in the substrate will let us delegate most of that to AIs.

"Privacy also changes. What does it mean when anyone can open a window to view anything, anywhere? For one thing, the gateway software will have to be run by those AIs with rules about privacy and who has rights to it—like no viewing inside unauthorized houses or other private spaces. We have these new talismans, and the gateway software will be watching and listening in the area of the wearer at all times; for now that is just for voice commands and wifi, but eventually the software will be able to recognize people and situations that might turn violent, and intervene before any damage is done. When everyone is monitored, that data is private and to be used by law enforcement only when authorized by a judge. Who might also be an AI, routinely… but what we lose in privacy we more than get back in freedom to move, and protection from violence.

"So to get back to the central discussion. Who makes the law for our judges and AIs? How do the people control their universal government, which might start with the people in this room, but grow to include ten billion people over a thousand planets?"

"What we have now seems to work well," Prof. Wilson observed, drily.

"Because," Ben said, "we all agree on most things, and we want the same outcomes, and we're too busy to worry about someone else's job. But that won't last, and we'll have major disagreements, where one faction wants one thing while another thinks the opposite is better. And we need a way to efficiently decide such disputes. Back on Earth, democracies elected representatives who traveled to large halls to discuss and vote on laws. We will have the universal Net, which can guarantee who you are and what your authority is, and a way of including anyone interested in the debates on any law. You can participate and vote on the Net."

"So we were talking about 'liquid democracy'…" Justin said, raising his eyebrows.

"Liquid democracy, also called delegative democracy.[2] This is the new type of democratic-republican system we are looking at. The basic idea is that every citizen has a vote on every law or issue, but for practical reasons they delegate their vote to a representative, who bundles together all the votes delegated to him or her and casts them as he or she thinks best. The key difference between this and republican systems we are used to is that there is no fixed term for a representative, and citizens can take their proxy back at any time to give to another representative, or to vote themselves directly. Thus 'liquid'—citizens can react to what their representative is doing, even down to revoking their proxy during a speech on the issue that sways them. Citizens who want to participate in every issue can; most people will give their proxy to a representative they trust and only occasionally consider switching. Participation in debate and the writing of legislation would have to be limited to a practical number of representatives who hold the most proxies, but a citizen would be free to watch the process and communicate ideas to their representative.

"Proxies can be limited or full. For example, I might delegate my vote on defense matters to Samantha, who is hard-headed enough to impress me as a wise choice for that, while giving my proxy for research funding to Steve, because he'll always be better at that. There's no pre-election period where a government can suck up to voters and spend money unwisely to get elected, then act as they wish for years after. The people can intervene quickly if they don't like the way things are going."

"Who chooses the executive, and what about those bureaucracies?" Prof. Wilson asked.

"The executive would be elected by the representatives, and have to work to keep their confidence, as in a Parliamentary system. We are intending the powers of the executive be limited this time—in the unlikely event of a war with an outside power, there would of course be emergency needs. But the huge bureaucracies for defense, agriculture, education, tax collection, and all that would all be unnecessary. A dispersed, connected, and footloose people with replicators won't need assistance surviving, and no external enemies exist that we know of. The executive government may never need to be more than a few dozen people."

"So, let me get this straight," Prof. Bubna said. "I have my talisman. I am always being monitored by AIs in the substrate who authenticate my identity and let me vote or select a representative to vote for me, and I can watch deliberations and vote on them if I choose, or send my representative a note to suggest something. If I don't like his vote, I can take away his proxy and give it to someone else. Or I can just ignore government and trust other people are paying enough attention to keep it from running wild."

"That's the idea," Ben said.

"Sounds good to me," Bubna said, and got up and left.

"I think we know which option he chooses," Justin said. "I like this idea, but wonder how we will get there from here."

"Well, I guess it's like the economic plan," Samantha said. "We implement it in stages. With corrections if something goes wrong."

Michael McCulloch stretched and got up to leave. "I'm a fan of the idea. But it means we have to build an incorruptible Net. And those AIs had better be set up to keep tabs on each other; we have to build them with checks and balances themselves. To correct each other, and to reprogram them if necessary. If we want humans to maintain control."

"Humans have had the power to destroy the species for over fifty years," Ben said, "and it was just luck that they didn't. While there's a risk to appointing robotic watchmen, there's an even bigger risk to continuing down the path of humanity confined to a single planet rigged with doomsday devices controlled by multiple incompetent governments. I'm willing to take the chance."

Great Wall

Justin went looking for Michael McCulloch the next morning and found him in the Grey Tribe's computer tent, which was the nexus for their work on the new Net. Michael was looking over a programmer's shoulder reviewing code.

"Got a few minutes?" Justin asked him. "I'm interested in your thoughts on eliminating the various Great Walls."

"I think getting rid of them is a great idea. The Chinese were first, but now most countries are doing it. Some are filtering and blocking the Internet to defend themselves from cyberattacks and spying, but for most the real reason was to keep their people from seeing unfiltered news and opinion that might threaten their government's control on mass opinion."

"We're working on the list of requirements for joining us. One is the end of Great Walls. Do you think that is a reasonable demand?"

"Well, maybe not," Michael said. "Look at the Swiss—they put theirs up to prevent the NSA and other spy agencies from hacking in. They would be wary of taking it down unless they knew the cyberspying was going to end."

"So how can we ask governments to free up people's access to international communications?"

"Don't demand an end to national walls," Michael said. "Put it as calling for an end to content restrictions that are political in nature. Block malicious probes, but not web pages. In the long run it won't matter, since everyone will have access to our version of the Internet, which won't be so easily blocked or bugged." He patted the programmer on the shoulder, and turned back to Justin. "Let's walk."

They left the tent and walked aimlessly. The morning fog was beginning to clear. "So we should ask for an end to filtering of normal search queries and message traffic?" Justin said.

"For now that is less offensive to nationalists than asking for what sounds to them like letting the NSA run wild. No need to push for something that will happen anyway in time."

"I'm worried that we will have trouble getting the people on our side if our message is blocked by controlled media."

"Talking to Steve," Michael said, "I gather there's almost no limit now on the tricks he can pull with the software in substrate space. We can pipe our messages directly to anyplace on the planet."

"But I think we'd have more credibility with people if they get unbiased news reports from trusted sources as well," Justin said. "Could we recruit some news people to write up our story here before the shit hits the fan, so we're ready with news stories confirming what we say?"

"Hmm. That's a good idea, and I know at least one reporter who's worked with me on Grey Tribe stories. She stood up to threats from her government and put up with our security to get the story."

"Sounds ideal. Can you get in touch with her?"

"Will do," Michael said. "Her name is Amanda Sundaram-Smythe, and she has a lot of credibility from years at the BBC. Her mother was a professor, her father immigrated to London from India. Amanda married a Lord Smythe for a few months before she divorced him and kept the hyphenated name. Quite the character."

They had meandered to Michael's tent. Michael's tent-mate Amy was puttering on a computer inside. "So," Justin said, nodding toward where Amy sat, "how are things with Amy?"

"Well," Michael replied. "She gets me out of my funks and back to the real world. I sometimes forget I'm an animal, too, and she is reminding me."

"She's doing a great job on the administration and record-keeping. Maybe she would be a good president."

Michael laughed. "Could happen. If the job is about tracking details, she'd be good. But she can be hotheaded. Maybe not the ideal Commander-in-Chief, too many people would get blown away."

"I'm going to vote for Ben," Justin said, "when the time comes."

Emerson Wilding and his recent companion, one of the Grey Tribe programmers, walked by, and Emerson nodded and said, "Good morning. How's it going?"

"Very well, thanks," Justin said. "We're plotting to decide who gets to be president. Or whatever we call our Fearless Leader."

"It should be you, of course," Emerson said. "You've led us this far and done a good job. Right, Carlo?" He nudged his companion.

"Si," Carlo said, nodding vigorously, "molto bravo! Very good!"

“Thank you,” Justin said. “But I’m not running. Let’s see how all this goes first.”

“And, Michael,” Emerson said, “Thanks for getting the entertainment server up. We were getting bored without anything to watch or read.”

“Not my doing,” Michael said. “One of the kids raided his own stash and put it up, and others have added to it. We’ll eventually allow direct access to Earth internet, but for now we have to be careful and dip in for short periods.”

The Second Department

In a blast-proof concrete building on a military reservation near Beijing, elements of the Second Department of the People’s Liberation Army met to discuss progress on Project Paifang and the action plan prepared for obtaining the technology agents had identified at the California university. The first agent’s report had been discounted until the reaction of US Homeland Security and other intelligence agencies had made it clear whatever had happened there was viewed as highest priority; since then, many agents in positions in the US defense labs and research universities had heard hints of a new project to weaponize the academic work in quantum computation.

So when their first effort to duplicate the quantum computer that had been used at the university failed because the major part of the effort —gallium arsenide plates—had disappeared from a secure storage area, it had only increased the Second Department’s view of the importance of getting the technology. Security cameras showed the plates had simply vanished, a technology more advanced than their agent had seen.

Every scrap of intelligence was examined, and more agents infiltrated the campus where the first event had destroyed parts of two buildings while the students involved had disappeared. Agents gathered information about the students from records, Internet searches, and casual interviews with students who knew them. Their families were similarly researched, and their homes entered and bugged. Their agents found Homeland Security bugs already in place.

The general in charge of the meeting, Li Yongchung, reviewed the project file briefly, but his mind was considering how he might escape this duty before complete failure. *Singapore is pleasant*, he thought, before sighing deeply and opening the meeting with a statement: "President Liu has taken a direct interest in this project. His eyes are upon us. We must not fail."

The intelligence officer in charge said, "We have very limited ability to act within the US, especially in the closely-watched area near the university and air force base. We had planned three operations for five family members of the students presumed to be involved. Our analysts have rejected one of those operations because of continuous surveillance by Homeland Security."

General Li's assistant—who he considered a threat to his career—jumped in and said, "But the Vietnamese operation has no such problem, correct?"

"That is correct," the officer said. "We want the operations to be simultaneous, late evening in California and afternoon in Vietnam. The parents in LA are in a wealthy neighborhood where we can act without much chance of interference."

"Do all of you believe holding these people hostage will be useful in getting cooperation from the students?" General Li asked, looking around the table at the young men—and one woman—eager to climb to his level. "Why would you think that? They have acted against their own government. Why should they bargain with us for old relatives when they are already on such a course? You don't see their government holding the relatives hostage. They could be tortured and used as bargaining chips, but the US hasn't done that."

One of the younger men—he thought of him as the shark—said, "The US government is afraid of bad publicity. They maintain the illusion that the people rule, and it is still possible to create a backlash against their President Stanton if they are seen to violate their own laws."

"Yes, yes," General Li said, "they are decadent and dream of the days when they were the most powerful country on Earth. But I am wondering whether this operation, even if it succeeds, will do us harm in the long run. Maybe the students will not care what happens to their relatives. Maybe they will care and find a way to hurt us badly for doing it instead of handing over useful information. But I'm okaying it, because the president wants something done, and this is the best of the ideas you've shown me. Execute as planned."

Kidnapped

In a quiet canyon north of Beverly Hills, two black vans pulled up at a sleek modern house tucked into the hillside. Dark figures fanned out and three climbed the fence to the enclosed pool area. All was quiet until their command displays showed the men were in place.

When the signal was given, glass was cut and doors opened. Agents went inside, followed by the muffled thumps of gas bombs that could be heard on the recordings reviewed later. Minutes passed. One gunshot, then a fusillade over a few seconds. Screaming.

The recordings caught agents withdrawing in confusion. "He has an AK-47!" one said. "Jerry's hit in the neck." Then they heard the sound of sirens coming up the canyon drive, and the agents took their wounded and left.

* * * * *

In a village in the hill country of Vietnam, Steve's father was about to leave his home after lunch when men pushed their door in and grabbed his wife. They shouted at him to get down on the floor and cooperate. He backed up into the next room and grabbed the axe from behind the door. He could hear his wife screaming and he charged back through the door with the axe in the air, aiming for the lead man.

Shots from two rifles took him down. As he lay dying, he wondered who would go to the trouble of attacking him.

* * * * *

Samantha's father Elton and mother Jessica spoke to the police in their kitchen. Elton said, "We were in the study getting ready to watch a movie when we heard the sound. Must have been the glass being cut, plus I think I had heard other odd noises that added up to people outside."

"So it's lucky we were in the study, where the gun safe is." Jessica said. "Elton had the big semi-automatic out in just a minute, though it seemed like a lot longer because we could hear them inside the house, coming down the hall."

"So you heard them coming and just fired down the hall without asking them to identify themselves?" the young woman officer asked.

"They had broken in," Elton said, "there were lots of them, and it didn't seem like a good idea to tell them where we were by starting a conversation."

"Sounds good to me," said the male officer. "Good thing you had a silent alarm." His phone bleeped and he answered. "Martinez. Yes? … Really? … I'll let them know." He put the phone back in his belt. "Homeland Security is on its way—seems you're persons of interest so anything involving you sets off alarms. They want to investigate themselves. 'National Security.' We'll stay until they get here."

"Ah. That's interesting," Elton said, looking meaningfully at his wife. "But not surprising."

* * * * *

As reports came back to the operations office in the Second Department headquarters in Beijing, faces fell and the officer in charge wondered how he would write the memo that ended his career.

Red Lines

It didn't take long for word of the kidnap attempts to reach the rebel camp.

Justin was asleep when his phone pinged at the arrival of email. He reached over and checked the email app. An email from the surveillance group with the intercepted transcript from Homeland Security in DC:

```
[Unidentified]: Attempted kidnappings in two loca-
  tions, one in California and one in Vietnam.
[Andrew Gao]: Our Chinese friends? Anything from
  NSA?
[Unidentified]: Message activity to one of their
  affiliated gangs in LA. Encrypted.
[Andrew Gao]: So what happened?
[Unidentified]: Samantha West's father shot them up
  and scared them away. Not the soft target they
  were expecting, so the parents are fine. Steve
  Duong's father was killed and his mother injured.
  If they were trying to get hostages, they blew it.
[Andrew Gao]: Not too bright, our Chinese friends.
  Should we step up security on the other family
  members?
[Unidentified]: We have round-the-clock sur-
  veillance on Justin Smith's family, which may be
  why they weren't hit. We should probably take them
  into custody for their protection.
[Andrew Gao]: That's a lot of people to hold.
[Unidentified]: The White House wanted them in
  custody last month but we argued them out of it.
  This makes them look smart.
[Andrew Gao]: Set it up.
```

It was almost time to get up anyway, so he hugged Samantha. As she stirred, he said, "Wake up. News from Earth. Your parents are safe but somebody—the Chinese—tried to kidnap them."

"What?" she said, blinking. "My parents? What happened?"

"We'll find out more later. But there was a kidnap attempt and your dad scared them away with a gun."

"Yikes. I never thought they'd need those things. My mother didn't like having them in the house."

"Well, get up. We need to get moving—the Feds are talking about rounding up our family members for protection."

"Can we call them?"

"I think we should be ready to bring them over right now. If they're bugged we can't even talk to them safely."

Samantha rubbed her eyes and got up. "They may not appreciate being moved. My mother is used to easier living. Even Daddy likes his hotels high-end."

"I'm sure they realize how dangerous it is for them now. Oh, and the other news is worse—the word is that Steve's father was killed."

"How awful. Did he get the email?"

"Yes. I don't know if he's seen it yet."

They dressed and washed up, and made their way to Steve's tent. Rasna was there.

"Steve around?" Justin asked.

"Just got up and went to wash up before breakfast," Rasna said. "Should be back any second."

Steve came around the corner with his phone in his hand. His face was blank.

"Steve, we just heard," Samantha said. "We're so sorry."

Steve said nothing until he was closer, then said, "My father is dead. Or probably dead, this report could be wrong."

Rasna took his arm and said, "What happened?"

Justin repeated the information from the Homeland Security intercept, and said, "Apparently the Chinese thought it would be useful to kidnap some of our family members to give them some leverage in dealing with us. They somehow figured out who we are and who our close family are, and went after them. Not mine, for some reason, but Steve's and Samantha's."

"I'm so sorry, Steve," Rasna said. "I should try warn my parents."

"We are thinking we need to get our families here to be safe," Samantha said.

"If the Chinese wanted to force us to help them, they failed badly. I wonder if they are going to try again since we're on the alert now. Which is why Homeland Security is going to take our families into custody. Your parents might be in less danger. Maybe they should take extra precautions, though."

"We need more information," Steve said. "Like where is my mother, and what's happening to her?"

Justin said, "Let's go check on everybody we can and see if we can bring them over now."

They walked toward the communications tents while Rasna went to pick up takeout breakfast for them.

"It's just hard to believe," Steve said.

"I know," Justin said. "For one thing, we could level Beijing in an hour."

"Faster, actually," Steve said. "I mean, why would they think I would give them anything? Even if they had my father, I wouldn't help them. My father would agree. We aren't fools—if we help them, they kill us anyway. Sooner or later."

"I hadn't thought that far ahead," Samantha said. "But I remember something about the Danegeld and the Dane. If you give in to extortion, you end up paying forever."

"I hope my mother is okay. I'll ask her if she wants to come, but I think she will refuse. I understand, she will still want to be near family."

They reached the communications tents and started setting up the gateway for viewing. It was Sunday afternoon in California, and they found Samantha's parents at home. Unfortunately they had company —men and women with 'HOMELAND SECURITY' shirts were everywhere, looking for evidence. Elton and Jessica sat on the couch and held hands while agents moved around them.

"At least they're still there," Justin said. "We may be able to talk to them if we can get them to someplace more private."

Steve said, "I still don't feel safe using the object moving program on people, so we should try to open a gateway to get them. But that means it has to be a private place."

"They may be wary of letting them out of their sight," Justin said. "I would be. If they've been told about our abilities. But then again, maybe that's a big secret."

Steve started up another program and said, "This is the surveillance app. I can get the point where the sound is generated and detected just an inch from the ear." He moved a joystick carefully and a dot moved close to Elton's ear. Steve got a headset and handed it to Samantha.

Justin said, "Whisper to him. Tell him we know Homeland Security is going to take them into custody any minute. And we think they'd be safer staying with us for a few months. Tell him we can open a gateway in the guest bathroom and we'll pick them both up if he nods yes."

Samantha put on the headset and whispered into the microphone. "Dad, it's me, Samantha." They saw him start, then his face went blank. She repeated what Justin had said, and her father thought for a moment, then nodded slightly.

Samantha whispered, "We're watching you. Try getting up and heading for the bathroom. Nobody seems to be paying attention to you guys, so tell Mom to follow you a minute later if you don't come back."

Sam's father whispered to her mother for a minute, then got up and headed back toward the bathroom. No one paid any attention to him when he went in and closed the door. Steve moved the window down the hall and through the bathroom door, opening it to door size, and clicked a button.

"Psst, this way," Justin said, and Sam's father turned around and stared at them.

"Come on, Dad," Samantha said. "We'll get you first and then Mom. Just step across."

He looked wary, then slowly stepped over the threshold. "What is this?" he said, looking around, while Steve clicked to turn the gateway back to one-way viewing only.

"New Earth," Justin said. "Fifty light-years from Earth, but very much like it. Welcome."

Sam's dad went to her and they hugged, then he said, "We were so worried about you. And they had so many questions about you. We told them what they already knew."

The gateway window blurred as an object passed through it. It was Sam's mom, and after she closed the door behind her, they repeated the process. She came immediately when she saw her husband standing next to Samantha.

"Mom," Samantha said, "it is so great to have you here, safe." The family huddled together, and Sam's mother sobbed quietly.

* * * * *

They turned their attention to other relatives. Steve's mother was not at home and they would need time to find out where she was in the hospital, so they moved on to Justin's family.

They moved the viewer around inside their home but no one was there. "Check out on the patio," Justin said, and Steve moved toward and through the wall. Turning the view, they spotted Justin's parents sitting at the patio table next to the gas grill, sipping from wine glasses. Steve moved the window forward and turned it to two-way.

"Mom, Dad," Justin said. They turned to look.

"Justin?" his mother said.

"It's me." He got closer to the window. "There's been an incident. The Chinese tried to kidnap Samantha's parents. They may have killed Steve's father. Homeland Security has orders to take you into protective custody."

His parents looked at each other. "They watch us all the time," his father said. "It was hard enough living with that."

"We really think you should stay with us for a few months until things settle down," Justin said. "Samantha's parents are already here."

"What about your sister, and your grandpa?" Justin's mother said. "Are they safe?"

"We hope so," Justin said. "They don't seem to be interested in them. Let's get you out of there now and we can warn Emily to lay low with the kids."

"Do we have time to get some things?" his mother asked.

"Not much," Justin said. "Only what you absolutely have to have. We can retrieve some of your stuff later." His parents went back into the house and came out minutes later with a tote bag.

"Okay, we're ready," Justin's dad said. They stepped through the enlarged gateway and hugged Justin.

Justin's dad said, "We need to find a way to tell our employers we're taking a vacation."

* * * * *

Rasna's parents in Silicon Valley were happy to hear from her, but worried by the news. After a short discussion, they decided to move in with friends nearby temporarily until it was clear they were not targets.

After the new arrivals had been fed and settled in temporary quarters, Justin and Samantha walked back to their tent. "It's getting dangerous," Justin said.

"No kidding," Sam said. "How much longer can we keep this up? When the governments of the world want what we have and will kill to get it?"

"They haven't bothered us for months. But it does look like word is spreading that we have the greatest prize a government could want.

We might think harder about going on the offensive. Taking out some of their capabilities. Showing them what we could do if they mess with us again."

"Maybe transport Dylan to that prison planet?" Samantha smiled thinking about it. "I can go for that."

"We'll watch him closely when we find him. I meant showing the governments we can hurt them. Without being so public about it that the population panics."

"They just killed Steve's dad," Samantha said. "Maybe the population *should* panic a little."

Chapter Four: Project Arrow

Dylan's Machine

A week after the kidnapping attempts, Justin dropped in on Steve's office to see how he was doing.

"I've checked with the others on the Council," Justin said, "and we all agree we have to demonstrate that we can retaliate if they attack us."

"Now that we run programs in the substrate," Steve said, "there's really no limit to the size or speed of destruction we could cause."

"I'm talking about things that strike at the heart of what the security people are doing, but without being visible news events that would scare normal people. What can we do like that?"

"Well, I just got an alert about gallium arsenide plates from the watch program I started last time we looked for them," Steve said. "A new one at the same site in China as last time, and a new site in Colorado. I was just doing some research on the locations." He made a window full-screen to let Justin see more of it. It was a map of rugged terrain in the mountains, with the nearest city, Colorado Springs, on the eastern edge. "Not far from NORAD, under Cheyenne Mountain. Looks like somebody built a fab inside a mountain."

"It's safe to guess it's the program Dylan is running to duplicate the Vortex so he can run it with your software," Justin said. "Let's take a look around."

Steve brought up another window and clicked a few times. A window opened showing a bulky gray and white cabinet in what looked like a factory; similar machines were arranged in lines, as he dollied back with the joystick. “Looks like a fab,” Steve said, “and a big one.” He changed the view again, and they could see a long way down the room between support pillars. “There’s about a kilometer of rock above this facility. Even the biggest thermonuclear bombs wouldn’t touch it.”

“Where are the people?” Justin asked.

“A modern fab is almost completely automated,” Steve said. “The small number of staff will be outside the fab floor, monitoring and troubleshooting.”

“Can we find them?” Justin said. “I think we just found a great way of demonstrating that they shouldn’t mess with us.”

Steve joysticked around the facility until they found the outside hallways and offices. They saw a few workers at desks looking at screens. A break room had a few more, talking in a group. Steve took the view back toward what looked like the entrance, and off to one side they could see walnut paneling around a larger door. “That looks like an important person’s office,” Justin said. “Go in there.”

Inside they found a reception area. A woman in an Army uniform was watching a video on her phone screen. Next to her was another set of doors. Behind the first, they found Dylan, focused on another screen. “The man himself,” Justin said. “Give me a minute to think about this. We need to get all these people out of the way. And then we can trash this place.”

“Shouldn’t we save the grid plates first?” Steve said.

“As you pointed out,” Justin said, “we have lots of them and they are no longer needed since you can upload programs directly. Destroying them is good enough.”

“Okay. So now what?”

“Open a talk window in front of his face and right in front of me. I want just my head in the frame.”

“Give me a minute,” Steve said. He adjusted the view until they were looking straight into Dylan’s face; he was concentrating hard on something. “Okay, go stand in front of the platform so I can get just you in the frame.”

Justin prepared himself for his performance. He was shaking a little from anger, which came back when he remembered how Dylan had treated Samantha, and betrayed them all. He focused on the message. “Open it any time.”

On the click, Justin was staring straight into Dylan’s eyes. Dylan jumped, and Justin said, “Dylan. How you doing, buddy? Dropping in for a visit.”

Dylan jumped up and backed away from his desk. “I guess I shouldn’t be surprised.”

“No, not really,” Justin said. “We have some scores to settle. Starting in fifteen minutes, when we’re going to destroy that cave you’re in. I advise you to warn everyone and get yourself out of there before time’s up. Got that?”

“You can’t do that. There are hundreds of people here and there’s only one road out.”

“That’s why you should hurry,” Justin said, signaling Steve to cut the connection. The window disappeared. Justin rejoined Steve in front of his monitors. “Let’s go warn the group in the break room, just in case Dylan runs without stopping to tell anyone.”

The workers looked shocked when Justin appeared to them, and each one’s face changed in a different way as they absorbed the warning.

"Fifteen minutes?" Steve said. "Is that enough?"

"We'll watch and make sure the last stragglers have made it out," Justin said. They could hear klaxons sounding, so someone must have reported the threat to security. "On the off chance Dylan's trying to take anything with him, let's see what he's up to."

Steve took the view back to Dylan's office, but he had already left. Following toward the exit, they found him about to get into one of the few carts parked there. "He's got a briefcase," Justin said. "Can you zap just that to here?"

"I'll try." Steve pointed and clicked, and an outline appeared around Dylan. "We definitely don't want all of him. Or should I just zap him into the Sun?"

"As satisfying as that would be, no. Try to get just the briefcase here."

Steve clicked some more and the outline changed each time, ending up around the briefcase. With a click, the briefcase appeared on the platform and fell over with a thunk. "There you go," Steve said. On the monitor, Dylan looked startled and looked around in helpless anger before getting into the cart and driving away.

"That will be interesting to look through, but for now let's check on the evacuation." Other workers from the fab were starting to arrive at the fab entrance. Steve moved the viewpoint quickly up the underground road toward the entrance, passing through Dylan's cart and others before settling at the entrance to watch.

Justin checked the time. "Thirteen more minutes. Of course we really wait until everyone seems to be out. Do we have a way of checking?"

"Not really," Steve said. "It's a big facility and it would take hours to look through it completely by viewer. And I still don't have a way to look for people as objects, like with DNA detection. Next year maybe."

“Okay,” Justin said. “We'll do what we can and hope no one gets left behind.”

They watched and waited while the rate of people and vehicles leaving grew, then after about ten minutes declined. Steve spent the time checking scans of the area and setting parameters in a substrate-resident program for mass motions. Ten minutes after that, they had seen no one for several minutes.

“It's time,” Justin said. “Take it down.”

“This is much like what we did to the quantum lab,” Steve said. “But in this case, instead of support beams, I'm shearing the granite support pillars.” Steve clicked on the screen. The last thing they saw of the entrance view was a cloud of dust, then the window went black. “The cave was about a kilometer square, with the whole mountain above supported by about ten thousand granite pillars, now giving way.” Steve changed some numbers in boxes onscreen, and the black window turned into a view from high above the mountain. Dust was rising from an irregular square outline where they could see motion. “I am guessing the mountain above is settling into the space below as a unit, sliding along new fracture lines around the edges.”

“Interesting,” Justin said. “It's a good thing we're the good guys. Is there any way we can find Dylan again?”

Steve returned to the view of the entrance, now obscured by dust, and panned back rapidly. They passed carts and other vehicles heading away. When they saw a guardhouse up ahead, the vehicles were piled up behind the gate, where many people had parked and were looking back at the rising cloud of dust, talking. As the view got closer, they could see Dylan at the center of a group of workers.

“I have an idea,” Justin said. “Be right back.” He left for a moment and came back with a small ziploc bag. He opened it and took out a tiny cube, which he placed on the platform. “We've produced a few tiny talismans for human implantation. This is a good chance to test it out.”

Steve stared for a moment. “But I’m not ready to try anything like that yet.”

“He’s the ideal subject for human experimentation,” Justin said. “He’s a rat as much as a human. It’s plastic coated with silicone, and it shouldn’t hurt him if you put it in a fat deposit.”

“The software won’t allow transport into a solid. But I can override that, I suppose. Let me look.” He started clicking and opened another window. The view showed Dylan, growing closer until his coat buttons looked like dinner plates. Then Steve carefully pushed the joystick forward. The view grew dim as they passed through layers of clothing. Then a murky red. Very slowly turning a fine control knob, Steve moved around the area looking. The window started to glow a faint amber color. “This is most likely a fat deposit.”

“It has blood vessels,” Justin said, “but it’s not very sensitive and nothing critical is nearby. I say we go for it.” And just as he finished, Dylan apparently moved a bit, because they were looking at darkness. “Pull back a bit, and hit it as soon as it turns yellowish again.”

Steve turned the fine movement knob the other way. He reached another amber zone, and clicked the mouse. Justin checked the platform, and a glob of something had replaced the cube. “Pull back and let’s see how he took it,” Justin said.

Steve used the joystick to pull away and up. Dylan’s face appeared in the window, still talking. There was no sign of distress or alarm.

“Here’s the talisman reference number,” Justin said, giving Steve the baggie. Steve opened another program and typed it in.

“So I set this to observe and track?” Steve said.

“Observe, track, and record everything near him. I want to be able to find him wherever he is and follow his every move from now on. We’re going to make sure something goes wrong with every attempt he makes to follow us."

"This is a very bad thing," Steve observed.

"They would do it to us if they could," Justin said. "They would kill us, and take the technology and use it for this and worse. I'm willing to do one wrong thing to prevent millions of worse wrongs. But we don't have time to worry about it right now, we can listen in on him later. Let's check out the site in China."

Steve redirected the viewpoint to the other location in the alert. The view changed, and again they were looking at some kind of factory interior. The container in the center of the view was attached to a large machine.

"Let's do something similar here," Justin said. "I'm guessing these guys had a lot to do with the kidnapping attempts that got your father killed. We need to show them what we can do. Start by looking around for people."

"Let's try this direction," Steve said, moving the joystick forward. The view soon reached a wall and went through, but they were now outside, looking at a gray urban landscape. "Oops, wrong way." He moved the stick back, and they went back through the building to another wall. On the other side was office space, and people.

"Can we get an overview of the area and find out what the web knows about this facility?"

"Sure," Steve said. He clicked on an icon and a new window appeared on the other monitor, which loaded a map centered on a cluster of buildings. The city around was laid out as a series of concentric squares, and the buildings were labelled everywhere but near the one they had tagged. "Do we have any information about where their spy headquarters is? This probably isn't it but I bet it's nearby."

Steve did some typing and clicking in a search window. "Two sources have it as this compound." He opened another map window with the outlines of buildings.

“Now we just need somebody who speaks Chinese,” Justin said. “Let’s see who I can round up—wait here.” Justin left and headed for the communications tent, where he asked around. He was quickly directed to a woman named Meiling in the Grey Tribe area, who followed him back while he explained what they needed her to do.

“Find some official-looking people in the more luxurious part of the building,” Justin asked Steve. “We’ll want them far away since we’re taking down a whole cluster of buildings.”

Steve joysticked through the entrance and stopped at a guard desk. “How about the guard here?”

“That should do. We want him to sound the alarm and have everyone leave the area.”

Justin coached Meiling on what to say. “Just tell him that the whole reserve—military area—is about to be bombed and they only have ten minutes to evacuate. Then smile and tell them we didn’t appreciate their last gift.” He made her repeat it in English. Then he showed her where to stand.

“Three, two one—you’re on!” Justin said as Steve clicked the mouse. The guard looked up and froze. Meiling spoke, and it sounded lovely. Then she smiled and finished. Steve closed the connection.

They watched as the guard picked up the phone and called frantically. The person on the other end apparently was having trouble understanding, because he had to repeat several times. Meiling translated—“He is saying ‘Bombs in ten minutes! Evacuate the base!’ over and over.”

Apparently the call was routed to someone who finally believed and told the guard his message had been received, because he dropped the phone and started shouting. “‘Get out, everyone!’” Meiling translated. An alarm sounded.

They watched as word spread slowly. People started to leave the building, most looking undisturbed, apparently thinking it was a drill.

“Let’s go back and warn people in the fab, too,” Justin said, and Steve returned to the fab where they had detected the grid plates in progress. Meiling was getting into her performance now, and this time she added a bit before the connection was closed.

“What did you add at the end there?” Justin asked her.

“‘Free minds! Free China! Freedom Now!’” she said. “Letting them know what we stand for.”

“I hope that doesn’t confuse them about who we are,” Justin said. “But I think the people involved in trying to kidnap our relatives will know.”

They returned to watch the streets outside the intelligence buildings as people continued to leave the buildings. Steve worked on setting up his program. As the minutes passed, they realized people were not leaving the area, but standing in the road looking back at the buildings.

“Too many people, too close to the other buildings,” Justin said. “And I’m betting only this one is really cleared. Well, it will do for our demonstration. Can you collapse just that one?”

“Sure.” He clicked and deleted several lines from his screen, leaving just one. Then he clicked on a button. They watched as the building in the center of the screen imploded and dust billowed out to blot out the view.

“Next,” Justin said, and Steve returned them to the fab building and joysticked to the outside entrance. People were still leaving, so they had to wait. Finally the flow stopped and they watched as emergency vehicles arrived and firemen started to walk toward the building.

“Oops. Now, Steve, before they get too close.” Steve clicked, and with a whump sound, the building collapsed.

“That was fun,” Steve said. “Can we keep going?”

“No,” Justin said. “There’s a good chance somebody got hurt in all that. We don’t want to get used to it.”

* * * * *

General Li responded to the urgent message and made his way to the meeting room where the others assigned to Project Paifang had gathered. After the botched kidnapping attempts, he had taken the opportunity to shuffle the staff and remove some of the less thoughtful men who had supported the plan. Its failure had resulted in a painful rebuke straight from President Liu, and it was only his solid reputation that had kept him in his position. It was good to get rid of the shark and his friends. The replacements were more circumspect about consequences.

“So we have two of our buildings destroyed after warnings from an apparently beautiful young lady who appeared in the air,” he said. “We’ve lost number one fab and the old headquarters building. While the building we are in now was probably their intended target, the message is clear. It is a response to our unwise action, and their care in warning our people first is admirable.”

New staffer number two, a young woman, spoke up: “Two people did not hear the evacuation order and were seriously injured. One is near death. There are still several missing.”

“Nevertheless, they showed consideration one does not show in warfare. We foolishly killed one of theirs. I am believing they could easily have destroyed the city or crippled our defenses. I will take to the president’s staff my advice: we should continue research toward duplicating their technology, but we will have to take a different route, with some other form of quantum computation. They have warned us not to follow them too closely."

*****

Dylan Foster spent the next several days trying to get support for a new plan. The shocking destruction of a multibillion-dollar Defense Department project had clarified the stakes for the White House and Joint Chiefs. Since it appeared the rebels could detect attempts to duplicate the Vortex-class computers, that approach would have to be scrapped. One of his other ideas would have to become the primary thrust of the project—starting dozens of small projects in different universities around the country that were already doing quantum computing research. His name and office were now authorized to direct every branch of the military and security agency to assist, and he began to coordinate the full power of government, one directive at a time. He would get back at the rebels, one way or another.

Prof. Wilson

"It is fitting that the first use of our new community building should be for a talk by our Professor Emeritus, Walter Wilson," Justin began. "And let's start by giving those great guys in Facilities a hand for putting up such a nice building." He waited for the applause to die down. About half of the community was here. "Isn't it nice to be in a real building and not a tent?" More applause. "And now, welcome the Professor." More applause.

Prof. Wilson got up and took over at the lectern, giving Justin a hug before he went back to his seat.

"So this is the beginning, the inaugural lecture of a new center of learning. It's been suggested that it be called 'The Wilson Center,' and other wits have had their fun with 'Wilson Institute of Technology,' or 'WIT.' Also in the running are 'Wiltech' and 'Wil U,' which would just increase the temptation to joke about the school motto being 'Make It So.' I don't think so! Names should await major donors, as when

Harvard was named after John Harvard, who left the school 780 pounds sterling and 320 books to start their library. We should probably ask for more than that…

"When the time comes and we can be open without fear of attacks, we will have scholars here from around the world—or worlds—studying the new technologies and using them to make great strides in other fields. In this lecture I will outline some of the areas of research I think will be most affected by the gateway.

"First, I must caution you not to let any of this speculation get back to people on Earth, since we are still in a delicate state with them. If you are communicating with relatives or friends back on Earth, do not talk about our bright future and the incredible things we can do with gateways. Or at least not yet. Because until we have a peaceful arrangement with them, Earth governments will only feel more threatened by inflated accounts of our capabilities. We've decided that for some time in the future—possibly years—the full import of the gateway technology will have to be kept secret from those on Earth. This is both for our defense and to limit the disruption on Earth itself.

"This is the first session of many to come, and you are reminded that other than the bare fact of gateway transport, other developments to come are to be discussed only with others cleared for it. Those in this room, mostly.

"We intend to create a new university here which will do both research and teaching with access to the new tools the gateway offers. I imagine that later, when full use of the technology is public, this will become a thriving center for scholars and students from everywhere —Earth and colony planets. Millions will participate online. But there will always be a need to meet here, face-to-face, to establish ties and work informally.

"Question?" said one of the older Grey Tribe programmers. "Where does the money come from to run this new university?"

"That is always a good question to ask," Prof Wilson said. "We haven't established an economy yet, and it's unclear how this colony will generate revenues, other than a tax on design patents and copyrights yet to be established. For now we steal it. Don't look shocked!—consider it a very small tax on corrupt Earth governments to establish a much fairer system.

"But to continue—Many of you are the right people to form the core of the teaching and research we will be doing someday. When the current struggle is over, I hope many of you will stay on to help us. And so consider as you listen how you might participate, as I go over these research areas.

"A note on where we are. When Steve did his search for close planets most similar to Earth, with atmosphere, climate, gravity, and light characteristics suitable for human habitation, he found this planet, 51 Pegasi c, which we are calling New Earth. What he did not know—because he didn't think to look it up!—was that this star system is famous in astronomical history.

"51 Pegasi b was the first exoplanet ever detected around a normal star, because it is so massive and so close to its star that the star jiggles with the planet's 4-day orbital period. It was dubbed a 'Hot Jupiter,' and many similar massive planets were soon detected orbiting close to other stars. When more sensitive methods were developed, it was found that most stars had planetary systems, most systems had many planets, and terrestrial planets were incredibly common.

"It was thought when the first 'Hot Jupiter,' our new neighbor 51 Pegasi b, was found that it must have formed far out in the accretion disk where conditions are right for formation of gas giants like Jupiter. Theory at the time had this star's thicker accretion disk exerting enough drag on the new giant to gradually decrease its orbit until, today, it is far closer to its star than Mercury is to the sun, orbiting in only 4 days. It was also thought that the gradual inward sweep of a giant planet would surely have ejected or swallowed all smaller planets and left a barren system. Later simulations showed that much of the material in the accretion disk would re-form behind the migrating giant and allow smaller planet formation to continue, in many cases. As here with 51 Pegasi, where we have found at least five more planets that accompany New Earth.

"Not only have we answered that question, but we now have the technology to observe millions of stars and planetary systems as they form. While we don't have a time machine, by looking at large numbers of examples in different stages of evolution, we will easily be able to tell what the general rules are. We can sense the composition of the insides of stars and the cores of planets…

"The 51 Pegasi system is high in 'metal' as astronomers define metal, meaning it has more of the elements beyond hydrogen and helium, notably carbon and oxygen. These heavier elements were formed by processing in earlier stars which then ejected material in supernova explosions. Because the 51 Pegasi system is somewhat richer in these elements than the solar system, New Earth has more water than Old Earth, and more vulcanism, but simpler tides from the lack of a large moon.

"Preliminary work by our biologists suggests life began on New Earth somewhat later than on Earth. Plants are similar to what might have been found on Earth during the early Cretaceous period, with photosynthesis based on a chemical quite similar to chlorophyll. While there is some mid-sized ocean life, they have found no large land animals—just exoskeletal creatures like crabs or primitive insects. They speculate that a fairly recent mass extinction from asteroid impact[3] killed all land creatures, leaving only plant seeds and spores and smaller sea creatures. Fossils might tell the story, when we have time to search for them. Greater access to remote viewing has helped survey the planet better, and refinements to gateway technology will provide undersurface scanning abilities.

"We lucked out when Steve picked New Earth, since we came here without a thorough investigation of the planet and its possible hazards. We now know we have no natural enemies here, and Earth plants will grow in local soils, so we can look forward to local produce someday. But we are going to need more planets quite soon to offer to the Earth-bound in need of space and freedom.

"Steve's preliminary scan identified dozens of likely planets within 500 light-years, where he stopped searching. Now that he has help with the software, I can announce that a team using much more detailed criteria, and doing automated mapping via gateway, has found at least a *million*—yes, a million—planets in our galaxy alone that meet the criteria of human-friendly star, climate, atmosphere, orbital stability, and length of day. Before any colony would be started on each, a lot more research would have to be done—unlike the rushed way we arrived here. But there is room enough for humanity to expand for thousands of years without having to build a Dyson sphere[4] or Ringworld[5]—and we now have the tools to do that, if we needed to.

"But so many other scientific fields will be enormously enlarged by the new tools:

"Astronomy and cosmology: Instead of finding windows in the electromagnetic spectrum where we can observe the rest of the universe despite obscuring dust and clouds, we can directly sense objects out to the edge of the current universe and be certain of their composition. This will provide far more reliable data than we have currently.

"Biology: with millions of alien biospheres to investigate, comparative biology will accelerate. Just as with stars, we can see snapshots of millions of different systems in different stages of evolution, and trillions of life-forms. The Earth's catalog of life will be tiny by comparison.

"Archaeology: We don't know yet if we will find dead alien civilizations and their artifacts, but I would guess we will. Steve has tried searching locally and found no evidence of energy-using civilizations in 500 light-years, but there may be some out there—which we will carefully avoid until we are more established ourselves. We don't know if a typical civilization finds the substrate technology and expands, finds it and disappears into it as an uploaded civilization, or if they never find it at all and we were just freakishly lucky to go down that path of inquiry. Something to look forward to… but in any case, archaeologists and paleontologists on Earth now have a tool to look deep into soil and rock for remains, without digs or disturbance.

"Medicine: The gateway is already the ultimate scanning tool, allowing viewing in realtime of any location in the body. There is talk among the biologists of using this scanning ability to capture chemistry in motion—the ability to watch and guide DNA replication and cellular processes. More immediately lifesaving ideas include detection and elimination of disease organisms and cancers throughout the body in one pass; microsurgery by software which could operate without external incisions; and ready availability of transplant organs by duplication, which I understand is already a controversial idea.

"Brain Science: With the ability to scan and store the complex arrangement of the brain exactly, we may now look forward to a day when its operation can be understood completely. And even before that, we may find a way to simulate a particular brain's operations in a substrate AI program. It is just possible we will be able to upload ourselves with our complete personality and memories at some point. I, for one, will welcome our new post-human overlords!

"Physics and Chemistry: With the detailed knowledge of particles and their interactions which can be derived from querying them, many of the mysteries of physics and chemistry can be investigated in detail. Superconducting and superfluid materials. Dark matter and dark energy. Custom-made forms of matter and nanomaterials. Direct sensing of condensed-matter objects like neutron stars and pulsars.

"Earth and planetary science: With direct sensing of the structure and composition of Earth and other planets, our guesses from external data can now be confirmed or disproved. It is possible detailed mapping of faults will lead to strain relief programs to eliminate earthquakes as a hazard. Weather can be directly sensed and global warming possibly controlled by reducing solar heating of selected areas. Damaging storms can be monitored and disrupted.

"Computer and cognitive science: The availability of infinite space and power for computing in the substrate will open up new possibilities for intelligent programs and modular intelligence. If the Internet seems to have started to build a kind of world intelligence of connected data and processing, the universal Net and substrate computation will be a jump to a much higher level. Which may end up looking like Teilhard de Chardin's[6] Omega Point, the collection of all knowledge at the endpoint of the universe—but such quasi-religious, philosophical ideas are speculation about a far future.

"Engineering and architecture: The replication and creation of new materials can extend to any scale, so ultimately even the largest structures can be built by substrate engineering and design. Though it's far from clear yet what new infrastructure and buildings will be required in a new world of material abundance and instant transport, design and construction of nearly everything will change.

"Space exploration: The gateway would seem to eliminate the need for actual spacecraft or starships. Why spend time traveling between hospitable planets when you can step directly from one to another? Why explore using ships and probes when you can view, sense, and manipulate anything you want from a safe distance? But if people want to, ships can be built and powered by gateway tech, and transported immediately into harsh environments. Some people may want to travel in real space as a hobby, or for recreation.

"Humanities: Aside from the major effects gateway technology will have on human civilization, it is likely we will soon encounter alien civilizations, or at least be able to study their remaining works and records. This will provide far more examples of cultures and cultural evolution in many more contexts than we have records of on Earth, and when combined with studies in evolution and exobiology, augment studies in history, linguistics, and psychology.

"So there's going to be an immense amount of crunchy new research for anyone who can let their imaginations roam. We speculate about alien civilizations, and Steve tells me he has seen evidence of such civilizations which he has not pursued because he was worried that even casual observation might give away our presence here somehow and bring down a hostile reaction. Steve worries that other civilizations using substrate technologies may have been there a long time and know how to subvert or damage our own use of it. So until we know more, we plan to play safe, stay local, and avoid interaction. By 'local' he means in the Local Group,[7] which contains our galaxy, Andromeda, a few other large galaxies, and about 50 dwarf galaxies. There are upwards of one trillion stars in the local group, and probably more planets. So while planets so similar to Earth we can live on them without much effort are a tiny fraction of all planets, that still leaves 'only' some millions in our neighborhood.

"That's my talk for today. Please email me if you want to be put on the interest list for future meetings. Questions?"

Prof. Bubna raised his hand and asked, "If we are ultimately thinking human intelligence will be uploaded to the substrate, why go to the trouble of expanding and colonizing in the years before that?"

"Humanity is in great danger right now, loaded up with terrifying weapons and hostile governments who could wipe the entire species out. Or for that matter, an asteroid could strike, or a nearby star go supernova, wiping all life from the planet. It may be decades, if ever, before we figure out how to upload humans into the substrate, and it is far from certain that we would be safe there, given we have no idea what civilizations may have preceded us on this path or what attitudes they might have toward the new kids on the block.

"There is safety in diversity, and the more habitats we live in, the safer we are from complete destruction as a species."

"I thought you would say that," Bubna said. "I'm not quite ready to go virtual myself, but I'd rather be alive as a simulation than dead for real."

"How do you know you're real now?" Prof.Wilson said, raising an eyebrow. He smiled as a few people chuckled. "Any more questions?"

Dinner Party

Justin had been too busy to spend much time with his parents in the weeks since they had arrived. When he did run into them, he was usually on his way to an urgent meeting with someone, and he had to excuse himself quickly. Even at meals, he rarely saw them until it was too late to eat with them, and they had started to go to the second mess tent on the expanding edge of the town. So Justin had started to feel guilty, and he wasn't surprised when he ran into his mother and she insisted that he and Samantha come to dinner that evening.

Justin and Samantha rapped on the doorframe of the deluxe tent his parents were assigned to. His mother greeted them and showed them in.

"This is very nice," Samantha said. "I haven't see anyone else with a tent that looks so well-decorated. Where did you find art?" She pointed to a painting of grass and trees hung from a tent rail.

"One of the young men from Italy brought his paints," Justin's mother said, "and he gets the backing from shipping crates. Very creative, and the first art inspired by the scenery here."

"We have no decor," Justin said, "since we've been a little busy and eventually we'll have real buildings. And furniture."

"No reason we have to live like Neanderthals," his father said. "It doesn't take much time to make it more homey."

Justin rolled his eyes, and decided to change the subject. "I understand they have you two listening to intercepts all day."

"Not all day," his father said. "Just a few hours in the morning."

"It's usually dull," his mother said, "but once in awhile you hear something really interesting, and get to write it up. Like a few days ago, when someone in a meeting of big-shots in the military mentioned 'the destruction of our lab' and someone told him not to talk openly about it."

"We think they've been told someone has bugged their offices so they should keep the most sensitive subjects to encrypted email for now," Justin said. "Which we can read over their shoulders, but it's a clever way to make it harder for us to listen in without telling the staff about us."

Justin's mother had set the table with appetizers, and directed them to sit down while she made drinks.

"Where did you get the guacamole?" Samantha asked.

"The kitchen had a few avocados left," Justin's mother said. "I asked them to make some, and they did."

"Delicious. I'm missing variety lately," Justin said.

"You're not kidding," Samantha said. "And they're purposely making the lowest common denominator in food, because if they spice it up some people complain. The Indians complain because there's not enough vegetarian, and everything is too bland for them. And so on."

"The problems of a communist society," Justin's father said, "where the state—that would be you, Justin—provides goods without knowing what people actually want."

Justin laughed. "More like having a one-restaurant town. That will change, and when Steve gets the replicator working we'll all be able to order whatever we want."

"So when is Steve going to open up development so he doesn't personally bottleneck everything?" Samantha said, looking at Justin.

"He's working on a way of supervising what goes into programs without having to write them all himself," Justin said. "He's used some modules added by the Grey Tribe programmers. The worry is security—that someone will insert a Trojan Horse that could give them control over the apps. He's thinking through how to authorize use without allowing abuse. Which is a hard problem."

"He's an amazing young man," Justin's father said. "But, Justin, you are, too. Without you, he would never have been able to do the things you've done together. I'm really proud to see you leading people and making mostly the right decisions under a lot of pressure. Your mother and I are so proud of you."

"Yes, we are," Justin's mother said. "You've grown up and become a fine person. I may have had my doubts when I had to nag you to clean up your room—"

"Thanks for mentioning that!" Justin said, laughing. "I cleaned when necessary. It's more efficient that way."

"—But I should never have doubted you," his mother continued. "And Samantha, you're just as impressive."

"Thank you, Mrs. Smith," Samantha said, "it's hard to keep up in this crowd."

OS

The next day Justin found Steve at his desk, as usual.

"How is progress on the OS?" Justin said. "Everyone wants to know when you'll let some of our crack programmers put up more apps. You need help."

"Progress is slow because I have so many urgent tasks. But it's taking shape. I've duplicated and fail-safed the boot loader program so there is now a pool of such programs waiting, and the first to grab a token gets the task; this is to provide faster service and to weed out any loader that has been damaged. Loaders also stop and check the other loaders periodically, and kill them if they don't pass checksum, so in case a stray error or conflict with another computation damages one, it is quickly replaced with clean code."

"So who gets to upload programs?" Justin asked.

"The loaders will monitor the area around talismans that have the 'programmer' authorization and load programs properly presented by the user, with a biometric authentication check—eventually DNA scan—to assure identity. Authorized programmers are you and me, so far."

"Me? I wouldn't dare load or run my code. I don't know enough yet."

"But if anything happens to me, you may have to."

"That brings up our succession plan," Justin said, "which we don't have yet. It somehow has to be connected with government, so the authorized government can direct changes to the AIs and the rules they follow—the law—without leaving any way for bad guys to take control."

"I expect this will grow out of the OS as it becomes more a rule-based system," Steve said. "The OS has many jobs. It decides if the user has permissions to run a particular app. It supervises the apps and runs them with necessary permissions, and checking any local conditions—say, for example, a user with a gun wants to be transported to a region whose regional law prohibits weapons without permits. The OS checks legal conditions at the target, determines there's an object matching a gun template on the user and the user has no regional gun permit, and concludes the user cannot be transported unless he or she leaves the gun behind. Eventually transport can be screened to prevent life-forms that might become pests or plagues in a different region. The idea is to start with a simple OS to manage the apps, and make it smarter and smarter about how it does that. And only programmers can upload apps or instruct the OS."

"Where do the AIs come in?"

"AIs are glorified apps that are treated like users by the OS," Steve said. "They are authorized to use certain apps in certain ways, but not to code their own programs—at least not yet. The runaway scenario of AIs programming more advanced AIs and creating a superintelligence is unlikely, but we want to make sure we control any such advance. Think of an AI designed to teach children; at first it just knows how to present lessons and keep track of progress, and it has access to presentation and monitoring subroutines to communicate with students. At this stage it is much like systems already in use, and still needs human teachers to assist in tutoring. As more and more modules are added, the AI gets better at judging the emotional state of the student and performing as a human coach would. At some point only a few students require human help to progress."

"That sounds great," Justin said, "but where is the part where you don't have to program everything?"

"I am working on a sandbox that allows others to come in and use an interpreted language to program simple apps that use only modules I've approved, and can only sense and act on the real world in limited ways. So then I can have others create custom always-on gateways, for example, which we're going to need soon for the colonization program. I can't set up a thousand gateways by myself and get anything else done!"

"So other people will be able to write and upload these limited apps?"

"Yes, that's the idea," Steve said. "They won't be allowed to use the full power of substrate programming and their code won't have any way of attacking the OS or the loaders, so there's no way to write a virus or a Trojan and get it to execute."

"And when might we have that? And have documentation so other people can start learning how to write apps?"

"I have the framework of the OS up. So far it looks like a Unix kernel.

I should farm out the interpreter coding to a language person—it might end up looking like MultiScheme, or LISP, since we have so many of those guys. Give me another few weeks."

In Council

The Council had convened to discuss the strategy again after intercepts showed increasing discussion of the rebels' destruction of Chinese and US defense facilities.

"As word of our abilities has leaked to the upper echelons of most of the world's security and intelligence establishments, the likelihood of a dangerous reaction increases," Justin said.

"We need to confront them directly and open up diplomatic channels," Ben said. "I think it is time to tell them what we plan and why it's in their best interests to go along."

"It's a shame you can't just talk to them on social media," Samantha said. "We could have a Facebook page laying out our program."

"They control the DNS servers in the countries who really need to listen," Michael McCulloch said. "No one outside the neutral zones would let their citizens see our pages or Tweets. And the Dark Net has been wiped out, too."

"Samantha," Justin said, "would you be willing to compile a list of all the diplomatic contacts for all of the major players? Like an address book of the top few diplomats from every country, plus others for the security establishments?"

"I could round up some help and try," she said, "but I think most important people have no public addresses."

"Well, do your best," Justin said. "We'll include in our messages a request for better contact information. They'll want us to know how to reach them quickly. And for now we don't want to go public, and they don't want us to, either."

"So what are we going to say in this private-to-hundreds-of-people message?" Ben said. "I think we should directly state, since they already know, that we have taken action against China and the US to prevent them from attacking us, and that any further efforts to develop technology to attack us will result in larger strikes against their defense facilities."

"In case any of the smaller players gets ideas," Justin said. "An attractive prize brings out the most aggressive power-seekers. We have to make it clear there's a new sheriff in town, and things are gonna change."

"A suggestion," Prof. Wilson said. "You want to scare them but not so much they panic. You want to sell them on the benefits of agreeing with us. One of the things they most fear is an informed population, so one of the threats should be to reveal their weakness in public. Another thing they fear is loss of their own positions if the government changes or is defeated by a superior force. So offering them a face-saving continuity—even if the reality changes—might persuade them more than demands they let go of power."

Steve cleared his throat and said, "I have been working on an idea. We can destroy their facilities one by one, but if you want to really change the equation, why not take away their most dangerous weapons? The nuclear warheads. It would be easy to use the search capability to find concentrations of U-235 and the other isotopes in warheads. We can transport them to someplace safe and tell them we've done it, and threaten to make it public."

"I think that would make the stakes clear," Ben said, "and has the additional benefit of immediately making the world a safer place. And it makes us safer, too." Heads were nodding in assent.

"Where would you store them?" Samantha asked.

"Someplace far away in space but stable, like one of Jupiter's Lagrange points.[8] We could destroy them instead, but we might need them later ourselves."

"Notify them that we're doing that and add a threat that we will make it public if we don't come to an agreement with the major powers," Ben said. "Warn them that any hostile action will result is further destruction of their weapons and defense facilities. Tell them we will stop any aggressive attack by one nation on another, and any state that tries will be punished."

"I have some ideas," Michael McCulloch said. "How about ending all bans on encryption, and all harassment of Grey Tribe members and organizations? How about the political prisoners being released?"

"Keeping in mind we don't want to tip our hand," Justin said, "so we might not want to demand too much until we have them agreeing that we can do a better job maintaining the peace than they do. We're not going to leave the security states with many excuses to continue oppressing their own people, but we don't need to let the millions of people who work for the security forces know their lives are going to change, just yet. We want them to heave a sigh of relief that they can relax and stop worrying about the Russians, or the Chinese, or the Americans…."

"We want to sound like responsible guardians who will help them secure their people," Prof. Wilson said. "And preserve the jobs of all those security people. Until some later time."

"So what are our action items here?" Justin said. "Ben, you and I will draft the statement. Steve, you work on the getting the warheads identified and the software set up to snarf them all at once. Samantha, we need those contacts to put out the statement and get things going on diplomacy. Michael, you guys draft a document on what you'd like to see to free up the Internets—we'll push that point later. And how are things going on getting news people here to document what we're doing?"

"We're talking with the BBC reporter—she's interested. There are some conditions to negotiate on our approval of her transmissions and the like. We have feelers out to some other reporters from neutral countries, but she's the best."

"Good, keep working on that," Justin said. "I have a feeling we're going to be going public sooner than we might like. We'll need to have everything ready before sending out the statement, so it may take us a month or two to prepare."

Bubna shifted in his seat and said, "One more item. We stopped shipping in supplies from the Swedish warehouse a month ago because of concerns that the CIA might trace back our grid order to a middleman who knew the address of the warehouse. We're running low on some items and surveillance shows nothing unusual happening there. The guards are wondering why the warehouse is filling up."

"So you're suggesting it's safe to start getting our supplies again?" Justin said.

"Maybe not safe," Bubna said, "but necessary. If we're going to send out messages drawing more attention to us soon, it might be wise to pick up more supplies before we do. Then we can endure a long period when we're unable to resupply."

"Okay," Justin said. "Make sure you scan the area before opening the gate to make sure nothing unusual is happening."

"Of course," Bubna said. "We always check first."

Part Three: Arms Control

Chapter Five: Ominous Quiet

Air Force One

Justin took a look at his email and found a note from his mother: "I noticed this coming through on the Dylan Foster feed and thought you would want to see it immediately. I get a kick out of seeing the lengths they will go to to try to avoid our eavesdropping." He opened the attachment:

```
TRANSCRIPT

Intercept from vicinity of Dylan Foster.
Location: Air Force One over Washington, DC

Identified Attendees:

President Elizabeth Howard Stanton
Director National Security Lab Dylan Foster
Defense Secretary Sheila Edwards
Homeland Security Secretary Lewis Jackson
National Security Lab Liaison Christine Immerman

DYLAN FOSTER: Madam President, thank you for pick-
```

ing me up and agreeing to meet under these circumstances. Your staff put this together remarkably quickly.

PRESIDENT: I've read the analyst's reports on what happened to your lab and the Chinese intelligence building. I thought these people were dangerous before, but your precautions are more than warranted. They may be more of a threat to our security than the Soviet Union when they copied our hydrogen bombs.

DYLAN FOSTER: They can listen in on virtually any of our offices and destroy or steal at will. I have reworked the plan for Project Arrow to recognize that. From now on, all research is going to be distributed to hundreds of smaller labs working in different, overlapping areas of quantum computing.

HOMESEC SEC: Given their ability to intercept every machine we've tried to build and their increasing capabilities, we agree that Mr. Foster's plan is the only one likely to succeed, though it will take time.

PRESIDENT: How much time?

DYLAN FOSTER: We can't predict when a breakthrough will happen, since we're asking our teams to find a new way of reaching the same capabilities but using different quantum computing pathways. We've recruited nearly every major researcher in the field, and even started new teams under the brightest stars in other areas of physics and computation. So our chances of a speedy breakthrough increase just by having so many teams at work.

PRESIDENT: But how long? Give me an estimate at the most likely time it will take for one of these teams to succeed.

DYLAN FOSTER: Two years. And when one team does

well, we'll redirect many of the others to adopt their approach and speed up development.

DEFENSE SEC: But until you succeed, we're completely open to attack. All of our defenses could be destroyed in a few days. And we'd like to know how we're going to recover from the complete destruction of our 'super-secret' underground facility.

PRESIDENT: We'll pull some magic in the budget and get your facility replaced, Sheila. But I think you should approach the matter as an opportunity to rethink big, expensive facilities. They don't seem to do well with this new mode of warfare.

DEFENSE SEC: We are revamping the parameters given to our analysts to encourage decentralized and duplicated facilities, with failover. This will take time to be reflected in our requests.

PRESIDENT: Unless we get this technology for ourselves, there may be no point in fixed defense facilities. So getting back to how we do that as quickly as possible. Or how we remove the threat they present to us.

DYLAN FOSTER: I was having difficulty getting cooperation from the CIA and the NSA for followup on the grids we found being built for them in Germany. Thank you, Madam President, for directing them to cooperate. Unfortunately they were unable to trace back through the maze of shell companies and agents who ordered the grids, but there is a team at the NSA doing data-mining of shipping and commercial orders to try to find any anomalous patterns.

PRESIDENT: Does the CIA need me to authorize extraordinary rendition[9] for some of those agents? It can't be that long a chain.

CHRISTINE IMMERMAN: Unfortunately the agents can't be found. They were warned and appear to be in hiding.

PRESIDENT: Well, any that turn up should be shipped here and questioned until we have the next names in the chain. I want to emphasize that all necessary resources should be used to track them down.

DYLAN FOSTER: Yes, Madam President. I'll make it clear to them that we need more people on our teams.

PRESIDENT: Lewis, anything to add?

HOMESEC SEC: We're monitoring the campus and their friends and family, at least the ones who are left. Rumors are rampant, but as far as we can tell the rebels haven't contacted anyone. We're still trying to plant agents in the Grey Tribe but we have trouble finding agents who have the right background to pass for Grey Tribe types.

DYLAN FOSTER: [Laughing] It takes years of obsessive training, and if you succeeded, they'd no longer be good agents. Sorry, I didn't mean to laugh. But you really don't understand these people like I do.

PRESIDENT: I have to admit I didn't like the idea of bringing you onboard, Mr. Foster. But you have done more in a short time than anyone who's risen through normal channels. And your knowledge of these people may prove to be vital to controlling them.

Mission: Impossible

Dylan spent a few days settling into a new rented office on the beltway in Maryland, chosen to be inconspicuous and far from any government facility. It was in a mostly-empty strip mall which featured a good Thai restaurant, which would be handy for lunch. He brought along his staff—the ones who were willing to work with someone obviously targeted—and they settled into corporate housing rentals.

His new plan would keep direct communications to secured, encrypted cell phones and anonymized Internet connections. He hoped this would limit the rebels' ability to listen in, and that they would lose track of the transfers of orders via multiple encrypted emails. If they found him, he would have to go to more extreme solutions, but for now this was as much as he could practically do.

Christine Immerman drove up to meet with him, and they took a walk through the mall parking lot to a fast-food joint where they settled on an outside table near the drive-through, where the noisy environment would probably make listening in more difficult. Then Dylan handed her a secure cell with headphones and picked up his own, dialing to connect. Hers rang and she answered it, putting on the earphones.

“Whisper into the phone handset and I'll still be able to hear it,” Dylan said. “Any listening point would have to be either in your ear or at the handset to catch anything.”

“I hope this isn't going to be typical of meetings in this new era,” Christine said.

Dylan held out his hand and checked the sky. “The rain has stopped, at least. So here's what I asked you up here to talk about—we have a lead. I didn't want to call you or send a message because every site they know about is probably being monitored. I'm not sure you can be too paranoid with these people.”

“So what is the lead?” Christine said.

“Last week I got a message from the NSA team. They did finally succeed in finding anomalous patterns of commerce for the kinds of materials the rebels would likely be using, and came up with a list of suspicious sites where large quantities of goods were delivered, but little was picked up."

"That's progress," Christine said. "I hope I was helpful in getting the NSA's White House Liaison to impress on them the president's desire to find these people quickly."

"That may have helped," Dylan said. "They seem more eager to help now than before. But I've handed the problem to the CIA, which has local assets. They've already done some effective ground surveillance to rule out all of the sites but one, a warehouse near Stockholm which surveillance confirms only receives shipments. Further investigation shows a shell company leasing the warehouse and a contract labor company providing staff and security, which confirms that it's likely to be theirs. So I have directed the CIA to plan an action to get a SEAL team into place inside the warehouse when the gateway is opened to retrieve their goods. Because of the high probability they are monitoring the whole area around the warehouse, I have instructed them to build a tunnel from a warehouse a block away that will come up under theirs."

"That sounds extreme. Won't the locals notice?"

"This may be our only chance to penetrate to their base of operations," Dylan said, "so we can't take any chances. And the CIA has done ops like this before—of course you rarely hear about them because they cover their tracks. Local governments don't want to reveal the CIA's operations even when they find out about them because it would make the local authorities look incompetent."

"So what is the plan of action?" Christine said. "We will have to run it by the president and NSC for approval."

"The plan is to have the team ready and a ramp built in the tunnel leading up to the floor of the warehouse, with charges set to cut through the floor. They'll have a micro-cam set up through a wall penetration, and when the cam shows the gateway open, the floor section will be cut loose and fall to the ramp, opening the way for the team."

"I used to love *Mission: Impossible* reruns as a child," Christine said, smiling faintly. "This sounds like one of their plans."

"It's risky, but I'm quite sure a more direct approach will fail. We need our people inside the building while the gate is open, and any sign of activity outside the building will warn them off."

"What are the team's orders? If they penetrate the gateway, what then?"

"I'm asking the DoD to give the team a backpack nuke," Dylan said. "They'll cross over and establish a secure area around the gateway computer, and try to capture Steve Duong and return him. If they fail at that, they leave the nuke set to go off and return."

"We want Steve Duong," Christine said. "I'm not sure the president will approve of using a nuke—too many things could go wrong. It's bad enough if our team is caught in an operation in a neutral country, but a disaster if they're carrying a nuke."

"Nuking them is the only way to be sure. Any conventional explosive a man could carry might not get them all."

"I'll support your request, but understand it's not likely to get the green light. The president wants this technology for us. Blowing the inventor and his friends away won't give us that. Of all the ways this could go wrong, the worst is having one of our nukes go off in a neutral city, and second-worst is our people being caught with one."

Dylan slumped. "But if the team fails, we may never get another chance."

"So make sure they don't fail. The CIA has a lot of clever devices that might be useful. Ask them for access to their labs."

* * * * *

In the surveillance tents on New Earth, an operator noticed there had been no transcribed words from Dylan Foster's bug program for some time. The video showed him sitting with a woman outside a fast-food joint where noise levels were high—cars were driving by only a few feet away. It seemed odd to her that they would eat together while wearing earbuds, so she made a note of it in the file. The note went unread in the forest of reports.

Jim McDonald

Justin remembered his talk with the gruff Homeland Security guy, Jim McDonald, after Homeland Security arrested and held him. As the hazards of confronting Earth governments increased, he wished he had someone to advise him who was experienced with the way they thought. And since McDonald was someone who had helped him escape at considerable personal risk, he decided to have the surveillance team try to find him. He composed an email query to the crack team in Surveillance asking for research on current whereabouts of Jim McDonald with what he could remember—was his title Director of Threat Assessment at Homeland Security?

The next day he had a report in email. McDonald had retired and moved to a small mountain town in North Carolina. The employee newsletter had even run pictures from his retirement party. His new address and pertinent data had been retrieved from credit reporting web sites. He considered what he should say—selling McDonald on joining the cause without giving too much away. *Not that it matters, now that half the spooks in the world know about us.*

He opened the web app that allowed him to call for a window to anywhere, and pasted in the address from the email. He was shown a map view of a small house; he selected a point inside. The viewer showed him an interior view. He scrolled around until he spotted Jim McDonald tapping on a pad computer and drinking from a mug.

Justin clicked on the button to make the window larger and two-way.

McDonald looked suitably surprised but controlled his reaction.

"Mr. McDonald," Justin said. "We found you."

"So you have. And call me Jim. I'm not official any more, just Jim."

"That's why I'm calling. We are running a pretty successful operation here. We have a ground-floor opportunity for a security specialist."

"See the world. Join the Army!" McDonald said. "I remember when that sounded good. I'm a bit old for a new posting."

They talked about the developing situation, and McDonald asked for an hour to think it over. Justin signed off and set an alarm.

When the alarm went off, Justin was reading more surveillance transcripts. He put that aside and opened a new call to McDonald.

"I'll join you guys for awhile," McDonald said. "I've been hearing rumors about what you've been up to, and it sounds a lot more interesting than what I've got going here. So sign me up."

Justin could see a pair of suitcases and some grocery bags on the floor behind him. "That all you need?" he said. "Let me open a real gateway window for you." Justin adjusted the size and parameters, and the gateway window enlarged to create a doorway. "Hand me your bags."

Jim handed him the baggage one piece at a time, and then Jim himself came through. "Nice way to travel," Jim said. "None of those long waits at Security."

"It's good to see you again. I want to thank you again for understanding what we're trying to do."

"I think you're fools to go up against it, but one thing I do know is that our government is getting crazier. Someone needed to do something. You have a better shot at changing things than anyone has had in a long time. I'll help you out until you no longer need me."

* * * * *

The Council met to hear from its provisional new member, Jim McDonald, who had spent a few days reviewing intelligence files and then prepared a report on security issues. Justin sat between Samantha and Prof. Wilson and listened.

"The threat of immediate duplication of gateway technology through cloned Vortex computers appears to have receded," Jim said. "The players have given up trying to duplicate the machines, since we can detect any such efforts immediately. The longer-term worry is that they will find another form of quantum computing that is not so easily discovered. Steve tells me he can't detect quantum computing per se. Care to comment, Steve?"

"There's no way to search for quantum computation generally," Steve said. "We can search for certain arrangements, types of particles, chemical elements, and other concrete factors. So we'd have to know what is special about the physical embodiment of the machine they are using before we could find it. And there are so many possibilities, some of them involving silicon chips like the billions of others."

"That's why I'm suggesting we identify and keep watch on the people most likely to be working on quantum computing," Jim said. "There aren't very many and we know from their published papers and web sites who they are. Dylan Foster is known to have recruited such researchers. If we watch them, we can find out what they are doing. And disrupt their work if necessary."

"I agree that's a good idea," Justin said. "But our people are already too busy with surveillance to take on a lot more."

"Steve tells me has has some plans in that area," Jim said. "An object tracking program, which would let you select a person and automatically follow them even in motion."

Justin looked at Steve, who nodded. "We could definitely use that,"

Justin said. "We can't risk implanting talismans in all the people we'd like to keep track of."

"Once you've identified an object," Steve said, "the program checks constantly to gauge how the object's boundaries have moved every millisecond or so. It could lose someone, but only if they were hit by a truck or something."

"Okay, let's set that up," Justin said. "What other actions do we need to take to reduce our risks?"

"One of the problems you have," Jim said, "is being a big fat target. It was worse in a sense when the few Vortex machines you had were the only devices that could open gateways. Now you have the talismans and apps to open them wherever you might be, but all of you are still in one place, so you're still a temptation to those who would want to remove you from their list of worries. You won't be safe until the weapons you have at your disposal are too dispersed to be taken out in one blow. Which means you need to do what the nuclear powers did—send out the equivalent of submarines to maintain a credible threat of retaliation. Multiple sites on multiple planets, any one of which can take over from this camp if necessary."

"But—" Justin thought for a moment. "We wouldn't have the time and people to split up into separate colonies for some time."

"I can see that," Jim said. "I'm telling you that all of you located on one spot on one planet are too easily taken out. It's too risky to open a gateway to Earth where some government or terror group can toss in a bomb. You shouldn't be using any single location on Earth where you predictably open a gateway. You won't be safe to open gateways to Earth until there's nothing here you can't afford to lose."

"That makes our supply depot in Sweden a big risk," Bubna said. "But we need regular deliveries of all sorts of things."

"I think you need to rethink that," Jim said. "It might be safe enough for now, but make plans to change. It should be much safer to transport goods at random from commercial warehouses. Less convenient because somebody has to identify and check out each one individually, but until you have peace with the Earth governments and have redundant facilities to retaliate, I'd recommend you stop using your Swedish warehouse."

"We're monitoring the surrounding area closely," Justin said. "We'd catch any effort to get close to the warehouse. But I see your point, and we'll work on a plan to change to random sourcing. Now that we can transport objects instead of opening gateways, it would be much easier for a few people to use the object move program to collect the supplies we need. But the losses will be noticed."

"If you work from a large number of warehouses," Jim said, "the losses will be chalked up to normal shrinkage. Stuff disappears all the time in transit, more often than not by insider theft."

"Okay, we get away from using the Swedish warehouse. Another item for our lengthening list of urgent things to do," Justin said.

Quinn

Justin waited for a reasonable hour in California, then pulled down a menu and selected Quinn's entry for his next call. The preview showed an empty desk, but soon he heard rustling sounds and Quinn came into the frame. Justin clicked to start the two-way call.

"Mr. Quinn," Justin said. "Is the coast clear?"

"Clear enough," he said, sitting down and turning on an e-cigarette. "I've put my receptionist on an afternoon-only schedule. Almost all my business now comes from you people anyway, so I don't need her much. So what's up?"

Justin remembered the first call he had made to Quinn using the gateway—Quinn had obviously been surprised, but only asked how it was accomplished when Justin called the next time. Justin told him the story intended for outsiders—it was a triumph of remote sensing. But he had had to discuss transport from the Swedish warehouse later on, so Quinn knew they were able to pull goods through the gateway.

“We've had some security issues come up.” Justin said. “Thanks for getting the word out about the grid plates stolen from the German fab —we have confirmation that your agents covered their tracks well and weren't identified.”

“They're used to using single-use identities and mail drops,” Quinn said. “If they weren't careful, someone would have put them out of business long ago.”

“But we have some improved capabilities that make it less important to use a single transshipment point. We've built up a stock of prefab buildings and and computers. And it is a security risk to continue using the warehouse in Stockholm. So you should stop ordering supplies for the time being, aiming for a cutoff date at the warehouse about two weeks from now.”

“Does this mean my fees will go down?” Quinn took a long drag on the e-cig. “And how will you get supplies?”

“We'll still need your assistance,” Justin said. “While we won't spend as much on supply orders through you, we'll pay you a continuing retainer. The heat is about to be turned up on all of us, and we want you on our side.”

“Sure thing. Cash always makes friends.”

“How would fifty thousand a month do for you?” Justin tried to look like it mattered to him.

“Make it seventy-five. I have lots of fixed costs. Overhead,” Quinn said, taking another drag.

“Seventy,” Justin countered. “Don't be greedy, and you'll have some ground-floor opportunities I can't even tell you about yet."

"Sold," Quinn said. "I've been honest with your funds despite a certain lack of oversight in what I've been spending. I have to admit it's interesting working with you guys. I'd like to see more of 'Wanda.'" Wendy had taken the pseudonym Wanda when dealing with Quinn. Justin could tell from his emphasis that he knew it wasn't her real name and wanted him to know he knew.

"She only needs to come by to drop off cash," Justin said, "and I understand you're holding quite a sum for us already."

"True, the suitcase she dropped off last month was enough for several months. I just enjoy seeing her outfits and listening to her stories. I'm a lonely man."

"I'm sorry to hear that. I'm afraid there's a chance you'll have to bug out at some point if our security is breached. If that happens, we'll help get you out."

"I have contingency plans for everything," Quinn said. "You give the word, and I disappear for an extended vacation."

Justin picked up an envelope from his desk and clicked on the button to open the window to matter. He tossed the envelope through. "Here's a gift, kind of a good-luck charm. Keep it with you at all times and we'll be able to talk to you wherever you are."

"So you really can go through one of these things. I appreciate the confidence you've shown in my discretion—I could probably turn you in for a big reward."

"Probably," Justin said. "But then you'd be a loser who gave up a much greater reward."

"Or you could just be a dreamer who's about to get stepped on."

Autonomous Drone

Dylan approached the gates of the CIA's complex in Langley in his brand-new government car, which was as neutral as it could possibly be. When he tried to look at the car, his eyes slid right by—it was so dull his brain refused to process it. He assumed this was a good quality for a spy's car, and after they checked his name off a list and let him drive in, he was disappointed to see the parking lots filled with older vehicles in a variety of colors and styles.

He made his way to the building where he was supposed to meet his contact from the CIA's Office of Technical Services, where the agency developed and tested custom devices for their field agents. He was told to wait in the lobby, and soon a short, chubby man approached him.

"Dylan Foster?" the man said. "I'm Edwin Zwicky. Call me Ed. I'm one of the people who fit agents for missions."

"Like James Bond's Q."

"Not really," Zwicky said. "I'm not the head of the organization, I just match the mission with the equipment. I don't decide what we research or build, but if you have a special need, I know who to go to for it."

"I assume you've seen the tentative mission plan."

"Yes. Our people will no doubt want some changes—the SEALs are terrific at stealth and fighting, but not all are as smart as you seem to think. You need to keep the plan simple and the number of decision points down. Too many options and they start to get confused."

"We'll work on that with the CIA and the SEALs," Dylan said. "What I need from you is some special hardware. The most powerful bomb you can fit in a backpack, with a dead-man's switch—if our team is taken out, I want their base destroyed."

"That shouldn't be too hard. With modern explosives such a bomb is quite powerful."

"The plan calls for securing an area around the gateway then finding and capturing their key personnel, especially their chief scientist. It would be helpful if we had drones that could search the area and immobilize the people we want while neutralizing others."

"Our capability in that area has already leaked," Zwicky said. "One too many convenient deaths in the Mideast. We have small remote-controlled drones that can search for and follow targets using facial recognition. Targets can be taken out using bullets, poison pellets, anesthetic darts, or explosives. The poison pellets are designed to dissolve and escape detection by autopsy in less-advanced countries."

"That would be ideal, but do you have anything that's autonomous? That can decide and act on its own?"

"Those are still considered too dangerous for use," Zwicky said. "There have been accidents every time we've rolled them out. The software still needs work."

"But in the scenario where the team is overcome or forced to retreat, I'd like to have something that will continue the mission even without a control signal."

"I can take that up with my superiors. We might be willing to release one for your use, provided it is programmed to do nothing on its own unless it loses its control signal. Sort of a hybrid."

"That would work," Dylan said. "I want a backup plan in case the team fails."

Father and Son

Justin and Sam visited his parents for dinner. After drinks and flank steak first prepared and frozen in some industrial kitchen on Earth, they settled down to talk at the table just outside their door.

"I'm looking forward to real barbecue," Justin's father said.

"Chef Peretti is planning on a barbecue picnic for the Fourth of July," Samantha said. "We have a fervent minority who love grilled meat. I'm not sure what he'll do for the veg contingent. Grilled eggplant and Portobello mushrooms, maybe."

"That's the great thing about American culture," Justin said. "It expands to include almost everyone else's. Or you could call it cultural appropriation, or co-opting everything."

"The Indians especially are used to celebrating everyone's holidays," Justin's mother said, "so they adapt what they enjoy and discard what they don't. Speaking of which, we should get these containers back to disposal." A small social insect which looked and acted much like ants had discovered that sugars from Earth were highly edible, and were becoming a problem in the camp. Some foods had to be kept in sealed containers or a swarm of the creatures would soon find them.

"I'll help you clean up," Samantha said, unknowingly continuing a custom practiced for thousand of years. Samantha and Justin's mother gathered up the containers and utensils and left.

"This is a good time to tell you something important, son," Justin's dad said, straightening up.

"What? We had the talk a long time ago."

"Not that talk," his father said, "Another talk. Just as important. About being a man."

Justin squirmed. "Really? Does it look like I'm doing it wrong?"

Justin's father laughed. "Of course not. You've chosen to undertake a risky and important project. You're more of a man than most men twice your age. And you have a woman by your side who I'd be proud to have as a daughter. Who, by the way, you should marry right quick now."

"We're thinking about it. When things calm down a little."

"They may never calm down," Justin's father said. "If you're both sure, get it done. We're here, her parents are here, and your friends are mostly here. Why not now?"

Justin rolled his eyes. "These next few weeks are going to be just a little busy! Ultimatums, threats, and hate campaigns directed at us. Maybe in a few months when we've won."

"Sometimes you take a leap in the dark," Justin's father said. "Maybe it's safer to wait, but if you wait circumstances may surprise you, and you may regret not acting while you had the chance. Your mother and I got married when I didn't have a job and she was still in school. Her parents wanted us to wait—I think they suspected I'd end up as a bum on Skid Row. But being together helped us both succeed."

"I'm feeling that with Samantha. It's much easier to go out there when she's behind me."

"And when you have children," Justin's father said, "your focus will change. I remember when we had you and I first held you. There was nothing I wouldn't do to make your life better. Whatever selfishness I had left burned away, thinking of you, and then your sister."

"It's early to talk about kids. Of course we want some. But this is hardly the time or the place—"

"Like I said, it's never the exactly perfect time for anything. Let me tell you a story…" Justin's father sat back and looked up at the unfamiliar constellations.

"My dad, your grandpa, sat me down about 25 years ago and gave me this same talk. I was seeing your mother and looking for a real mechanic's job while changing oil at Jiffy Lube. Her parents were dubious and I can see why, but my dad reminded me that he had married my mom while he was in the Army and stationed at Fort Bragg. Her parents thought she was too young and didn't want her to leave town or marry a guy who might be sent to war, but my dad was very persuasive. My mother got pregnant and had me while they were living together on base, and soon after, he shipped out. But you know what happened—my mother died of breast cancer, and he cut his overseas posting short to get back to help his parents raise me. The moral being, you never know how much time you will have, or what might happen to upset your plans."

"I remember," Justin said. "Kind of a grim story."

"I may not be around much longer. But you're all grown up, and I know you can take care of yourself. You probably realized a long time ago that you're a lot smarter than me—"

"I wouldn't say that!"

"But it would still be true. I remember when I realized I was on my own about some things my dad didn't understand—so I had to take responsibility for those decisions myself. He wasn't some wise elder who could guide me, but just a man who was sometimes wrong. That's where you are now. I'm just the guy that fathered you—you're the one who will run the show from now on. You have outgrown my guidance."

"I still listen to you. You have a lot of wisdom and experience."

"But you'll decide for yourself, and you have been doing that for a few years now. It's good, that's how it's supposed to be. I get to tell people that you're my son, and that's enough."

Chapter Six: O Fortuna

Doomsday Book

Justin and Steve worked side-by-side at the consoles again for the first time in months, setting up command macros for their contingency plans.

"I had to do some research to remember all of the isotopes that could be used to build a nuke," Steve said. "U-235 is the famous one, but I decided to be safe we would look for high concentrations of all the radioactive elements. So we're seeing some noise like thorium-based reactors."

"How can you tell a bomb from a reactor?" Justin said.

"A reactor tends to have a low concentration of the radioactives, comparatively, with additional moderators that are controllable and promote the reaction when present. I set up the screening using a low-end estimate of critical mass in a volume small enough to be a likely bomb, but that may pick up some reactors. Which we'll also keep a list of, just in case—we want to keep a watch program on them in case someone decides to raid them for fissile materials to make a bomb. Now we go through the list and scan the surroundings to sort them out."

"So let's take a look," Justin said, double-clicking on the first result. A window opened with a map background. He clicked again. "Closeup with density scan." They saw what looked like an x-ray of three dark wedges with surrounding medium-density materials and a high-density shell. "That sure looks like a bomb."

"It will more often than not require viewing from several angles to be sure," Steve said, "but that's already certain to be one, so check that the object boundaries are reasonable and hit the 'bomb' button."

"There are thousands of these to go through, you know, so let's get clicking. It may take days." Justin adjusted his chair for a long stay.

* * * * *

"Here's something interesting," Steve said. "A high concentration of uranium isotopes, near critical mass and density, but a kilometer underground."

"I remember reading a story about natural reactors.[10] Where naturally-deposited radioactives were close enough to critical mass that they generated a chain reaction with enough heat to melt the area, and isotopes that proved it had happened on later examination."

"I'll save the location in the 'oddities' file."

* * * * *

"Another find," Justin said. "This one looks like a bomb, and it's in Brazil, which isn't supposed to have any. The next eleven are in the same area."

"Let's pull back," Steve said. "Oh, I see—they're on planes. Could be loaners from another government. In any case, they're warheads. I've plugged this program into the object tracking program, so wherever they go, their location will be updated."

* * * * *

Hours passed. They stopped in the late evening and returned to the task the next day. Finally the end of the search list approached.

"So what's the final census?" Justin asked.

"The old nuclear powers had about the number of bombs expected from published sources. One country that supposedly has them had none. Five countries that supposedly don't, do. And I didn't try to sort out the ones at sea, but they add up to about what's documented for all of the naval powers. But the ones in Antarctica—wonder what that's about?"

"It won't matter in a few days," Justin said. "Whatever plans someone had for untraceable attacks or retaliation are about to be cancelled."

Mobilis in Mobili

Justin took the podium while Ben handed out copies of the statement they'd hammered out together. "This is what we've come up with as a general threat and invitation to join our new Commonwealth," Ben said.

"We're about ready to assemble the package of files to deliver along with our invitation," Justin said. "It will include data files locating all of the bombs and warheads we'll be removing, which I suspect will cause heartburn for some governments who've been lying about them, but too bad. Plus locations of reactors of all sorts and military infrastructure—that's a hint that we are already thinking about going after them if we don't get cooperation. And as sweetener, the early survey results on about a hundred planets perfect for colonization."

Members of the Council—except Bubna, who was late—murmured in response. "I worked with Michael and the Grey Tribe people trying to find diplomatic email addresses and public keys," Samantha said, "but not many countries make them public. Diplomats mostly use encrypted cables, not email."

"We do give them a secure return channel, though," Michael said. "Our public key and a site in a neutral country where they can post an encrypted message. The smart ones will tell us how to message them securely."

"So if we're sending this to every major country's government in the clear, isn't it likely to leak?" Samantha asked.

"Almost certainly," Justin said. "But there's not a lot we can do about it. We have to start a game of offering something most countries will want, to set them against the countries who maintain the nuclear stockpiles and think of themselves as great powers. The faster we get agreement from the majority of smaller countries, the faster we win with the big guys."

"You threaten them," Ben said, "then you offer them an easy way out. We keep demonstrating what we could do—bad cop—then we show them the benefits of opening the stars to human colonies, and ending stagnation and poverty—the good cop."

"Come with us, or get left behind," Prof. Wilson said. "Either way, in a much safer world. Sounds like a good deal when it's put that way."

"As further proof of what we can do," Justin said, "we moved one warhead already and took video of the cruise missile it came from, then we show the removed warhead sitting on Mars next to an old Mars Rover. That's not where it's going to stay, but we just wanted something with visual impact."

The Invitation

```
The Provisional Council of the Commonwealth of
  Humanity invites the governments of Earth to join
  in a new security agreement for the benefit of all
  the people of the Earth.

For over eighty years, the world has lived in fear
  of nuclear catastrophe, and despite generations of
  arms control agreements, the use of even a frac-
```

tion of the remaining arsenal in war would destroy our civilization, built over thousands of years of toil by our ancestors. War might even end most life on Earth. Even a few thermonuclear devices exploded high over major continents would generate EMP sufficient to damage power grids and destroy most computers, plunging the world into a new Dark Age. The risk of accident or insanity is too great to allow these devices to be held by fallible governments.

Thus we are removing all nuclear weapons from the Earth and storing them in a safe place. This begins a new order for humanity, where the constant threat of warfare is ended, and the assurance of peace and freedom allow every human being to develop without fear of violence or hunger.

We will share the benefits of the new technology with everyone who joins us. We estimate there are at least a million planets suitable for human colonization in this galaxy alone, and we can give your citizens instant access to them, just by stepping—or driving—through a gateway. We've included survey data on just a handful of the planets we've identified. There will be no shortage of room or resources.

The technology we control allows us to guarantee the borders and security of all states that agree to join with us. These are the conditions every state must agree to:

- The end of aggressive action against any other state. Warfare begun by any state will result in the destruction of that state's war capabilities.

- Non-state groups who use weapons to promote their cause through terrorism or guerrilla warfare will be removed.

- All bans on encryption and punishment for political crimes will end. All political prisoners will be released within one month of agreement. The

UN's Universal Declaration of Human Rights will be respected.

Governments that agree to our conditions by midnight GMT 31 May will immediately be allowed to bid for colony planets, and will be protected by our security guarantee. Those who do not agree will have their defense capabilities further degraded until agreement is reached. In the interest of continuity and order, we will not make our existence public until the deadline, and we request countries that sign the agreement hold their public announcement until after the deadline.

We urge you to carefully consider the great advantages of our offer. The world's governments have been unable to eliminate the risk of nuclear weapons; after decades of effort there are more of them than ever, in more countries than ever. We have already eliminated that threat for you, and we are all safer as a result. Joining with us will bring even greater benefits to all.

* * * * *

Steve ran the programs he and Justin had set up to transport the list of bombs to a storage field at the Sun-Jupiter Lagrangian point, where they would settle into a stable orbit with the Trojan asteroids. The program completed in a few seconds, and he opened a window to check the area. The screen was dark, and he had to step up the gain to see the ranks of bomb cores dimly. A few people observing clapped, but no one cheered.

Michael McCulloch was given the honor of hitting 'send' on the invitation packages. The mass mailing went to thousands of email addresses of upper-echelon government officials, diplomats, and the remaining monarchs and dictators.

Michael checked the site they had specified for replies. Something arrived there, but it was a notice of bounced mail. In a few minutes there were dozens of those. Finally a response—from an official in

Vatican City, asking to confirm if they had correctly replied as instructed. Michael sent a note back in the clear.

"I don't think anyone will digest this and reply in less than a few days," Prof. Wilson said. "There will be a lot of meetings and reports and consultation between governments before we get answers back."

"I would think so. But the smaller countries will surely find the idea of a whole new planet of their own enticing," Samantha said. "If they think they will be able to transfer their rule to a new planet, we can let them believe that."

"One of the carrots we offer," Justin said, "is more territory and more subjects to rule. But they will be unable to enforce their rule fairly quickly. I'd expect the smarter autocrats to figure that out."

"Autocrats are wily within their network of influence," Prof. Wilson said, "but on the whole not students of history or economics, which is one reason their countries do poorly. I expect they will send troops along with the colonists. But they won't be able to send gunboats to control their troops."

Justin and Samantha continued to talk to Prof. Wilson while Michael kept a scan of texting services and the Web going. The full text of their letter appeared attached to a public tweet only ten minutes after they sent it, but was widely assumed to be an interesting forgery.

An hour later, only three more messages had come in, all saying the message had been received and would be carefully considered, though one also asked (in French) if it was a practical joke.

Justin realized he would need to call on the leaders of the world directly. He took Ben aside and they began to discuss what to say.

Amanda Arrives

Amanda Sundaram-Smythe nervously waited to be picked up in her apartment in the Marylebone district of London. She had received an encrypted email from Michael McCulloch of the Grey Tribe a few weeks before, and took it seriously as an opportunity to do another great story on him and the groups he was associated with. As the negotiation over conditions and story approval continued, he was more open about the rebel group he was now with, and she began to correlate some of the odd recent news items with his group's activities.

Michael had suggested what to pack—items suitable for a camping trip or safari lasting weeks, at least. She made sure her prescriptions were filled and tested her laptop and recording equipment with her travel charging kit. She left behind most of the makeup and packed sensible safari clothes, with one little black dress just in case. She had dropped off her cat with friends who already had two.

The appointed time arrived and she stood on the Persian rug near her luggage. Nothing happened for some time, and she started checking her phone for email in case there was a message. Then the quality of sound in the room changed, and she looked up to a window with Michael's face looking back at her.

"Hi," Michael said. "Sorry I'm a little late. You ready?"

"Yes," she said. "I must say this is remarkable. It's like I could reach out and touch you."

Michael clicked something out of sight. "There, now you really could. Let me open this to walk-through size." He clicked again, and the view expanded. Now she could see past Michael to a doorway—tent opening—with blue sky above and tan canvas below. "Come on through," he said. "Hand me your bags first."

She handed him one bag at a time, then stepped through herself. She felt nothing as she passed from one world to another. The incessant background noise of London faded away, and it was quiet except for voices in the distance.

Michael showed her to her accommodations—a tent built like a room, with high walls and sturdy framing. She had seen similar tents on assignment in Middle East war zones—some soldiers lived in them for years.

"I know it's nearly lunchtime for you, but it's dinner time here," Michael said. "Let's round up some of the Council to meet you. We set the date to pick you up unaware that it was going to be momentous for other reasons—we have to do a kind of teleconference with the White House and other leaders after dinner. So you'll have something to record almost immediately."

They walked toward the center of the camp. Michael hurried their step when he seemed to recognize a striking young couple—a tall and rangy young man, and a lithe auburn-haired woman—up ahead. "Wait up," he said, "Welcome Amanda to the camp. Amanda, this is Justin Smith and Samantha West."

Justin shook her hand, while Samantha demonstrated her mastery of the double air kiss of European greeting. They were stereotypically Californian in their white teeth, tan skin, and glow of good health.

"We're glad you're here," Justin said. "We need someone to explain us to the world. We're going to change things for the better, so we expect to be the subject of mountains of propaganda and false stories planted by threatened interests."

"You can rely on me to report what I see and hear honestly," Amanda said. "I assume that's why Michael came to me. I have made governments uncomfortable before."

"We've just made ourselves known to all the governments that weren't already after us," Samantha said. "So you couldn't have come at a better time. After dinner we will drop in on the Oval Office for a chat, then the Chinese president, then the EU Commission president. We'll fill you in on what we've offered them during dinner."

"Has it occurred to you," Amanda said, "that governments run by old men and women who have clawed their way to the top through a forest of political obstacles will find it hard to accept a small group of young people and techno-geeks as equals for negotiation?"

"It has," Samantha said. "We'll have our older Council members up front for the meetings. And they know we have a technology they will have to take seriously. If they don't, we'll have to demonstrate why they should."

"I have a lot of questions for all of you," Amanda said, "but also some advice. While I can help by reporting your story as straight news, you may need a lot more help getting the sympathy of the population. I know just the person, if you can afford her fees. Daniella Pink—She will make your stories so irresistible that even the media in controlled countries will want to cover your personal journeys."

Diplomatic Calls

One of the media-savvy Grey Tribe guys had arranged the chairs in the meeting hall of the community building just so, and put marks on the ground for standees. A camera had been set up to record the view the people in the Oval Office would see, and another pointing the other way to record the view into the Oval Office. Extra lighting had been brought in to compete with the daytime on the other end. Amanda stood to one side out of view of the cameras, readying her own equipment to record the event.

"How is the time?" Justin asked the technician.

"Almost 10 AM DC time," he said. "The president is scheduled to be in the Oval Office meeting with security advisors, and surveillance shows them arriving now."

“Okay, can we get everyone to their places, please?” Justin shouted to be heard. People began to move toward their marks. Justin planned to join Ben standing in the center, so the chairs behind were separated into two groups. He had planned the arrangement to show their diversity and balance—the two older professors on either side, two middle-aged hackers (one male and one female), Steve Duong seated slightly in front of the others, and Rasna and Samantha seated on the ends. They all agreed it would be better to keep spectators away, since they could view the video of the event and Justin didn't want any outbursts or crowd noise. At the last minute he decided it was important to have someone familiar to the Chinese, so he sent someone to get Meiling, the young Grey Tribe programmer who had performed the warning messages to Chinese state security, and he placed her in a chair next to Samantha. The fact that she was pretty would probably help with young Chinese men.

Finally everyone was in their places, and the show was on.

The large viewing window opened, and they were looking at the president's desk from the west side of the office. The president was behind the desk, with three men seated in chairs in front of it. Standing behind were several others. They had all turned to stare.

“Madam President. Greetings from New Earth,” Justin said. “I'm Justin Smith, and this is my colleague, Benjamin Franklin Ramirez. We are sorry to break into your meeting, but we have sent your government a message and we'd like a few minutes to discuss it with you directly.”

President Elizabeth Howard Stanton looked coldly furious for a fraction of a second, but then her face smoothed out and her eyes narrowed. “I've just been briefed on your ‘message.’ This government does not deal with terrorists, and if you continue on this course you will all be declared enemy combatants. You two are American citizens, so the penalty for treason will apply.”

“We have a technology we know you have tried and failed to duplicate. What we offer is civilian use of the technology, which will revolutionize world trade and make the world a more prosperous place, and we will take on the burden of keeping the peace around the world which the UN has failed to do."

A white-haired older man—the Secretary of State, Justin remembered —was visibly angry, and said, "You have already meddled in the delicate balance that has kept the peace for fifty years. You have left us defenseless against nuclear attack."

"There can be no nuclear attack," Ben said, stepping forward. "All nuclear and thermonuclear weapons have been removed from the Earth. No one else has them now, either. And no one will ever have them again—we've set up automated watches to make sure nuclear materials are not produced in amounts and concentrations suitable for weapons. Something the UN could not do."

"We've received few replies to our message so far," Justin said. "One of them was from the UN Secretary General, requesting that we cede our technology to the UN as the properly constituted body for safe-keeping and peaceful enforcement purposes. What was our answer to that, Ben?"

"No! *Hell,* no!" Ben said. "They have been a corrupt and ineffective organization since they were founded. While some agencies have done good work, they have mostly served the interests of the worst governments on Earth. We may not be perfect, but we will be a better steward of the human rights of the world than they have been."

"You are asking us to trust a small band of rebels with the security of our country and the entire world," The president said. "You can see why we would have trouble agreeing to that. Why should we trust you?"

"Because we're not giving you a choice. If you agree to our terms, your government can continue as before to deal with domestic affairs, and your citizens will have access to our technology. With resources freed up from security and defense spending, you can rebuild infrastructure and improve education. Everyone will be better off, and safer."

"And if we don't agree to your 'terms'?" she said, spitting out the last word.

"Other countries will get first crack at the colony planets. Your defense facilities will be slowly reduced to rubble. Your economy will begin to fail as others use the new technologies to create new industries and better products. You will be left behind."

The president looked into nothing for a few moments. Then she smiled slightly, and said, "I have read the dossiers on every one of you. I know you think you are doing great deeds for the world—I always wanted to save the world when I was your age! But the world is a complicated and dangerous place. We will consider what you propose and open diplomatic channels to work out some sort of arrangement, if that seems possible."

"We would be happy to discuss this further," Ben said, "and we understand the many consequences of what we propose will require time to evaluate."

"But," Justin said, "we need a tentative agreement by the deadline, so evaluate quickly and make a decision. We won't give you any more time than the rest of them." And he signalled to close the window.

Samantha came up to Justin and hugged him. "I was convinced," she said. "Great job."

Amanda approached and said, "That was excellent material. How soon can I use it in a story?"

"Excerpts, maybe," Justin said. "The bit about nuclear weapons is still a secret and we can't allow you to mention it until it's more public."

"I understand,“ Amanda said. "I will say that this is a far bigger story than Michael sold me on. I'm very happy to be here for it."

"Well, we're not done yet," Justin said, raising his voice. "We've got Brussels up next, and China in ten hours."

White House Lawn

Dylan was at his desk when his special secured cell phone rang. He got up and started walking—he had personally written the protocol for communications about actions against the rebels, who appeared to be able to listen in at any known location.

"Foster here," he said, answering once he was out of his office.

"Foster, this is the president. We just had a visit from the rebels, who made a point of interrupting my briefing this morning with a little show. Now I've brought my people out to the White House lawn for an impromptu stroll as per your instructions." Dylan could hear her breathing hard and a lawnmower in the distance.

"Which should make it more difficult for them to listen in," Dylan said, walking around the edges of the strip mall parking lot. "We have no evidence that they've ever been able to track a meeting in motion. But I would advise caution in discussing critical matters in any case."

"I hear you," the president said. "I wanted to reinforce my instructions on your goals. We may have to play a long game of appearing to cooperate and waiting for an opportunity to turn the tables. I want it clear that we want that tech, and the inventor, and you are not to attempt to destroy them unless some other party is about to grab them."

"I understand," Dylan said. "Christine already made your thoughts known. I will write you a supplementary memo when I get back to my desk."

Black Op

Dylan flew to Stockholm to meet with the mission team and supervise final preparations since the tunnel was nearly complete. When he arrived on site, the guard looked at his ID carefully before waving him into the garage where the team was meeting for a final run-through before entering the tunnel. The SEAL team ignored him, but a man wearing similar tactical clothing noticed him waiting and came over.

"Director Foster, I assume. Mitch Jeffers."

"Good to meet you in person," Dylan said. "I assume you have the implant controller and the drones. I'll need to review the programming of the autonomous drone."

"It's already loaded with the target photos and directives."

"I spoke directly with the president yesterday, and she made it clear that I was to personally check everything. She wants this technology above all, and she views destroying the rebels as less important—she's willing to wait longer if this mission fails to extract the key rebels. Which means that backpack bomb is out—"

"Henderson!" the CIA man shouted, "we have a change in the plan. Scratch the deadman package. And bring over the drone interface."

"Yessir," one of the men said, while another moved to take a large backpack from the piles waiting to be carried.

"That'll be a relief to the guy who was supposed to carry it and hold the dead-man switch," the CIA man said. "He was not happy with the idea."

Henderson walked over with a tablet computer. "Here's the control interface for the drones. The regular ones are shown." He clicked a button. "This is the autonomous program interface for the experimental one." Henderson handed the tablet to the CIA man.

Dylan stared at the screen full of dense code and buttons. "What does any of this mean?" he asked.

The CIA man looked at him. "You probably should have reviewed the documentation for the device earlier. But I am familiar with some of this—here's the trigger parameter for autonomy, number of seconds after loss of control signal, now set at sixty. The program starts here, continuing to travel as it was when under control for a minute, then starts a mapping pattern. Conditionals: when a target person is recognized, the special program takes over—it circles the target and views it from more angles, getting closer until ID is certain. If the shot is clear, it takes it. So the bullets or pellets or darts are fired. It waits a moment to make sure the target is down, and then proceeds as before."

"So this part is the targeting and choice of action?" Dylan said, pointing to a box in the middle of the page.

The CIA man double-clicked on the box and it opened into a new page. "Here's the list of targets and actions."

Dylan looked at the thumbnail pictures of his former friends and Samantha, who he had thought would be a suitable addition to his life. After each was the word DART, which stood for an anesthetic dart to knock them out for easy capture. "I think I can handle this. I need to check everything out—I'll bring it back when I'm done," he said, taking the tablet from the CIA man, who looked at him curiously for a moment before shrugging and heading back to the others.

His finger lingered over the DART button for Samantha. He tapped it and a menu showed his options. He stared at the more lethal options, then tapped DART again. Then he went to the option for Justin, and changed it to PELLET—a deadly poison designed to kill without leaving marks. He did the same for Steve Duong. If the mission failed, there was a chance the drone would bring his goals a bit closer by killing Justin or Steve, or both. And he had checked the specs enough to know the drone was designed to wipe its memory if it fell into the wrong hands, so the evidence of his changes would never come to light.

He saved the changes and went back up a level in the program to make a show of reviewing the rest of the programming, but no one was watching him.

* * * * *

The camera had been installed in the wall of the warehouse near Stockholm several days earlier by a remote-controlled robot introduced from the wall cavity below. In the days since, the gateway had opened infrequently, usually late at night Stockholm time. Finally the tunnel was complete, and the SEAL team and CIA handler had been waiting under the warehouse floor for eight hours when the camera finally showed the glow of alien sunlight through a gateway. The video showed the conveyer belt start up to move goods toward the gateway, and two men loading the crates onto the belt.

Dylan was watching the team leader's helmet-mounted cam feed from a van blocks away. He heard the team leader say, "Fire in the hole!" and a muffled sound of the explosives cutting the hole through the floor to give them access. Then a jumble of motion and smoke, as the two rebels ran back to launch themselves through the gateway. The team ran through the gateway, with sunlight and surprised young people on the other side. As planned, the team fired many rounds to scare off anyone near the gateway, and one of the technicians manning the console fell wounded. The team leader scanned from side to side, making Dylan dizzy as the camera moved with him, and signalled another man to release the drones. He threw them into the air, one at a time, and they took off in different directions.

"Oswald and Renner—secure the street outside!" the team leader shouted. More of the team made their way up the rubble-strewn ramp to the gateway and waited to enter.

Then the gateway disappeared, and one man who was partway through screamed in agony as he fell forward, part of his scalp and knee disconnected from the rest of him and left on New Earth. The secondary channels of the team members still waiting were filled with sounds of dismay and questions.

Part Four: After the Raid

Chapter Seven: Poison Pills

Target Practice

More people gathered near the gateway tents to inspect the forms of the soldiers frozen in stasis. Justin searched for Jim McDonald, and spotted him coming up the street at a trot.

“So,” Justin said, “what you warned us about last week—they sent a team in through the gateway.”

“Damages?” Jim said.

“One killed, one wounded, some displays shot up.”

“Did we get them all?”

“I think so,” Justin said. “Someone reported seeing drones in the air.”

“Let’s go—those could still be a threat. The government’s done some work on intelligent drones. Best to take them out. And search for any soldiers that might have escaped. Where do you keep the guns?”

Justin led him to the tent with the gun crates, where Jim surveyed their collection of weapons. "A shotgun would be better for handling the drones," Jim said, "but you guys didn't know that." He picked out a rifle. "Let's go."

They moved up the street at a fast pace, stopping at each intersection to scan left and right. Above one of the lanes they saw a black dot, and turned that way. It was a quadcopter with two camera eyes hovering about ten feet off the ground, so when they were a few tents away Jim stopped and aimed, signaling Justin to do the same. They fired a half-second apart, and the drone jerked and fell to the ground with a clatter of blades. As they got closer, Jim fired at it again and again until the body was tattered fragments.

As Justin and Jim returned to the main street, they saw several people from the crowd at the gateway tent coming toward them, but Justin shouted, "Just being sure the drones are dead. Stay where you are." They continued their search and came upon another drone hovering quietly, dispatching it the same way.

Coming back toward the center of the camp another way, they spotted a third drone a few blocks away, this one moving slowly down the center of the street about twenty feet overhead. The drone's camera lenses moved from side to side, as if searching for something.

"This one's moving," Jim said. "That's not good. Let's find cover."

They moved to one side and hid behind the edge of a tent. Looking around the edge, Justin saw the drone continue its slow pace up the street toward them.

Someone walked into the street from one of the tents. Justin realized it was Steve just as the drone changed its motion as its cameras focused on him. The drone circled him, dropping low, and Justin heard a shot.

Steve reached for his neck and staggered. Then he crumpled to the ground.

"Jesus," Jim said, and he and Justin left cover to aim and shoot. The drone fell and they pumped more shots into it to be sure.

* * * * *

They carried Steve to the medical tent, interrupting the doctor who was working on gateway technician Gunther's bullet wound.

"Drone shot him with something," Justin said. "Just a tiny wound, but he went down fast."

"Put him on the gurney. Let's take a look. Ah, I see. Pellet entry just above the collarbone." She felt for Steve's pulse and clipped some sensors to him. "That's not good. Shock or poisoning."

"He's critical to your effort," Jim said, "which is why they targeted him."

More medical staff appeared. "Get him into the operating room," the doctor said. Two guys rolled the gurney into a curtained-off room. "Stay out," the doctor said, pushing Justin back and closing the curtain.

They could hear noises and instructions as the doctor worked. A nurse came and went carrying vials and instruments. People who had heard the news started to gather outside the tent. Rasna came forward, pale and shaking.

Fifteen minutes later, the doctor came out, looking tired but smiling. "We got the pellet out before most of its poison payload had made it into the bloodstream. We have his heart rhythm stabilized and he's doing well on a respirator, so I think we caught it in time."

"How close was it?" Jim said.

"Another minute and he might not have made it," the doctor said.

"His heart was going arrhythmic and he wasn't breathing properly." Rasna had to be helped to a chair.

"What is the outlook?" Justin asked.

"Hard to say if there's been any permanent damage," the doctor said. "I'll be researching the symptoms and trying to analyze what's left of the poison to identify it. Most likely he will recover."

Wendy and Quinn

The Council met and decided to evacuate remaining agents on Earth and step up recruiting through the Grey Tribe to populate backup camps on distant sites on New Earth. The attack reminded them of their vulnerability, and moving capabilities away from base camp would allow the rebels to continue even if the camp were destroyed.

Justin and Samantha set up a call to Wendy. She was wearing cutoffs and a Mickey Mouse t-shirt, and her hair was a golden pageboy cut.

"Wendy," Samantha said. "It's us. Is the coast clear?"

"Yes. There's been some odd news lately which must have to do with you guys. Like last night's story on American special forces types appearing inside a Swedish jail cell. What's up?"

"Looks like the CIA was able to get a special forces team into our warehouse without our knowing, despite the surveillance," Justin said. "Apparently they dug a tunnel underneath. A group of them got through the gateway and killed one of ours. We closed the gateway before most of them could get through and Steve froze them in place and sent them to that prison cell, but not before they released drones. One of them shot Steve full of poison but it looks like he'll recover—but he's out of it for now."

"And the reason we're calling is that we want you to bug out now,"

Samantha said. “It’s going to get tense and anyone we’ve had contact with is in danger.”

“Your timing is good, since I just handed in my last paper. The term is over tomorrow. And I was planning to leave for Atlanta to spend the summer with a guy I met there.”

Justin and Samantha looked at each other. “Really?” Samantha said. “A guy? Tell us more.”

“George is a FedEx driver and musician, friend of my cousin’s husband. We dated for awhile when I was there, and we’ve chatted online since. The closest thing I’ve ever had to a boyfriend.”

“Would he be willing to come along with you?”

“I haven’t told him about any of this. I’m exotic enough without adding rebel financier to my feature list. So I have no idea. But I’m torn—I was looking forward to Atlanta again, where the spies aren’t as thick on the ground. But you think it’s not safe?”

“We think no one who ever knew us is safe, at least for a few months until this is resolved. We’ve offered the governments a new security arrangement—which is a surrender of their ability to wage war and intimidate other countries. We expect every government on the planet to try to find out more about us and everyone we knew.”

Wendy looked thoughtful. “Give me two hours to pack. I’ll call George and bring up the subject of the future. If he makes the right noises, we can approach him after I come over. His job isn’t so great that he can’t leave it for a better opportunity.”

* * * * *

Justin set the gateway to find Quinn’s talisman. The view showed a dark bedroom and a suitcase where he had apparently left the talisman. Panning around, they spotted a window with forest greenery and mountains above. Justin asked for a map view, and it showed a spot near the north shore of Lake Tahoe.

"Guess he's on vacation," Justin said. "Let's look around. I didn't tell him he should actually wear it around his neck."

"Nice view, though," Samantha said. "Makes me wonder when I'll ever get to go there again."

Justin joysticked down the hall and then down a flight of stairs to an open great room. Quinn was in the kitchen getting coffee. Justin got closer and then opened the two-way view. "Quinn, it's Justin. Is the coast clear?"

Quinn started, and looked back toward Justin's face looming above the kitchen island. "Surprised me. I guess that cube you gave me works."

"You should probably keep it on your person at all times," Justin said. "Like, with a chain around your neck, in a pouch."

"I'm not much for jewelry," Quinn said, "But I'll figure something out. Who's the lovely young lady?" Samantha had pushed into the frame hugging Justin from behind his chair.

"Quinn, meet my… *friend* Samantha," Justin said.

"Friend, huh?" Samantha said. "Try harder to find the words." Quinn chuckled quietly.

"Very close, treasured friend," Justin said. "Squeeze, concubine, holder of the key to my heart. What term would you like?"

"We'll talk," she said. "I think Mr. Quinn understands."

"Indeed I do," he said. "So what brings you here? As you probably noticed, I decided to come up to a friend's house at Tahoe to leave the scene in case something was up. I heard your warehouse was raided and some American special forces types ended up in a Swedish jail cell unexpectedly, so I decided to lay low for a few weeks."

"That was a wise choice," Justin said. "I was going to warn you to leave, but I had in mind your coming here to join us for a few months. We're turning up the pressure and lots more governments will be trying to find out about us. The warehouse was found out, and there's no telling what they can find out from the employees and tracing back from the shell company agents." He went on to explain the nuclear gambit and the offer-threat they'd made to the governments

Quinn kept stirring his coffee while he thought. "So that's what you meant by a greater reward. I could ask what's in it for me, but you probably don't know yourself. What would I do there?"

"We have a growing need for logistics experts. We can move anything from one place to another, instantly, over any distance—we're fifty light-years away on a pleasantly Earthlike planet, and we need to establish more bases to make ourselves less vulnerable to attack. We'll be opening up similar planets to colonists from countries that agree to our terms—and eventually to everyone, whether their governments like it or not."

"My specialized knowledge is in people and systems on Earth," Quinn said. "It would make more sense for me to use my knowledge to help you handle governments."

"You could probably do that," Justin said. "We'd continue to pay your retainer, of course, and up it some more for hazard pay. When we can go public, we'll have PR needs and you can help by spreading the word about the new system to your contacts. You could even start by setting up subversive trade networks—more leaks in the walls between countries. Hmm…"

"I am liking how that sounds, and I can think of lots of ways to cause them trouble by moving people and things around."

"So we can pick you up now, if you're ready."

"I just lugged my bags up the stairs. I barely unpacked, but I'd like to make a few calls to let people know I'm going to be gone and take care of suspending the business for awhile."

"So how about we come back in an hour?"

"That will probably be enough time. I'll be upstairs by the suitcases."

* * * * *

Justin and Samantha picked up Quinn first, and then Wendy, who had six large suitcases to bring across.

"Who knows how long I might be stuck here!" Wendy said. "I need enough changes of clothes to feel fresh. You two may be able to wear the same clothes every day, but I can't. Makes me feel… invisible."

Quinn took her hand and kissed it. "I very much doubt that you could ever be invisible, Mademoiselle."

"How very kind of you, Mr. Quinn," she said. "Old-school manners are so refreshing." Her smile was brilliant.

"How did it go with your boyfriend?" Samantha said. "George, was it?"

Wendy turned serious and said, "He wasn't dead-set against the idea of joining us. He was surprised to find out I was so involved in a conspiracy, but that didn't bother him, either. He wanted to talk to his mother and think about it some more. So I'm supposed to talk with him more in a few hours. He says he can't leave without giving notice and having his brother handle subleasing his apartment! So many details, but he didn't question the idea of running away with me. Which makes me happy."

"He's even less involved," Justin said, "so it's safe enough to collect him after you've talked more. Have somebody help you find his apartment by gateway so you can talk more, and let us know when he's ready to go."

Sickbay

After a morning spent at new recruit orientation, Justin and Samantha stopped at the medical tent to check on Steve. He was asleep in a bed tucked away in an alcove, and the breathing machine had been removed. Rasna was in a chair next to the bed, reading a book.

"Good morning," Samantha whispered. "How's he been?"

Rasna looked up and put the book down. "Better. He was talking and he ate some soup."

"That's a relief," Justin said. "Not just because we care about him, but we all depend on him to do his magic on the substrate programming. It would take us months to figure out how he does it."

Steve stirred, then opened his eyes and said, "You understand most of it, Justin. You're just a slow coder."

"How are you feeling?" Samantha asked.

"I feel old." Steve said. "Like I was beaten up, and everything hurts. But I'm hungry again."

"I'll go see what the kitchen can come up with," Rasna said. "Jello and a protein drink?"

"That would work," Steve said. "Cherry jello, not that lime stuff." Rasna left.

"So, old man," Justin said, "the doctor says you'll be back to full strength in a few days."

"She's optimistic," Steve said, "I'm realistic. I didn't really think about how important I was to keeping this thing going for the rest of you. I've been thinking about it."

"We've picked up most of the people left on Earth who were vulnerable," Samantha said. "Wendy and Quinn are here, and Wendy has a new boyfriend she's trying to recruit."

"And," Justin said, "we're following Jim McDonald's advice to randomize our supply sources and steal one crate at a time using your object-picker, not a gateway. That should remove any chance of another attack."

"There's still one weakness, though," Steve said. "If Dylan or someone else gets access to the substrate via a different form of quantum computer, they can attack us through a gateway. The parallel search capability is not so obvious, but if they find that, they can find us the same way I found this planet—by searching for the most Earthlike conditions nearby. And the Vortex computers are a weakness—they can be found by looking for their grids."

"What can we do about that?" Justin said. "We might need them in case something goes wrong with your boot loaders."

"We could transfer them to a safe place far from here," Steve said, "but then if we needed them, it would be because the substrate apps had broken down, and we couldn't use transport to get them back. Which means they have to be close enough to reach by conventional means."

"Oh," Justin said. "I think I see your point. So maybe on the other side of this continent. Which means we ought to have the capability to travel here. Maybe we should steal a few safari vehicles."

"We should have that in case of emergency anyway," Steve said. "Two all-terrain vehicles at least. And jerry cans of gas for distance driving."

"We can use the gateway to set up storage depots for gas and supplies along the way," Justin said. "This is starting to sound like a fun trip."

"Which we won't be taking unless everything is falling apart," Samantha said. "So get the road trip off your mind."

"It'd be nice to see more of the planet," Steve said.

"We've had the planetary survey team at work mapping it," Samantha said. "They've been using their remote recording capabilities to capture the most interesting spots—waterfalls, volcanoes, canyons, glaciers. They put out a highlights video last week."

"I didn't hear about that," Justin said. "How is that possible?"

"You're busy," Samantha said. "And we have the astronomers at work finding new wonders of the universe we can now see directly. Check the community bulletin boards on the server. There's quite a collection of viewing locations and photos."

"Later on, when I'm retired," Justin said. "From this job, at least. But I can think of uses for awesome sights—to display what we're offering the Earthlings."

Daniella Pink

Amanda added new stories on the removal of the nukes, the raid, and the attack of the autonomous drone to her release packet. She fleshed out the framework of each story with new interviews with Steve from his hospital bed and footage of the invaders as statues. She considered the danger of adding the videos of the dead Grey Tribe member bleeding in the street, with the outraged reactions of his friends, but decided to include it all and let editors sort out what to use. It could be spun as a dry report or made into a propaganda piece casting the rebels as underdog victims, depending on what was left out.

Samantha dropped by her tent. "We wanted to follow up on your recommendation for PR," Samantha said. "We have plenty of money, so we should be trying to buy the right kind of media attention. The governments will try to spin everything their way, so we need to fight in that domain as well."

"And now is the time," Amanda said. "Justin tells me I can release my stories after the deadline, when you are going public with the demands on the governments and the removal of all the nukes. You want your stories out and visible as soon as possible after that, before the public mood is set."

"So we have a few weeks," Samantha said. "Would you introduce us to that Pink woman you mentioned? We have to approach her quietly, and convince her it is worth the risk of working with us."

"I'd be happy to introduce you," Amanda said, "but how? I can't call."

"I can fix that," Samantha said, pulling out her phone. She opened an app and tapped a few buttons. A view window opened in front of her. "This is an overhead view of Piccadilly in London." She clicked again. "Now it's two-way for photons. Check your phone."

"Okay," Amanda said, getting her phone out of her carryon bag. It still had some charge, and it showed one bar of signal. When she brought the phone near the view window, the signal strength increased. "I'll try sending her a text." She tapped out a message: "Fab client for you, but hush-hush. When can you be in your office alone for an hour meeting?"

The wait for a response was short. "Darling! I love intrigue. I can clear the hour starting at noon."

Amanda's phone said the time was 11:40 AM in London. So Amanda texted back, "We will be there at noon. Close the curtains and let NO ONE in."

The response came back, "OIC. THAT kind of client! CU soonest."

Amanda took Samantha through her stories while they waited. "It's strange to see our real lives as news stories," Samantha said. "It's all true enough but leaves out so much."

"And when it's rewritten as history," Amanda said, "it loses even more. Be thankful if the history is anywhere close to what really happened. Everything is rewritten to fit the narrative of the historians writing it. Who tend to make whoever won look better than they were."

* * * * *

When Amanda's phone said it was noon in London, Samantha changed the target location of her gateway app to match the address Amanda had given her. The map showed it on a side street near Sloane Square. The view was of a crowded neighborhood and a brick building partly obscured by parked cars. "That's the building," Amanda said. "She's up the half flight and to the right."

Samantha used her finger to direct the view toward the door. The sign said, "Daniella Pink Agency," and she flowed through it into a reception area. "The office on the left," Amanda said, and Samantha directed the view through that door.

Daniella had silver-pink hair in a bob style with bangs, and large round glasses. She was at her desk picking at her pink fingernails. Samantha centered the view on her and got in closer before opening up the two-way call.

"Daniella," Amanda said. "It's me." Daniella looked up and saw them both in frame. "And this is Samantha."

"Hi," Samantha said. "Nice to meet you. I see you carry the pink theme through everything."

"It's important to be memorable," Daniella said. "People may laugh at first, but everyone knows who I am, and they recognize me in a crowd. I don't care what they call me, as long as they remember to call me." Her accent was refined, but underneath there was a slight remaining coarseness.

"It's actually quite striking," Samantha said. "My fashionista friend Wendy would love the look."

"Thank you," Daniella said. "But about this most unusual window. How does it work?"

"We have a lot to explain," Samantha said, "but you have to agree that anything we tell you is confidential before we can go forward."

"Certainly," Daniella said, scribbling on a legal pad. "Who is the client?"

Samantha explained who they were and their status as rebels asking other governments for cooperation. Daniella's eyes widened when they explained the gateway and how it could be used. She scribbled more when the attack was mentioned.

"...and so we had Amanda here to write the true stories so they could be released to counteract a barrage of propaganda from the governments," Samantha said. "Amanda says you could be very helpful in getting our story out to the public."

"I deal in images and stories," Daniella said, "crafted to gain the client an advantage with the public. What we call the media serve their own interests by entertaining so they can sell ads, and even the dreariest news reports are pitched to tell a story of human interest. The first thing people want to know when a horrific crime is reported is 'why did he do it?' It's my job to have the public seeing things from your point of view."

"We just want the truth out there," Samantha said.

"The truth doesn't win unless it's more interesting than the propaganda your opponents are spinning," Daniella said. "If their story is more interesting and understandable, their story will win. You must make your stories so compelling that people will identify with you and want you to succeed. Governments have gone from dry press releases to slick videos and social media in the past few decades—they have tax money to spend on agencies to promote their version of the truth, and a media too lazy to check up on the truth of what they say. You will have to spend also."

"We're very well funded," Samantha said.

"In this situation, I would need a large retainer upfront and direct access to an account for funding media buys," Daniella said. "Most of our coverage will be free because you are going to be the most interesting story on the planet soon. Our goal is to make it personal—to make each of you a public figure people know about. Then they will be interested in your ups-and-downs, who's boinking who, that sort of thing, as all primates are. And that's when you win, because you're no longer an unknown threat, you're admirable human beings just trying to do good for the world."

"Amanda has a package of stories she's going to release to the BBC June first," Samantha said. "If you agree to keep them confidential, we could send them to you for orientation. If you can generate interest and get more outlets to interview us, that would be great. We have to have an appointment and location like this one—private and at a known location. But we'd be ready to start interviews June first, when her stories go out. So if you'd round up interested parties for then, we'd make ourselves available."

"Let me give you some background on how this works," Daniella said. "Public relations as a business was invented by Edward Bernays, a clever American who realized he could manipulate popular feeling by planting stories and creating events the news media would be irresistibly attracted to. He started out using wartime propaganda techniques to mold public opinion, then did the same for businesses.

"Only a tiny minority of the public has detailed knowledge of current affairs. Those people are very important opinion influencers, but the vast majority of the population barely follows politics or the news—they are far more interested in whether the cute boy down the street fancies them, or whether their boss is having an affair. What we do to bring them into the story is bring it down to that level—to the primate level of social understanding.

"Bernays realized that if he could craft a compelling human story—even if it weren't entirely true—he could get media to run his creations for free as news. And if the broad public was caught up in the story, their opinion could be molded by the emotional elements of the story—who's the hero, who's the villain, could be changed at will, and an apparent consensus formed from emotional stories that struck the right chords. He called it 'the engineering of consent.'"[11]

"The person on the street has a vague sense that the government is a team that works for him or her. When it's really more true that the employees of government work for their own good, and any good to the public is the rare happenstance. Mostly the government taxes and hires and builds to satisfy the network of interests that keeps the politicians in office. If you're going up against governments, you have to be portrayed as the underdogs who are reforming the system so it's better. Democracies run on tides of opinion swayed by continuous government propaganda, and even in China molding public opinion toward one party faction or another is critical to keeping power.

"So we have to get each of your personal stories and make them appealing. It's good that you have a multinational group up there—we can use that by featuring your Indians more strongly in India, and so forth. People are most interested in people like themselves who did something completely unexpected—rebelled and took off for another planet. They'll want to know why, and if they like the answer, they'll take your side."

* * * * *

After Samantha closed the comm window, she turned to Amanda and said, "Whew. That was intense."

"She's quite something," Amanda agreed. "One of the best PR people in the world. She has contacts all over, even in Latin America and Asia. From intellectual journals to tabloid or entertainment news, she can get your story in it. It's like she knows exactly how to pitch a story to lock into the binding sites of the editors. And she's the maestro of leaks—she can have an idea planted in ten places in a few hours."

"Send me your story package and Justin and I will review it and get it to her," Samantha said, "minus the nuke story. Your canned biographies will give her a start on figuring out how to build us up as media stars."

Excision

Two weeks after the raid, Steve was back at work, and apparently back to normal. Prof. Wilson came by his office at the appointed time.

"It's time to get that implant out of you," Steve said.

"I'd like that," Prof. Wilson said. "How?"

"I've refined the object recognition program and tested it on plants and animals. I can remove a seed from a watermelon, and I can remove a pellet from a mouse. Without problems, I mean! And I've figured out how to substitute a sterile silicone gel for what I've removed."

"Sounds good enough. Where do I sit?"

"There is fine. You can see the gel is already on the platform over there, and I'll move the exact same amount and shape from the block into your head to replace what's leaving it."

Prof Wilson wondered why this informality and lack of a sterile operating room was disturbing. He knew they weren't necessary, but it seemed too casual. "Do I have to stay very still?"

"No," Steve said, "the object once recognized will be tracked. I mean, big moves would be unwise, but normal fine motion shouldn't cause problems. Here's the scan." He pointed at an image on the screen that looked like a more colorful x-ray. There was a small square object with tendrils just inside his skull, outlined in blue.

"Let me adjust some parameters," Steve said, clicking a few times, and the blue outline changed slightly. "It's identified a metal and plastic object, a centimeter square and a millimeter thick. The fine tendrils are nonmetallic tubes and conductors designed to interface with your neural pathways, which power the chip and let it read and control impulses. I don't think we should try to remove them—they won't do any harm without the control box anyway."

"Okay, that seems reasonable," Prof. Wilson said. "If they do, I gather I'm screwed."

"If they do," Steve said, "I'd have to be much more careful in removing them, and we're not ready for microsurgery yet. Shall I do it?"

"Yes."

Steve clicked. Prof. Wilson thought he saw a flash of light in one corner of his eye, but he felt nothing. Steve stood up and retrieved the beaker of silicone gel from the platform.

"See?" Steve said, bringing it over, and Prof. Wilson could see a black shape inside the clear gel.

"Amazing," Prof. Wilson said. "The plan is to use that as evidence, so we need to have it scanned and prepare a report."

"Already on it," Steve said. "I scanned it while you were waiting, and the files only need a little massaging. I'll package those up with videos of how you acted during the raid and a statement from Jim McDonald on how it was implanted. Together those will make a strong case. We'll release it to the crowdsourcing sites on the web and let them analyze the scans."

"And save the physical object," Prof. Wilson said. "If nobody needs it for proof, I want it in Lucite on my desk as a reminder."

"It's your implant, Professor."

Diplomatic Corps

As the rate of incoming responses to their message to governments grew, Justin and Ben could not keep up. They posted a FAQ to try to handle some of the common questions—then the neutral zone web site they were using to handle messages went down, overwhelmed by traffic and a DDoS attack. Hours later the attack had cleared, but Justin sent the FAQ out to the original mailing list to forestall some of the queries.

Justin chatted up some Council members, and without a formal meeting, it was decided to appoint Samantha Minister of State, and let her create a temporary "diplomatic service" to handle relationships with governments. That meant taking some of the volunteers off surveillance, which was also far behind, and giving them the task of answering.

"It's like being in customer service at a call center," Justin's father said during dinner later on, "but more verbose. The smaller countries like Tanzania and Nicaragua get right to the point. The big powers must have committees editing everything, and the resulting emails are long and never get to the point."

"I hear we have a few friends out there," Samantha said, "who are seriously considering going with us."

"Taiwan is very interested," Justin said, "as they should be, since the American security guarantee is worth a lot less these days."

"And the Vietnamese," Justin's mother said. "I had the nicest exchange with a man in their government. He was having trouble believing we had defanged the Chinese and Americans, so I sent him more videos of the collapse of the Chinese intelligence building. He was quite impressed, and said he would try to get us a positive response."

"We can expect a friendly reception from counties that have felt threatened by the great powers," Justin said. "It won't cost them anything to take a chance on signing up with us, and it could pay off. If we fail, they pretend it never happened. If we win, they were always our supporters. It's the big powers that will resist, since they have more control to lose."

"I have people assigned to countries they are already familiar with," Samantha said, "and gave them policy guidelines for responses. Which is all we can do—the personalities of our people will show through. I reminded everyone they're in sales right now, and the customer is always right—no comments on how thuggish their government has been, or how great it will be when their people are freed. For the countries that need it, we can offer aid and technical assistance, though I have no idea when we'll ever back that up. Some of the poorer countries have elite power structures that depend on regular aid funding to pad their foreign bank accounts, so we want them to think we might be able to replace what they get from great powers now. And maybe we can, or maybe it won't matter."

Foreign Body

Back on Earth, Dylan Foster was having a bad day. After he flew back from Stockholm, the stream of outraged emails never let up, as the repercussions of the failed raid had everyone involved looking for a scapegoat. He reminded the president and the rest of them that he had advised nuking the camp while they had the chance, but had been overruled. So the failure of the raid was not his fault. He hoped the autonomous drone had at least killed Steve or Justin, but there was no sign of that—the raid had apparently achieved nothing, and alerted the rebels to be more cautious.

He left his office at five to work out at the small gym in his corporate housing complex. He stretched on the floor mat and noticed someone had left a foam roller under the dumbbell rack. He remembered using one of his own, but had lost the habit when he was very busy with his thesis. He retrieved it and started to use it to massage his lower back, rolling his body on top of it. As it applied pressure, his back muscles started to relax.

When he turned sideways and started to roll over his side, he felt something odd as the roller passed over. He tried it again, and then probed the spot with his finger. *Jesus,* he thought, *what the hell could that be? I hope it's not a tumor.*

* * * * *

The next day, he checked in at the CIA-recommended urgent care near his office. An x-ray showed a shadowy square object embedded in the fat deposit above his left hip. The doctor was puzzled, but Dylan knew when he saw the hard outline of the object that he'd been chipped.

The next day, Dylan reported to an outpatient surgical center that did secret work for CIA agents, and they took out the object. On examination, it proved to be a tiny cube of plastic with dark lines through it —there seemed to be no electronic or other function. Dylan had microscans made, and then had it destroyed in the medical incinerator. He checked into a cheap motel and directed his staff to maintain silence in the office while they prepared to move to a new location he would requisition.

Chapter Eight: The Finish Line

Deadline

The midnight GMT deadline went by while Justin was asleep. His phone chirped as he was waking up, and he blearily noted alerts from the BBC, Bloomberg, and Reuters about breaking stories. He got out of bed quietly, hoping to let Samantha sleep, but she began to stir as he dressed. He left hoping she would return to sleep. The sun was not quite up yet but the sky was bright.

He got some breakfast and coffee and went to his desk. The BBC stories spawned more stories, and governments were being asked to respond. He had worked with Ben and Michael on an official statement announcing their existence and control of all nuclear weapons, and that had reached multiple news wires shortly after the BBC's release.

He opened a news aggregator, and this list of headlines came up:

```
BBC: Rebels Steal All Nukes!
Video Shows Warhead Near Mars Explorer
Grey Tribe Linked to Rebellion
Rebel Base on Exoplanet?
California Campus Source of Radical Conspiracy
US Homeland Security: Gulags and Mind Control Im-
  plants Alleged
Quantum Arms Race: US Secret Program
Diplomats Scurry, Rebel Talks Denied
China: Denies Killing Rebel's Father
Gateways: Colony Planets Abundant
BBC: Rebels Outlaw War?
```

He got busy responding to critical messages. Samantha dropped in after the sun rose, holding a mug of coffee and a muffin.

"Quite a splash," she said. "In a few more hours Daniella will be up, and we should launch the charm offensive. Our pictures will be everywhere."

"Not my favorite part of this," Justin said, "but I understand why it's necessary. We're never going to be anonymous again."

"Something you give up when you dare to change the world," she said. "I think you are more afraid of fame than you were of Homeland Security."

"Like a lot of guys, I grew up trying my hardest not to stand out," Justin said. "If you stand out, you're a target. Blending in is safe."

"So you're a target now," Sam said. "But you have your friends with you, and the world's most powerful weapon. You're doing the right thing, and we all know it. Someone had to stand up to them, and we did it. Together! When this is all over, they'll build statues in your honor."

"That's what I'm afraid of," he said. "I lose my freedom so that others can have theirs. Doesn't seem fair."

"Life is unfair. You had the opportunity and the courage to make it happen. So you did, because that's who you are. I wouldn't have it any other way, no matter what happens." She hugged him close.

More stories appeared in the feed:

```
NYTimes: Governments Say Nuclear Arsenals Intact
China Daily: CIA Source of Disinformation Campaign
LATimes: Rebel's California Connection
Japan: Gov't Has No Comment
Tiny Nauru Considers Alliance
BBC: Mystery Soldiers Explained
```

```
Florida Guru Welcomes New Overlords
```

Justin clicked on the last story and they read it together. “Oh, great,” Justin said, “Our first nutty supporter.” The ‘guru’ was calling on his flock to meet at a sacred convergence point to welcome the coming of the new order, which he claimed he had foretold in his writings.

He clicked on the BBC story, which turned out to be an expansion of an earlier story about armed soldiers appearing in a Swedish jail cell. They had refused to explain how they got there and were being held while the US government denied their involvement, but the BBC story added new material on how they had been stopped in their raid on the rebel camp and transported to the cell.

“Can we get Daniella to put some of the less ethical press onto this story?” Justin said. “It would be worth a large bribe to get one of those men to talk.”

“I'll suggest that,” Sam said. “It's not uncommon to have tabloids pay big bucks for exclusive stories. If it's a large sum they might find one of them willing to risk the blowback from the military. What's the highest we'd pay?”

“Fifty million, maybe,” he replied. “One thing we have plenty of is money.”

Stars

Samantha's daily conference call with Daniella Pink was getting longer every day. Wendy joined them for today's, and when she saw Daniella's outfit, she clapped. “You're perfect! Where did you get the glasses?”

“Eye Wonder,” Daniella said, “a little designer shop in Chelsea. When all this is over, I'll take you shopping in London.”

"That would be wonderful," Wendy said, "when all this is over."

"But until then, to the agenda," Samantha said. "Amanda's too busy interviewing to attend today, and she thinks she shouldn't see the sausage being made, objectivity and all that."

"That is wise," Daniella said. "Her kind know my kind is necessary, but they can't sully their virtue by listening to how we think. Might damage them for life."

"We had a huge response from the Internet crowdsource community on the scans and the program dump of the mind control implant," Samantha said. "As usual, some of it's wrong, but the controversy sucked in some true experts, who are now on record with their analyses. It was produced by a fab in Connecticut who does work for the security establishment. The program memory contained code related to known government viruses—it decrypts itself and begins processing neural data when it receives a coded radio signal."

"It's a dirty, rotten thing to do to someone," Daniella said. "To control their feelings without their knowledge. We don't have to get technical for people to understand. The conspiracy sites will eat it up. Especially since it's real."

"We could also have more digging into Dylan Foster's appointment as head of the National Security Lab," Samantha said. "I spent enough time as his girlfriend to have some additional dirt on his father, Wentworth Foster. He was one of those connected Silicon Valley VCs who used green energy funding from the Unity Party administration to make an even bigger fortune. He parties and networks with the superrich. It wouldn't hurt if Dylan came out looking like a beneficiary of influence-peddling as well as theft and extortion."

Daniella tapped notes into her tablet, and said, "The BBC story about him was already damning. Just curious—why did you ever go with him?"

"He was handsome," Samantha said. "You've seen pictures, he looked like Thor. What I thought was sophistication was entitlement, and I was too young to know better. He seemed interested in me at first, and he has a brilliant mind."

"I could have told you he was bad news," Wendy said. "But I think you were thinking with your—"

"We've all been there," Daniella said, "and done that!" She laughed. "I know I have, like a dozen times. I finally wised up and found a guy who makes me laugh and is there when I need him. Not the most bleedin' obvious stud in the room, but quite fine in that area. Just not showy."

"Well," Samantha said, "I got away without too much damage, and Justin is so much more my friend, and comfortable to be with."

"Which is how it's feeling with George, now that he's joined us," Wendy said. "He likes me for who I am. He doesn't expect me to be anybody else but me, and he doesn't mind my… quirks. He came to another planet to be with me."

"And that's commitment!" Samantha said. "But back to the agenda. The interviews you set up for Rasna and Prof. Bubna went over very well, I understand. Bubna tells me it's embarrassing."

"The Indian press is making them heroes," Daniella said. "They are making things up to create stories! I'm expecting a Bollywood movie project at any moment."

"Though having Steve as her beau kind of limits the opportunities for singing, dancing, and hiding behind trees," Wendy said.

"There's also a lot of activity in China," Daniella said. "Despite the controlled press. The appearance of Meiling at several secret sites turned into a legend that has gone viral on social media, with videos and pictures. Even the press has taken notice and featured her background story—expat genius programmer *and* a beautiful young lady, had a big part in inventing the gateway, etc. I didn't have to invent a story, they created one themselves."

"How are we doing in the US?" Samantha asked.

"Not so well," Daniella said. "Word is out that coverage is to emphasize the traitorous aspect of your actions. Even the gutter press is afraid to cross them, when their access to the Internet can be throttled at will by the FCC. So some of my suggestions have been taken up, but by the smaller sites, and it always starts with a condemnation of your criminal conspiracy, theft, and felonies. No mention at all of mind control implants and gulags."

Checkup

Justin was with Steve in Steve's office when Prof. Wilson dropped by for a scan of the implant location to make sure all was well. Steve set up the program, and the scan came up. Steve adjusted the depth, and did some comparisons to make sure the silicone gel had not migrated.

"Looks good," Steve said.

"You saw the email with the results of crowdsourcing the implant data?" Justin asked Prof. Wilson.

"I did," he said. "Very interesting that they could use the exact shape of the chip features to determine which process was used, and then which fab actually made it. And the code being encrypted like a virus —"

"That's a useful idea for substrate apps," Steve said. "We already have them duplicated so there are many copies and check them for corruption. If they were encrypted in a container as well, it would be harder for an enemy operating in the substrate to reverse-engineer them or subvert them. I need to add that feature."

"The most likely enemy in the substrate would be Dylan," Justin said.

"And we just got word that he had the talisman removed. We have so few people on surveillance now, nobody noticed until it was too late to set the object-tracker on him. So we don't know where he is, and his offices and apartment are empty."

"But he has to contact offices we are listening to," Prof. Wilson said, "so won't we find out where he is soon enough?"

"I think they are being very careful now to limit discussion of critical information," Justin said. "We're getting less and less. The surveillance has turned up a number of research groups he's been talking to and funding, but I doubt if we know them all."

"We know some of the groups he talks with," Steve said. "Why don't we set one person to work listening in on them for clues? Set up a database of known quantum computing researchers, find them, and track them. Set a facial recognition program on all of the video to look for connections, and especially for Dylan."

"I'll get Samantha to suggest someone,"Justin said. "Maybe she can spare someone from the 'diplomatic corps.' Meanwhile, I'll get Jim and some of his people to help move the Vortex machines away from here."

Safari

Jim McDonald took on the job of getting a few vehicles, personally selecting a pair of Bobcat 4x4 ATVs with a high towing capacity. Steve helped him transport a few tons of gravel from Earth, which rained down on a cleared area near camp—it was distributed so evenly that just driving over it with the vehicles tamped it down into a serviceable parking lot.

Jim had considered adding a helicopter to the fleet, but Justin vetoed the idea as probably a waste of time, since Jim was the only one at camp who knew how to fly one.

The Vortex machines were unplugged and strapped to a trailer platform for transport. Jim and Justin had used the surveying group's maps to chart a route that would be passable with an ATV towing the trailer, around the headlands of streams and bypassing rough areas. The route was 400 miles to reach a spot only 200 miles away, but deemed safest.

Then Steve set up a large gateway opening to the distant storage spot, and Justin and Jim drove the ATV through. Unhooking the trailer, they looked back through the gateway. The landscape around them was lush and rolling hills, far greener than the desert by the sea where the base camp was located. In the distance down a valley was a stand of tall treelike plants.

"Want to take off and see what's out there?" Jim said. "We have a Net box to connect us. We can drive for a few hours then open a gateway to return any time we want."

Justin looked around and considered whether being gone for a few hours would really matter. "Sure, let's do it," he said. "But let me send Sam a message."

"She's standing right there," Jim pointed out. And she had walked up to the other side of the gateway to watch them.

"Hey, Sam," Justin shouted. "We're gonna take a drive around and come back by nightfall. Okay?"

"Sure!" she shouted back. "We'll leave the gateway here just in case you turn back for some reason. Umm…"

"What?" Justin shouted.

"Can I come along?" she said.

* * * * *

They drove into the forest slowly. The ground was soft with decaying leaves, but easy driving. They passed through several natural clearings, and a stream meandered parallel to their route. The valley grew wider and the bottom flatter, and eventually they reached a scrubby plain. The river meandered away to the north.

“Further?” Jim said, and they nodded. They drove along the banks of the river until they reached a sandy area where another river joined it —and they could not cross. They got out and walked around, looking at the water flowing and the aquatic life it held—not quite fish, but spiny wriggling things.

“What’s this?” Samantha said, pointing at a ridge of stone with her toe.

“Let’s see,” Justin said. He traced the line of the ridge with his eyes, and saw an angle a few paces away. When they had gone all the way around the stone, they knew it was something artificial—a triangular stone slab without cracks or features. Except at the corners, which were inset with dark blue metal.

“This does not look natural,” Jim observed. “More like a foundation, or a survey marker.”

“I’m marking the location,” Justin said, tapping the map app on his phone. “We can scan it from camp.”

“So there were people—or something like people—here once,” Samantha said. “Maybe we should find out what happened to them.”

“But it’s probably time to go,” Jim said. “It’s getting dark, and we didn’t bring the guns.” So Justin opened a gateway large enough for the ATV, and they drove through it back to camp, not speaking.

That evening, Steve scanned the spot where they’d found the stone. It was the only unusual object in the area—a meter thick and uniform. They recorded what they’d found and sent it to the survey team to investigate further.

Show of Force

Weeks passed while the propaganda and diplomatic war continued. Taiwan secretly signed an agreement with the rebels, while Nauru, Argentina, Chile, Nicaragua, Angola, Tunisia, Vietnam, and Sri Lanka released public statements of interest. The Council met to discuss the plan for increasing participation.

"You'll notice," Jim McDonald said, "that the countries most interested are those who feel threatened by a nearby power, and never had nukes themselves."

"How many countries are leaning our way?" Ben asked. "If they've been talking with us and sounding positive, we want to show them some favoritism."

"I'd say most of the less powerful countries favor the idea," Samantha said, "but they don't want to risk offending a great power, or giving up the aid and security guarantees they have now. So getting them to sign will require a demonstration that their former security partners are on the way out."

"Steve and I," Justin said, "have prepared a demonstration which should impress some people who haven't been taking us seriously. Which is most of them."

"Now that there aren't any limitations in program space or speed," Steve said, "gateways can be as large as you want. We've come up with some ways to use that, and a long list of locations over cities to display what gateways can do."

"We've borrowed from Jordan Jacobs' work on gateway views of scenery around the universe," Justin said. "Thanks for doing that, Jordan." Jordan waved from the audience.

The plan came together, and the Council set a date for its historical resonance: the Fourth of July.

* * * * *

The displays were timed to start first on the East Coast of the US, then proceed with the setting sun around the world to finish in Europe. Steve started the program with a click of the mouse. They had set up a display in the community building so everyone could watch, even though it was early AM camp time. The view was taken from a point on the National Mall near the Washington monument, pointing toward the Capitol building. Other screens showed the major US new channels.

Visitors who arrived at the National Mall early to get a good spot for the concert and fireworks display were among the first to notice the light dimming. While the sun was still visible as a disk just before it set, only the edges of the sky near the horizon were still bright. The rest of the sky got darker and darker, until in a few minutes it was black. Stars began to show in the blackness.

“We've covered all of the big East Coast cities with visible-light-only gateways,” Steve said, “above the level of airplane flights and a hundred miles wide. The fade was cool, don't you think? Now they're looking at the star field from light-years away.”

The news channels were breaking in to report the phenomenon. Excitable newscasters found people to interview. Some of the people who had waited for hours decided to leave in a hurry.

“I think we should project the statement now,” Justin said. “Before people panic.”

Steve clicked. Above the Capitol, giant gold letters in perspective scrolled out their short message:

People of Earth!

> For too long you have lived in fear of nuclear armageddon and terrorism.
>
> Your governments have armed themselves and competed to build more and more destructive weapons. They could have destroyed the world many times over, and they used the need for defense and security to justify repression of your freedoms.
>
> We have a better plan.
>
> We have developed a technology that frees us all from fear. We offer the stars, and an end to war and suffering. For the next hour we will show you the universe that awaits us.

"This is set up like a good fireworks display," Justin said, "with the best saved for last."

Steve clicked, and a view of the Earth itself took up the sky, from a few hundred miles up. The dark gateway areas covered the Northeast, and some lights had appeared in the uncovered towns to the north, while the west was still in daylight.. After a minute, the view changed to a closeup of the Moon, with craters and mountains in sharp relief. Then it was on to Mars, with the Tharsis Montes volcanos lined up in a row and Olympus Mons looming behind them. Then Saturn took up half the sky, the rings running from horizon to horizon. Then they started viewing some of the planets identified as colony prospects—one world of blue oceans and green and brown lands after another. The pace quickened, and the sky was filled with a view of the Crab Nebula from close up, tendrils of plasma looping through the sky. The Pleiades from inside the star cluster. The Galactic Center, with tens of thousand of bright stars packed into a small area—the sky was filled with light from them, and it was as bright as day on the ground.

"It's a good thing this is visible-only and I've set a limit on brightness," Steve said, "or those people would be getting more radiation than would be wise."

The view expanded to show the entire Milky Way Galaxy from above, and then zoomed down to the center again, to a bright whirlpool of gas around a fuzzy point. "Most of the audience won't know what that is," Steve said, "but that is a realtime view of the accretion disk around the black hole at the center of our galaxy, which can't be seen from Earth because of intervening dust clouds."

The sky went to black again. "And now for the fireworks," Steve said, and clicked.

A pinpoint brighter than any star appeared above the Capitol, and dimmed as it expanded into a bluish-white, then yellow, then orange ball. "One of the larger US thermonuclear bombs," Steve said. "I refined my object-move program to move it to a highly-compressed volume, which was effective in setting off its fissionable trigger." As the orange cloud faded to black, two more went off side-by-side. "The explosion is actually happening a light-year away. It's a good thing this window only allows visible light through, or the power grid on the East Coast would be burned out, and most computers and electronics fried. If only a few of these weapons had gone off at this apparent height over the developed world, most of those living would have starved before the delivery and communications systems could be rebuilt."

"Is that the end of the show?" Samantha asked.

"That's it," Justin said. "We'll send out a statement for the media telling them what they saw, and the rest of the world will have the program before the show. But we thought the surprise value would be best used on DC itself."

The news networks showed a silent crowd. Scattered applause broke out, but most people who had viewed the show appeared to be talking to others. Reporters broke in to speculate and discuss the display with a panel of talking heads who didn't seem to know very much.

Steve set up the program to run the same show automatically for the cities in successive time zones, and the audience started to leave the Community Building to resume their night's sleep. The council members lingered to watch the news coverage. They had calculated that about a quarter of the world's population would see it directly, while most of the rest would see video coverage.

Ultimatum

By the time Justin and Samantha were awake and ready to read the news, the display was about to start in Asia, first over Japan, then China. Headlines from the news aggregator:

```
DC Reax: News Conference: "Faked Lightshow"
Astronomer: True 'Window' Parallax
Russia: All Nukes in Place
Spectral Analysis: Thermonuclear Blasts
Top Ten Colony Planets
```

"Denial with flashes of acceptance," Justin said, "as you'd expect."

"The governments are still denying," Samantha said. "So you may have to continue with demonstrations. Especially for the US."

Having been warned in advance, the Japanese media coverage of their display was spectacular and thorough. Interviews of Japanese experts and street observers were split between skepticism and hope that all the nukes were really gone.

Breakfast was subdued, and someone had set up a screen showing CNN's coverage of the Beijing display. The government spokesman admitted talks with the rebels were occurring, but denied that China would consider agreeing to the security proposal, which threatened Chinese sovereignty. Troop movements had been spotted by satellite, but the spokesman denied they were significant; merely exercises planned months earlier.

Sitting with Ben and Samantha, Justin said, "How many countries have agreed?"

"Twenty-one, including Taiwan's secret agreement," Sam said. "What do we do if China launches a conventional invasion of Taiwan?"

"We stop it," Ben said. "If Taiwan is with us, we've promised to protect them. So that would be the first test of our promises. We can't afford to blow it."

Steve and Rasna came by and sat at the end of the table. "Good morning, all," Rasna said. She received mumbled greetings in response.

"Steve," Justin said, "is there any way you can track Chinese missiles and planes in case they start an attack on Taiwan?"

"I've thought about that," Steve said, "since that was the primary reason they signed up with us quickly. I've set up a monitoring program that looks at every hunk of metal crossing the strait there, and flags it if the speed is abnormally high. I'm having one of the techs try to view each airplane to make sure they're civilian. So far, so good."

"Have we sent all the agreement countries the Colony Planets RFP?" Ben said.

"Yes," Samantha said. "There are around 200 countries and we have survey information on about that number of likely planets, some more desirable than others, of course. It doesn't actually make any sense to give Nauru its own colony planet, of course, but we're taking proposals. The more likely and populous countries will get first crack at the best."

"Don't forget," Justin said, "we need to keep in reserve the most perfect, tropical, sandy-beach planet for our penal colony. We want a place people would pay to vacation on. And then we want to be able to show how hellish it is when the criminals we send there have all their needs satisfied and nothing to do."

* * * * *

The day passed slowly, and the display marched across the Earth, reaching India, Russia, and Europe by the end of the day.

Steve and Justin were in Steve's office after dinner when they were notified of activity near Taiwan. Steve called up the monitoring program. "Missiles crossing the line," Steve said. "I'll turn on the missile shield."

"That stops them?" Justin said. "Can we check on other Chinese forces?"

"Yes, any metal object much faster than an airplane gets transported to the sun," Steve said. "Possible airplanes have to be allowed through, so we check each one of those to see if it's a scheduled civilian flight. And we're tracking ships in the strait. See these groupings?" He zoomed in. "Naval vessels heading for Taiwan. Can't allow that." He clicked on each and did some more clicking and typing.

The ship outlines disappeared from the screen. "Where did you send them?" Justin asked.

"They are arranged on top of the most-visited parts of Great Wall near Beijing. The aircraft carrier I sent to the park next to the Forbidden City in Beijing. Another bit of history for the tourists to enjoy."

"Any airplanes need handling?" Justin asked.

"Let's look," Steve replied. "Here's a few squadrons of fighters and bombers." More clicking later, he sat back as the outlines disappeared. "They're flying over Tierra del Fuego now. Most likely they'll find an Argentinian airfield to land in."

"Embarrassing," Justin observed.

"That's the idea," Steve said.

* * * * *

They sent video of the Chinese attack on Taiwan, and its rapid deflection, to the media. Already there were reports of the appearance of ships on the Great Wall, and video of the bulk of the aircraft carrier looming over the Forbidden City walls and groaning as it settled into the ground of the central park in Beijing.

"Do we have any easy examples to be made of insurgents or terrorists?" Justin said. "Might as well take some out to prove we can do it."

Jim McDonald had come in to watch. "The Islamist group in Chad has been in the news," he said. "Kidnappings and killings. Pick on them."

Steve opened up the maps and took a look. A web search for news gave them towns in the area, and he focused an overhead view on them. He searched through the area and zoomed in on likely camps. "Aha," he said. "Trucks with machine guns in the back. Anti-aircraft weapons. This place needs some cleaning up." More clicking and typing. "I'm removing all large metallic objects from this entire area, right up to the town. That should take care of vehicles and heavy weapons, as well as freeing the caged hostages. Biggest thing left would be a pocket knife. I think the locals will be able to take revenge if the guns are gone." *Click.*

"Can we send an alert to Chad's defense forces telling them it's safe to go in?" Justin said.

"I'll get that done," Ben said, leaving.

* * * * *

It was midnight camp time when Samantha came by with more reports. "We're up to 78 countries. The Taiwan thing had a big effect, and I think we'll see fifty more by tomorrow. Canada, Mexico, Japan,

Britain, and Germany have signed up."

"Okay," Justin said. "We'll give the holdouts a bit longer to think it over. Time to go to bed."

* * * * *

The next morning, a message from the Chinese president suggested a face-to-face talk. Samantha rounded up enough of the Council to be credible, and when the time came, they opened a gateway to his office. Behind the president stood an array of generals and officials.

"President Liu," Justin said, bowing slightly.

"Justin Smith," President Liu replied. While an interpreter stood with him, he was known to be proud of his fluency in English, since he had spent a few years at a university in London.

"We were sorry to interfere with your military," Justin said. "Taiwan has signed our security agreement, and we were obligated to defend them."

"We meant only to control territory which is part of China," the president said. "Surely we have the right."

"You think so, but the people of Taiwan do not agree. You will have to settle your differences without the use of force."

"What if Tibet seeks to leave China? Are we not allowed to prevent that?"

"We have not signed an agreement with China as yet. Those conditions could be negotiated. We would tend not to approve of the use of force by either side in such disputes."

"We are not happy with your interference. Yet we also noted you avoided the death and destruction you are so clearly capable of."

"We will do as little damage as possible in pursuit of peace and harmony."

President Liu looked to the left and right, noting the facial expressions of his staff. "Our Army is doubtful, but I have decided. We will make you a counter-proposal. We want colony planets in proportion to our population. And we require internal security and policing to remain completely under our control, but we are willing to accept overall your security proposal if our sovereignty is guaranteed, and you have a similar agreement from the US and Russia."

"Have your people contact me to discuss the wording," Samantha said. "We'll work something out."

"Very well," President Liu said. "We look forward to further talks."

* * * * *

"So, who's left?" Steve asked at lunch.

"We have 150 countries signed up," Samantha said, "and conditional agreements with 25 more that depend on signing up their enemies. All of the ex-Warsaw Pact are with us, and most of the EU, and India. Outstanding holdouts include the US, Russia, and France, plus a gaggle of countries that just seem too disorganized to respond effectively."

"Stage two demonstrations coming next," Justin said. "Just the biggest holdouts."

Samantha went with Justin and Steve to watch them set up more programs. "Okay, what do we have for the holdouts?" Justin said.

"First we'll box up the top of some major monuments," Steve said. "They don't move anywhere, but the upper stories will be put into stasis with a special optical passthrough, so light will go in one side and out the other. People will see blue sky where the tops used to be. I've got that set up for major buildings and monuments: DC loses the upper two-thirds of the Washington Monument, New York most of the Empire State Building, Moscow the onion domes of St. Basil's, other cities their tallest building. A half hour later, the optical cap goes on, blocking all sunlight. Which reminds me, when this is over, we can offer free street lighting—"

"Later, later," Justin said. "For now we need to seem threatening, not helpful." He took Samantha's arm. "So, Minister, would you compose a message just for the holdouts? Along the lines of, 'your monuments are unharmed but will not be returned until you have agreed to our terms.'"

"I will phrase that more diplomatically," she said. "As in, 'until you have understood the benefits of our proposed security arrangement.'"

"Whatever gets them to agree," Justin said. "We could be doing demonstrations for weeks, especially with the US."

Steve started the program, and soon the US network feeds were full of outraged Congressman calling on the Administration to declare war on the rebels, or to seek out and resolve the rebel grievances. The more thoughtful called for continuing negotiations.

Steve and Rasna

Samantha continued to report more signups, and the total of countries agreeing rose to 179, including Russia, Pakistan, Australia, and France. Remaining holdouts: The US and a scattering of small countries.

Justin dropped by Steve and Rasna's tent after dinner to report progress and talk plans. As he approached their tent, he heard loud voices. When he knocked on the doorframe, the voices stopped, and Rasna came to the door to greet him.

"How are you guys?" Justin said. "Is everything okay?"

"Rasna's parents want her to get married," Steve said, "and she is pressuring me to visit them to settle it."

Rasna flushed and looked down. "It's not like that. They've moved back into their house and they say Babuji—Father—is ill and would like to see the matter settled. Which I doubt—that he's ill, I mean—but they do want us to get married."

"Did you remind them that we are in the middle of delicate negotiations over global security?" Justin said. "And that your boyfriend just stole all the world's nuclear weapons? Can thinking about a wedding wait just a bit until the fate of the world is settled?"

"When you put it that way, it does sound foolish," Rasna said. "But my father's an engineer and he thinks in terms of getting the job done and checking it off his list."

"Tell your father Steve is critical to our operation and can't take time out for personal matters for months, at least," Justin said. "If he's an engineer, he'll understand that."

"I did try to tell her that," Steve said. "It's not that I don't like the idea. I just don't see a need to stop work to do it. There will be time later."

"It would be easier for me if one of you told them!" Rasna said. "It's hard to disagree with my father about anything. And my mother will cry or do something manipulative like that."

"If it helps, we can go talk to your parents," Justin said. "I can see why Steve doesn't want to talk to them until he's ready."

"Maybe tomorrow," Rasna said. "It's the middle of the night there."

"Okay," Justin said. "Could you excuse us while I talk to your future husband?"

"Oh, sure," Rasna said. "I'll take the trash out and see who's around."

Rasna picked up the waste bag and left.

“I wish I could copy myself and have the copy take care of those kinds of things,” Steve said. “Which reminds me—I forgot to mention it yet, but I implemented object storage. We can now scan anything and save its complete state at that moment to substrate memory.”

“That will be handy when you get the replicators built,” Justin said. “Until then, what’s the point?”

“I took the liberty of scanning myself and all of the members of the Council,” Steve said. “That attack reminded me that we are all critical members of a team, especially me. So I have a program tracking each of us and making regular backup scans, just in case.”

“Don’t you think you should have discussed it with someone before just going ahead?” Justin said, his voice rising gradually. “You copied people *without asking them?*”

Steve shrank a bit, and said, “It’s just data. If it’s never needed, no one has to know.”

“Eventually,” Justin said, “they have to know. And you have to do the same for everyone here, to be fair. Copy the whole damn camp.”

“I was planning to do that,” Steve said, “and all the important items we use. A library of things to be generated on command.”

“People are a bit different,” Justin said. “If you tell them that if they die, they can be brought back as they were at some past point in time, they might accept that. But it’s a choice they should make for themselves.”

“Okay,” Steve said. “This is one of those people things I leave to you to handle.”

Underground Arrow

Dylan Foster drove into the Taco Bell parking lot and picked a bench near the drive-through for his meeting with Christine Immerman. Since the chip had been removed, he had adopted strict security for communications, and it was no longer worth risking a physical meeting with anyone regularly in the White House, since they might all be tracked. Now they were relying on the encrypted cellphones with headsets, and Christine was supposed to leave her office and go to a noisy place where she could walk while talking. That would make it extremely difficult to intercept much of the conversation.

At the appointed time, he called. She answered, “Dylan, I hope this is really necessary. I found the loudest noise I could find, jackhammers doing roadwork on 7th Street. It’s giving me a headache.”

“It’s necessary,” Dylan said. “They may be able to track people moving, in which case they could be listening in on you now.”

“Well, I can’t hear myself, so good luck if they’re trying.”

“Getting on to my report,” Dylan said. “We have the staff scattered and working via encrypted cell only. The big teams are making progress, especially the group at Illinois who have achieved an eight-by-eight matrix of qubits. They’re trying to scale it up further, using an array of phosphorus atoms embedded in silicon. That makes for more qubits in a small space, so the chips used aren’t unusually large.”

“So the Illinois team is getting closer. Still, eight-by-eight qubits is a few orders of magnitude too small to get us where we need to be. Better than no news, but when will we have a weapon?” Immerman said. “We can’t wait for a solution. The president is under pressure to settle with the rebels to get their demonstrations out of the news. It’s fucking *dark* down here.”

“The work may take months or years. I have cloned their team at five other research labs to speed up the development of the approach."

"We don't have months or years," Immerman said. "We may have to at least pretend to agree to the rebel's terms. This means you will be officially fired and a new head of the National Security Lab put in place. We say we've stopped doing research and disbanded your project, but you continue under the black budget—we'll transfer your people over to some NSA program number. Sorry, but you have to appear to have been repudiated—maybe arrested for embezzling, we'll come up with something to publicize your disgrace. Meanwhile, your budget is going to be unlimited, since it's clear most of the weapons we spent so much on these past few years are now useless, so we'll stop spending on them. Not that we would stop buying them entirely—jobs for the districts, y'know!"

Dylan took a deep breath. "I understand. I accept the temporary need for public gesture so long as our basic agreement remains, and after I give you what you want, I get what I want."

"Fair enough. We officially break you and you go underground, but the agreement remains. Anything else?"

"I've also set up 'clean room' teams of students," Dylan said. "They came out of physics and computer science with no association with quantum computing, in case the usual quantum researchers are being watched. I have hopes for entirely new theoretical approaches. There are hundreds of four-person teams."

"That's very nice but hardly reassuring," Immerman said. "As you said once, breakthroughs can't be planned. I think your other approach sounds more likely to be useful in the near term."

"But we could get lucky," Dylan said. "These are the smartest kids I've ever seen."

* * * * *

On New Earth, a member of the surveillance team watched her

monitor as Christine Immerman put away her phone while walking slowly back to her office. The lipreading software combined with the voice pickup were able to decipher much of what she said despite the noise, and the transcript looked important enough to rush to Justin.

Hunting Qubits

Justin finished reading the transcript of one side of a phone call by Christine Immerman, apparently talking with Dylan, who had so far escaped their tracking program. He walked over to Steve's desk to discuss it.

"We have some word on what Dylan's up to," Justin said. "Some people at Illinois have got an eight-by-eight matrix of qubits working." He handed Steve the transcript and the report on the research team at Illinois. "This was the approach they were known to be using."

Steve read it and looked thoughtful. "I may be able to do a search for an arrangement like that. No way of distinguishing silicon chips in general, but the arrangement of phosphorus atoms is distinctive. This is an old approach which suffered from noise issues—I'll read up on it and see if I can find more specs on their hardware."

"Doesn't sound like they are anywhere close—'months or years'—so you have time. But notice she's saying they are planning to pretend to fire him and stop research, but he's going to go on trying. While they pretend to agree to our terms and stab us in the back as soon as they can. Bad faith."

"You think the other governments aren't going to try to develop the technology?" Steve said. "I would imagine secret quantum research is going to be a preoccupation of all the great powers."

"We set things up so that governments would get out of the way peacefully, and their power would fade naturally over time," Justin said. “Doesn't seem like they want to fade away quietly.”

Jim McDonald came by, and they filled him in on the transcript.

“One thing is obvious,” he said, “we need to keep an eye on all the world's quantum computing researchers, not just the ones in the US. I'll put somebody on adding the rest of the researchers to the database of academics we're watching.”

“Even if we lack the people to look at all that data,” Justin said, “recording it gives us a chance to look backward when somebody does come to our attention. So record everything.”

“Notice how we're starting to sound like the NSA?” Jim said, laughing. “‘Record them all, and let God sort them out.’”

Stasis

Justin went around to other members of the Council to see if the apparent plan of the US government to agree to terms made any difference.

“No,” said Ben. “They may still need a push to go over the hump.”

“I see no reason to ease up on them,” Prof. Wilson said. “They should be more afraid of what we might do than they are so far. The pretense that they control the situation continues.”

“They haven't freed political prisoners.,” Michael McCulloch said. “Civilian encryption is still illegal. I say fry ‘em.”

“The most powerful are the last to give it up,” Jim McDonald said. “If we don't make an example of them, the rest of the world will see it as license to test us.”

So when Justin returned to Steve's desk, the plan was executed with the click of the mouse. Reflective stasis fields appeared around all major government buildings in Washington, DC, while the darkness lifted as the light shield over the city disappeared.

Steve had farmed out the task of calculating the coordinates to outline the major buildings with rectangular prisms. The White House and executive office buildings were surrounded by one large box; the Pentagon disappeared into a mirrored cube a kilometer high and wide that also covered its parking lots. The reflective surfaces were everywhere around the Mall, and thinned out until the last one around the CIA's headquarters in Langley.

Meanwhile, major US military bases around the world got the same treatment. There were casualties when a transport plane in mid-landing at a European base crashed into the stasis wall, exploding on impact and sliding down the frictionless surface.

Since it was a work day, hundreds of thousands of Federal employees were frozen inside their buildings. The news reached the network in minutes, but the understanding of how many facilities had been frozen took some time to assemble. Panic began on Wall Street, with traders selling into what had already been a weak market, and the dollar tumbled.

"Release the statement," Justin said, and Samantha sent a message to her people.

```
Facilities of the Federal Government of the US have
  been placed in a stasis field for 24 hours. No one
  inside the fields has been harmed, and they will
  be unaware that any time has passed when the
  fields are removed. The Security Agreement has
  been signed by more than 190 countries, and as the
  last remaining great power, the US has a responsi-
  bility to join with the rest of the world in ac-
  cepting this beneficial new arrangement.

If the US government does not approve the treaty
  and sign our agreement within 24 hours after the
  stasis fields have been removed, our next step
```

```
will be to permanently remove all of the facili-
ties now preserved in stasis, crippling the func-
tioning of the US government.
```

The statement reached the wire services in minutes. The networks interviewed people in the US who were outraged and shocked, but a few were willing to admit they enjoyed the feeling of revenge as the powerful were brought down. In the rest of the world, the numbers were reversed—many were openly celebrating the blow to the US.

Justin called up a window to talk to Daniella Pink. "Justin. Everyone," she said when she saw the window. "It's after dinner here but I came in to keep in touch. You're becoming wildly popular as people all over the world realize you're winning. The polls in most of the world show approval of your actions. Everybody loves a David vs. Goliath story, and they've resented the American swagger for a long time."

"How long until they see us as the Goliath and want us gone?" Justin said, turning to look at the others in the room.

"You usually have a honeymoon of a few years," Daniella said. "If you're planning to let people do what they want and not interfere, they'll continue to think of you as a benign force that removed the threat of war. If you start bossing people around and threatening them, then you'll soon be seen as the oppressor."

"About what I thought," Justin said. "Everybody happy?" He looked around, and saw mostly nods of agreement. Only Michael McCulloch was frowning.

Clean Room

Dylan made calls out of his cheap motel room while the world waited twenty-four hours for the stasis fields to end. When the time came, he had to explain to one CIA caller that a day had gone by—apparently the caller had been about to call him when the field froze him, and he had no idea he had been frozen. Dylan was quietly amused at the consternation of lesser minds.

Then he got the call from Christine Immerman. "It's going down as I said it would. Prepare to be publicly shamed. The president and her cabinet are in hiding, and the rest of us are to work from home until we're sure this is over."

A few hours later, the president and members of Congress went in front of the TV cameras to jointly announce signing of the treaty. The president was grim: "We've agreed to the conditions of entry into this security agreement only because we've been threatened. We expect the rebels to fulfill all of their commitments to the people of the US, including those on security and anti-terrorism."

So they can *act fast,* he thought, *at the point of a gun.*

Dylan made more calls to reassure his researchers that they would continue to be funded, and even have funding increased. The Illinois group had made another stability breakthrough, and Dylan sent them the Vortex source code he had stolen so their theorists could work out how to map the gateway functions to a new device type. It was obvious they were several generations away from duplicating the number of qubits in a Vortex-5, but with more money and more teams somebody could get closer faster, or so he hoped.

One of his "clean room" teams in California was making progress on a completely different technology which used lasers to address excited ions in a plasma. He realized they needed something like the mirror-controlled lasers used to cut connections on chips after testing, and referred them to an engineer at one of the companies that had mastered the technology to precisely aim lasers thousands of times a second.

Another team at Caltech had a masterful young theorist who was approaching the problem by viewing quantum phenomena as emerging from a universal cellular automaton. Dylan got them in touch with the laser group in hopes they could bring those ideas together.

Then he sent them the source code as well—it might contain more hints on how to open a gateway.

Enter Kuklov

Justin met with the Grey Tribe's Michael McCulloch and his assistant Alex Kuklov on the day of the US capitulation. Kuklov had arrived weeks after the original Grey Tribe exodus, but had rapidly become a spokesman for those who chafed under McCulloch's directives, so McCulloch had dealt with the problem by taking him on as an assistant.

"We understand why we're working with the governments," Michael said. "You wanted to lull them into a false sense of security thinking their domestic operations would go on as usual."

"That's right," Justin said, "which is why we didn't make many demands you guys wanted as conditions. They wouldn't have accepted an end to their power over their own people. The elite depend on the graft and the cartels that have been set up over decades and enforced by regulation. Do you think the media would have been fair to us if the media owners realized they would be losing their monopolies?"

"True enough," Kuklov said. "But our people want to see real progress in tearing down the Internet walls and freeing up information. The situation where our people are is still the same—we are watched and hounded. I left Russia to get away from secret police, and still they are everywhere."

"We're asking governments to accept a big loss of power and sovereignty," Justin said. "We have to give them time to adjust before pushing for more."

"There are actions we can take to disable some of the Great Walls," Michael said. "We can begin flooding the world with our own Net nodes which would let anyone bypass local controls."

"Are we sure our Net can withstand attacks from hostile elements?" Justin said. "Opening our Net up to the global population is a drastic step to take when we know there are governments out to get us. Could we perhaps wait a few months and see how it's going?"

"We've engineered it for security," Kuklov said. "The primary issue is not the Net, but servers connected to it, and we can isolate ours for safety. Letting the rest of the world use it to route around walled areas should be safe enough."

"So we install a firewall on our subnet and assume that will be good enough?" Justin said, sitting back in his chair. "Tell you what—do that and send out some Net nodes to your people in the countries with extreme walls. Just a test to see what happens, and make sure we can disable them if anyone tries to attack us through them."

Michael looked at Kuklov, who shrugged and said, "Okay. But we want to see more change and more freedom as soon as possible. We didn't work to see gradual freedom. We want it now."

Michael lingered at Justin's desk after Kuklov had left. "Sorry about Kuklov's pushiness," he said. "Our people fail to see why we shouldn't push the governments harder while we have the advantage. And I understand the impatience—he was a teenager in the Soviet Union, moved to Estonia, and enjoyed the burst of freedom there before the Russians stepped on them again. He ran out of places to escape to, and he burns to get back at the authoritarians."

"If we push harder," Justin said, "the existing power structures will fight us harder, and some of the trade arrangements people depend on will collapse before anything new is ready to take their place. So I understand what he wants and why, but it took decades for the world to freeze into these blocs, and it will take awhile to undo that without setting off a global depression."

"Well, you have to throw them a bone. Distributing the Net boxes will help, but some more dismantling of bureaucracies would feel better."

"Do you remember what happened when the US dismantled the single party and repressive bureaucracies of Iraq after they toppled Saddam Hussein?" Justin said. "That's an extreme example, but don't assume that when you remove a dictatorial state that peace and harmony will break out. Better to remove the source of their power and let the system evolve gradually toward more freedom. People who are used to being told what to do will tend to look for someone else to tell them what to do. Which means demagogues and divisive tribal politics can gain ground."

Part Five: Diaspora

Chapter Nine: Colonies

Multiplying

“So we won,” Justin said, “but there’s still a shitload of work to do.”

Samantha took a sip from her wine glass and looked at him across the table. More and more often they ate dinner at the small table in their tent to escape people who wanted to talk to Justin about Something Important in the mess hall.

“I think that’s one of the rules of life they hide from you so you won’t give up in despair,” she said. “The reward for succeeding is more work.”

“If Steve ever gets those replicators working, I’m going to copy myself and leave the copy with all the work. You and I can sneak away for a long holiday.”

“That would be nice,” Sam said. “Saving the world was important, sure, but where’s the ‘we time’?”

"And we know the US government and others are still plotting to stop us, if they can."

"For tonight, let's forget all that and enjoy the feast the chef came up with in honor of Bastille Day," she said. "Coq au Vin made with boneless chicken strips from a factory. Leeks au Gratin with fresh leeks, presumably stolen. And a chocolate mousse for dessert."

"It's very nice, though that's not the revolution we'd like to emulate."

"Too bloody," she agreed. "But there's another reason why tonight is special."

"And what might that be, my sweet?"

"I dropped by Medical today to check, and I'm definitely pregnant."

Justin had no humorous comment for that, and was silent for a moment, then said, "That's… wonderful! But how? Haven't we been careful….?"

"I got out of the habit of taking the pill when we left Earth. And it got messy a few times, and once you entered me again after you took the condom off, while we were spooning. Plenty of slip-ups."

"Well, it's a happy accident," Justin said. "At least it is if you think it is."

"It is," she said. "But you know our parents are going to want a wedding sooner rather than later. Even in the modern world it's embarrassing if you show during the ceremony."

A Million Worlds

The planetary survey group had updated their files again, and there were now over two hundred likely colony planets which had passed all the tests of habitability for humans and their crops. Final tests would require visits by teams of biologists looking for less obvious predators and pests, but the proposals from governments and private groups began to pour in, along with outraged protests from environmentalist groups in the rich countries demanding no pristine planet be "contaminated" by Earth life.

The survey group gave each candidate a number, and when Justin started to hear talk of the ruins on Planet 631, now dubbed Bee Planet, he took a look at some of the images that were causing the stir.

The images showed what had clearly been enormous habitations, looking like giant honeycombs made of some durable white material that gleamed like glazed ceramic. Up to ten stories high and miles long, the buildings (or were they excretions?) went on for miles, with collapsed bridges between them littering the ground beneath. There were no signs of the inhabitants, and the life remaining on the planet was either primitive plants or aquatic. Something had happened to kill off these creatures, but the only evidence remaining was the nearly-eternal shells of their dwellings.

Since its atmospheric composition was marginal, Bee Planet had been reserved for future study. Justin wondered how many of these dead worlds they would find, and how long it would be before they encountered a living civilization to rival humanity.

He went back to look through the genuine proposals received so far. As expected, many were less than thorough in following the guidelines laid out in the RFP, some just asking for any planet and giving no specifics on support commitments, recruitment policies, or level-of-effort.

Then there were extremely detailed proposals from major countries like India and China, which despite the few weeks that had passed since the RFP was sent out, showed that a large number of people had been consulted and took the process seriously. The Indian proposal even included suggested locations for permanent gateways near highways and rail terminals.

They had also received serious proposals from NGOs ("Non-Governmental Organizations," he explained to Steve, when he came in to look over his shoulder.) Separatists of various kinds wanted to establish planets where only their kind would be allowed; there were lesbians, ultra-Orthodox Jews, schismatic Muslims, polygamous Mormon sects, and neo-Nazis who were hopeful they could have a planet uncontaminated by discordant types of human. The lesbians attached a manifesto arguing that in vitro fertilization and sex-specific embryo selection would result in a paradise finally freed of oppressive patriarchy. Justin was interested in finding out how that plan would actually turn out, but decided to vote it down.

"What was wrong with that one?" Steve asked.

"The ultimate plan is for active movement between the colonies," Justin said, "and while a geography-based government might exert some control over who comes to visit or stay, we don't want to allow exclusionary colonies. Fine if they want to be majority-something, but we wouldn't allow them to banish people who otherwise conform to their reasonable rules of law. Being of the wrong race or sex is not an allowed reason for exclusion, under our basic rights law—it's right in the RFP. So encouraging this kind of thing would only lead to trouble, as it has on Earth."

"So we are encouraging people to colonize, but not to require isolation?" Steve asked.

"Exactly," Justin said. "We're not advertising it yet because it would discourage government investment in the colonies, but the purpose is to build a highly-connected network of habitations that will guarantee survival of our civilization as a whole. The colonies will be diverse, but not so separated they evolve into disconnected cultures. Human cultures will all be unified in the substrate. And here's Ben's comment on the lesbian separatist proposal—'unlikely all female children will want to be lesbians despite social pressure, sounds like a coercive and totalitarian idea that denies biological reality.'

"I was looking at the Australian proposal," Steve said, "which talks about establishing a mining industry for the economic base. That seems like a waste of time since I'll have the replicators done soon."

"That's another example where we are withholding information," Justin said, "so we have to gently discourage them or let them waste time and money on irrelevant activity. Maybe we suggest mining wait until further studies are done."

"Well, I've trained people to set up permanent gateways, so we're ready to go whenever the proposals are approved."

"Just between you and me," Justin said, "I think after the rush of government-sponsored colony efforts with careful scientific vetting, we'll just start doing the vetting ourselves and opening more wherever there's demand. I think there are a lot of people willing to be pioneers that governments won't want to allow to leave. So first we look like we approve of countries cloning themselves, then when it's too late for them to back out, we blow the doors off and let humanity stretch out. And by that time you'll have your replicators for them."

"So I should get back to work on that problem," Steve said, heading back to his desk.

Show Trial

Dylan heard indirectly about the plan to have him arrested and arraigned on charges of embezzlement. All for show, he was reassured. He protested via encrypted email—he had no time for play-acting, and there was a danger the rebels could find him and track him if he had to report to a courtroom.

The response came from Christine herself:

```
We're not going to waste your time or expose you.
  The arrest and trial will be done with a body
  double, and the video doctored with CGI and voice
```

```
replication software. Completely convincing and
undetectable—half the President's speeches are
done that way now. We have to use a real prosecu-
tor and a well-known defense attorney, but your
part will be short and scripted, and your speech
generated by software that changes the actor's
voice to resemble yours. You'll be sentenced to a
long term in Federal prison—where of course our
friends up above will never find you.
```

He wished he could get word to his parents that it was all a sham, and he was still doing important work, but there was no way to do that without possibly being tapped.

And then he realized that, as far as the world was concerned, he would be a convicted felon rotting away in a cell. If he was supposedly killed by another inmate, no one would ever know they'd disposed of him in whatever way was convenient for them.

He had just parked at the gym when his phone buzzed again. It was a message from the team in Illinois that had been making progress on the silicon-based approach:

```
All prototype devices disappeared overnight, along
  with much of the lab equipment. The department's
  servers and backups vanished, and the University
  central storage was destroyed. The Physics Depart-
  ment has shut down the project as too dangerous to
  host here, and Homeland Security is on the way.
  Please advise.
```

He sat in his car for a long time, then began making phone calls.

Wedding

When Daniella Pink heard about Samantha and Justin's wedding plans, she volunteered to make it rival a British royal wedding as a global propaganda coup. She suggested "a few extra special guests" and multiple film crews to give several media conglomerates 'exclusive' coverage.

"Don't fight me on this, Justin," Daniella said, starting to make a list. "This is a prime opportunity to tap into that primitive human impulse to identify with royalty. The media have been preoccupied with tensions between your people and the governments. This will get them back to the story of peaceful rule from above."

"How we plotted to take over the world and leave it ruthlessly alone?" Justin said. "I see what you're saying, it's great PR. It's just too much of a security risk to have too many people visiting us for the occasion."

"What if you keep the list down to a very few people from neutral countries," Samantha said, "and only one cameraman, the same one Amanda used. We can give exclusive interviews by gateway window. There are still efforts to get at us."

"And we are keeping it simple," Justin agreed. "It's the first marriage under our own law, so it's very simple indeed. Prof. Wilson will play pastor—he looks and sounds the part—and the contract is just between us. No legislature determined our promises to each other."

"No one cares about the legalisms, sweetie," Daniella said. "They want to hear the words and see you kiss your bride while your mothers weep. Fathers too, for that matter. A triumph of hope for new life over aging and death! It can be very simple and still look spectacular for the cameras. I know just the designer...." She started another note.

"Now, wait a minute!" Justin said. "'Designer'? What would he have to work with up here?"

"You'd be surprised what a great designer can do with flotsam and jetsam. You have plants there, no? Wires, string? And besides, you can help him get whatever he needs from Earth, though it's a shame you can't set yourself up as endorsers—'By Appointment to Their Majesties Justin and Samantha' would be fabulous marketing."

"Let's not push the royalty analogy too far," Samantha said. "We're thoroughly common."

"You two are more refined than some of the royalty I've seen," Daniella said, "trust me. One of the Princes was notorious for chewing with his mouth open at state dinners."

"I'm not even elected yet, much less royal," Justin said. "And it gives the wrong impression of what we are about."

"You're not going to let me have any fun, are you?" Daniella said. "Very well, it will be relentlessly middle-class. But you can still do with some style. Get your friend Wendy to help you find the right dress, Samantha—if you keep her from overdoing it, she'll make you look fantastic. And music..." She added more notes to the pad.

* * * * *

The wedding had taken on a life of its own since they had talked to their parents and set the date. Word got around, and somehow it leaked to the media on Earth. This produced another round of in-depth stories of their lives and their families, this time minus the reminders of their dangerous rebellion.

Life for the vast majority of the people had not changed. The US had at first denied holding any political prisoners, but eventually most were paroled to 'responsible' parties. The smaller dictatorships had to be reminded of the agreement they had signed, but continuing pressure by rights groups backed up by demonstrations of force when necessary had freed most of the known prisoners. The many Net nodes set up by Grey Tribe members inside walled Internets had made routing around the walls much easier, and the governments had made no moves to block them.

The world had settled into an uneasy new normalcy. And the wedding would be a show to legitimize them further in the eyes of the masses, who were more concerned with personalities than politics.

* * * * *

Daniella's designer friend Marcus arrived with a full load of sample books and ideas. It had to be explained to him again that they wanted a very simple arrangement and that he would have to use local materials, with perhaps a few additions transported from Earth. He rejected the chairs from the mess hall as "too colorful"—since they were various colors of plastic, Samantha could see his point.

They fetched him the day before the wedding to complete his design. The field overlooking the beach was cleared, and rows of white chairs transported from his supplier put into place. The bulk of the greenery was native, but orchids and yellow daffodils imported from Earth made up for the shortage of showy native flowers.

The aisle between the rows of chairs led to a simple bower entwined with native vines and white flowers. Lacking formal clothes, camp guests wore everything from Hawaiian shirts to lacy sundresses. The day was warm and sunny, and the guests transported from Earth were overheating in suits and formal dresses, but the mix looked good on camera. Marcus had brought formal English morning coats for Justin, Samantha's father, and best man Steve. Daniella herself came in a flowing pink gown, and looked around the camp curiously as Justin escorted her and her husband to the wedding site. "This is it? The source of the force that disarmed the world?!" She laughed and seemed delighted.

"This is Steve Duong," Justin said, pulling Steve toward them. "He's really the force that disarmed the world."

"Nice to meet you, Daniella," Steve said. "Justin exaggerates, but I did do a lot of it."

Wendy approached them. "Close to time," she said. "Justin, your grandfather is here with your parents, down front. You might want to say hi to him before this starts."

"Oh, right!" he said. "Daniella, you have a place reserved down front.

Let's go see my grandpa!"

* * * * *

Finally the music started and the guests took their seats, at first slowly, then quickly. The DJ was a Grey Tribe member from Germany, working with a playlist provided by Daniella and Marcus of Bach, Handel, and popular love songs performed by string quartets.

Justin waited next to Prof. Wilson under the bower, and the processional music started. Rasna and Steve appeared from over the rise and walked slowly down the aisle, splitting when they reached the bower to stand on either side looking back.

Then, after a pause, Samantha and her father walked slowly forward in time with the music. Her gown was lacy but restrained and elegant; her auburn hair was swept upward and held in back with white flowers. Justin took it all in—his mother starting to sob, his father next to her looking back to see Samantha, Samantha's father holding her hand as they walked down to the front.

Amanda's cameraman had set up video cameras at several points, then moved around taking stills with a big-lensed camera. The few guests from Earth included the Minister of Foreign Affairs from Taiwan and the Indian Minister of Science and Technology, as well as a British pop star client of Daniella's.

Justin followed Prof. Wilson's lead and made it through the actual ceremony. Prof. Wilson quietly instructed Steve to produce Samantha's ring, and Justin put it on her finger without too much of a struggle, while Rasna fumbled a bit before realizing she already had Justin's ring in her hand. She handed it to Samantha, who slipped it on Justin's finger.

Then Justin and Samantha were kissing, and it was over, with much clapping and cheering as they joined their families to smile for the cameras.

* * * * *

Daniella had arranged for the live video feeds to be streamed by Net and edited and mixed for broadcast, and the ceremony was seen by millions live, and billions later. She reported that their approval numbers had risen further, especially in the US, where the aftereffects of negative government propaganda still lingered. More than sixty percent of Americans polled now approved of their actions.

Replicator

A few weeks later, Steve asked Justin to come take a look at the replicator software. Justin came by with a mug of coffee to sip. Steve had built a Lexan box a meter on a side with a stainless steel floor next to his desk.

“What's with the box?” Justin said. “Why not just instantiate the new object wherever the user wants it?”

“While testing I wanted some protection against explosions or dangerous gases,” Steve said, “which came in handy several times. The other reason is that having a talisman embedded in the floor of the box tells the app exactly where it is and tells it which account the box is associated with for design charges. Having a specific location for scanning and instantiating simplifies the user interface—put something in, press the ‘scan’ button; take it out, press the ‘new’ button, and you have your meal or whatever. Having to specify what's being scanned and where to put the copy are additional steps in a UI for more sophisticated users.”

“So any dummy can use this like an appliance,” Justin said. “That makes sense. Where is the matter coming from to create new objects?”

“That was a harder problem,” Steve said. “I thought I could just store the same data in substrate cells and the result would be the same object, but it's not quite that simple—the amount of data that has to be written to create even an atom is enormous. It's far simpler and faster to find complex components of the object, like atomic nuclei of a certain isotope, in other locations and rewrite the external connections to relocate them and orient them toward their near neighbors in the object. The atoms are relocated from late-stage stellar atmospheres that contain all the elements."

"In amounts that are lost in the noise by comparison to a stellar mass. Okay, so you won't be eroding anything important by accident."

"Right," Steve said. "And the same for disposal—an object can be eliminated by transporting its components into the same stellar atmospheres. No mess."

Justin looked around and noticed the bowl of fruit and a row of identical stuffed bears. "This is what you've been testing it on?"

"Those and these," Steve said, pointing out the cage next to him. Several white mice crawled over each other. "We now have more mice to test with than we started with."

"So you can copy living things?" Justin said. "Cool. But scary."

"I used the more complicated UI for testing it on people," Steve said. And a second Steve came out from behind the curtained-off area, grinning.

"My god, Steve, really?" Justin said. "You did it. But you can't just dispose of your test subject when they're human!"

"If it's me and I consented," the second Steve said, "I don't see why not. All that is lost is the memory of experience unique to the copy. And there's a good reason to have more of me around—there's too much work to be done for just one of me."

Justin considered this. "You could also scan the copy before disposal, and when you instantiate them later, they'd have the memories created since you made them."

"Correct," Steve said. "Nothing has to be lost. In science fiction, there's usually a way to merge the copy's memories into the original's, but we don't have that kind of ability—yet."

"I don't suppose you've mentioned any of this to Rasna," Justin said. "She may not take it so well."

"I'll tell her the whole truth," Steve said. "She's being pressured again by her parents, since you two went and got married in front of the whole world. With my assistant here, I can take a week off and we can get married while he handles the work, and that will make her happy. For everyone else, I have a cover story. It turns out I have a twin brother, 'Larry,' who's just arrived from Vietnam and has poor English skills, so he won't talk much."

"You had better program the software for normal use so it can't scan or duplicate people," Justin said. "People would try it and chaos would follow."

"I thought of that," Steve said. "The story will be that living things are too complex for it, and the software will refuse to work if it detects signs of life."

"Wise choice," Justin said. "Though we will know better, and I can see a benefit to starting to keep scans of everyone, just in case. Someday literally everyone, so accidental death would be a temporary problem."

"That someday is not so far away," Steve said, "but we have a few years of setup before we'd roll out something that big. But I can quietly start a program to store scans of everyone who passes through a gateway or gets transported. And as the number of people who have talismans expands, more and more people would be backed up."

"And please keep that secret," Justin said. "The Council should know soon, but no one else needs to until we start bringing back accident victims."

"Is it ethical to withhold that even for a few months?" the second Steve said. "How will a bereaved family feel knowing we have held back from restoring a lost loved one?"

"The psychological effect of that knowledge would be unpredictable, and we're already changing things faster than people might tolerate. Store the data and we'll announce we have it at a later date."

"Okay," Steve said. "But we need to get a big library of foods and material goods scanned in before this will be ready for the public. How are we going to tackle such a big task?"

"The library of objects could be like Wikipedia," Justin said, "user-built and free to all unless the design is copyrighted. That kind of crowdsourcing system is a Grey Tribe problem. Let's build a few more of these replicators and announce them to the camp so they can get started thinking about design."

Steve turned to his keyboard and typed in a few commands, then clicked the mouse. A second replicator box appeared next to the first. "See?" he said. "It's really quite handy. Build once, copy thereafter." 'Larry' nodded in agreement.

Reverse Engineering

Dylan was on a treadmill when he got the message to call the clean room team he had set up at Caltech. He called them while still cooling down.

"Anderson?" he said, "I got your message. What's up?"

"We've had a breakthrough!" Anderson said, breathless. "Will had an insight and we just succeeded in opening a pint-sized gateway. To the parking lot, but we can see though it."

"That's great news," Dylan said. "It will give me something positive to report to the president's people. They have been pushing for any sign of progress."

"Will says he can see how it all works now," Anderson said. "We're trying to find out how to set coordinates."

"Be careful you don't allow matter through until you know what you are doing," Dylan said, thinking of his burn scars.

"We know that. The first opening was to vacuum."

"How stable is the hardware?" Dylan asked.

"It works fine for hours at a time," Anderson said. "We solved the overheating problem with a new cooling system for the lasers. Since then, few problems."

"I'm coming out," Dylan said. "I want to work on it myself. And get those people from Cal to come down as well. They can miss a term."

"Yessir," Anderson said. "Are we still supposed to keep this secret?"

"More so than before. Not a word to anyone. The people who have published in the field are probably under surveillance. You guys will be famous soon enough."

Civil Unrest

The first colony planets were opened to science teams selected by the governments of India, Taiwan, Britain, and China. Steve personally set up the exploratory gateways, typically on military or scientific sites convenient for the exploring teams.

One of India's three awarded planets had to be disqualified when a biologist discovered an omnivorous soil-dwelling worm capable of drilling through boots in seconds and undeterred by the biochemical differences of Earth-evolved life. The biologist who made the discovery paid with his life, and was memorialized by having the planet named after him—his body had been stripped of flesh in minutes inside his protective suit. Second-guessers noted that the armored hooves and the low population density of the above-ground animal species that had been catalogued should have been a clue to the presence of such a ferocious predator, but since the worms were normally quiescent in soil their presence had gone undetected by remote viewing.

That and similar incidents led to a change in protocol, with those teams that had not already done so adding decontamination and backflow-prevention airlocks to be used until planets were deemed free of hazardous organisms that might be able to thrive on Earth.

But most of the planets originally surveyed turned out to be as free of hazards as they appeared, and the colony teams began to move. Steve set up the first few connecting gateways himself and then handed off the work to others. In India, wide gateways were set up along highways, near train stations, and in areas with dense populations of subsistence farmers who would be most likely to jump at the chance to occupy new lands. In China, gateways were located in military reservations at the government's request, and regiments of troops were the first colonists. Taiwan got a single planet with a gateway near Taipei, and teams of scouts were sent in first to visit all the likely sites for cities.

The US was lagging, and negotiations continued. Factions in local governments rejected proposed sites, and concerns about traffic overloading and safety dogged the talks. "It seems that fear of unlikely or easily-managed problems is greater than desire to open up new territory for people to use," Samantha said.

"The US is a late-stage oligarchy," Ben commented, "sclerotic and resistant to change. Nay-sayers have been given a legal platform to halt physical progress for so long that it's hard for their governments to get out of the habit of stopping everything when a loud interest group squawks. If it might have an effect on someone's sinecure, you can bet someone will file suit to stop it."

"It's interesting to note how differently the idea is treated in different cultures," Justin said. "The Indians just check to be sure families have the suggested supplies and let them walk through. The Brits send in organized teams with expensive equipment and vehicles. The Chinese send in soldiers first, then farmers, not even checking for equipment. Like they assume those who are unprepared deserve what they get, or will get help from others."

"Each government is unconsciously trying to clone its society and power structure," Ben said, "which shouldn't surprise us."

At a gateway in northern India's Assam region, a local warlord came down from the hills with his troops and attacked the government forces surrounding the gateway area. Some of his forces made it through before the gateway could be closed. "Enterprising of him," Jim McDonald noted, "but a losing idea, since we're obligated to remove any guerrilla forces." Jim and Steve took to the console to find and transport back all the armed men who had crossed over, and then put the warlord and his army that remained massed near the Earth side of the gateway into stasis fields. Video of their reflective statues made the news networks. "They took a chance, they lost," Jim said. "Someday we'll unfreeze them, but for now they serve as a useful warning to others."

Most of the smart pioneers had phones and solar power panels, and Net-cell interface nodes had been placed on the other sides of the gateways, so early colonists were able to report what they were finding on social media. This only increased interest from those who had been fearful and stayed behind. Every day more people crossed over, and after a few days some of the new planets had tens of thousands of colonists spreading out around the founding gateways. As in the Wild West in the US, law enforcement was an afterthought in many of the colonies, but most colonies remained peaceful and only a few outlaws caused trouble.

Meanwhile, Kuklov and McCulloch had put the Grey Tribe and kitchen staff to work scanning raw and prepared foods for the replicator project. The object database built up, and others began to add common household items like furniture and bedding. The menus for selecting items for replication began to get complex, and one person got to work simplifying the menu structure and adding most-recently-used lists to make it easier. The day came when the replicators were useful enough to roll out so that everyone in camp had one, and suddenly the mess tent as focus of social life in camp began to decline.

Pattern Match

Dylan had been out in Pasadena for several weeks overseeing the growing project to build on his pirate team's success in opening at least a small gateway. Again he was stuck in a crummy-but-expensive old motel he chose for its convenience to the campus, and spent half his time keeping campus administrators from noticing how many unauthorized staff were at work in the basement labs of one of the oldest buildings.

The team from Berkeley had joined them and occupied two more rooms of the abandoned basement. Dylan had moved an old desk to one corner of Will's lab and set up his laptop there.

One morning after a wasted hour dealing with the accountants back in DC, Dylan called Will over for a progress report.

"What's the holdup now?" Dylan asked.

"The hardware won't support a larger gateway or higher-speed matter transit," Will said. "We have too few qubits and even a small object at low speeds strains the computational ability of our machine." Will was a shambling, overweight stereotype, and smelled for lack of recent bathing. Dylan had to hold his breath when Will was near. But he was a genius on par with Steve Duong, and had grasped much of what Steve had discovered after working through Steve's program code.

The better-groomed Anderson sat down with them and picked up the conversation. "The Cal team are working on a next-generation machine with four times the qubits. That should give us a fast gateway about a meter square."

"What's the ETA on that machine?" Dylan asked.

"Two weeks," Anderson said. "They're stuck waiting for laser assemblies." The lasers used to pulse ions to read or write data relied on tiny mirrors made of silicon attached to their base chip by flexible hinges; these mirror-array chips were difficult to make.

"Question for you, Will," Dylan said. "If we are having this much trouble with processing power, how is it that the rebels have been able to open large numbers of large gateways? They can't have built that many more machines."

"I'm guessing they have figured out how to move programs into the substrate itself for execution," Will said. "That should be possible, but I can't wrap my head around how you would address particular cells to do so. It's not like they're numbered. The gateway works by addressing the particles and cells relative to their patterns, but I don't see how to write new programs into cells. Yet!"

"Keep working at it," Dylan said. "Our need right now is to get the gateway large enough to be useful, and this new machine should do it. How are you doing on the search part of Steve's source code?"

"I think I have that coded for our machine," Will said, "but I haven't tested the code yet. There are sure to be bugs."

"I want to be there when you're ready to test," Dylan said. "Call me over."

* * * * *

“The search relies on a pattern match,” Will said, demonstrating the new program. “A template of the characteristic elements and local qualities is set up in qubits, and the quantum calculation returns one or a set of locations that come close to matching the template.”

“Have you tried it at all?” Dylan asked.

“The first thing that popped into my head was to set it up for nearby concentrations of U-235, since that must be how they found the nukes. The results were as you’d expect, views of atomic reactors.”

“We can use that to find out where they’ve stored the nukes,” Dylan said. “But let’s see if we can find their base. Can you set up a search for a gas with temperature and composition similar to Earth’s, with gravity close to ours, but at least a light-year away? The closest ones would be most likely.”

“Give me some time to work that out. The g-field is a second-order characteristic, so I’ll have to write a little code for it.”

* * * * *

Dylan was just finishing up a take-out Chinese dinner at his desk when Will called him over. “Okay, I have a list of likely spots,” Will said. “Here they are in order of distance.”

“Let’s open some viewports and see what’s there,” Dylan said. Will clicked on the first item, and they got up to look at the small gateway window that had opened in front of the machine.

“We need to set up a camera here,” Dylan said. “We need to record what’s seen and then we won’t have to come over here every time we look at something.” Anderson left them to get a video camera.

The view they could see was orange, and the vegetation was scrubby and black. “This doesn’t look like New Earth,” Will said. “On to the next."

Several tries later, Dylan called a halt. "They must have used a more specific search. We could be here all day looking at false leads. Can we add some terms to the search? How about G-class sunlight, and blue sky?"

"Sky color is beyond what we can do in search," Will said, "but the temperature curve of the light—the ambient photons—and a more detailed specification of trace gases in the atmosphere might narrow it down."

Anderson had returned with a video camera scrounged from the Cal group next door. "I'll set this up and plug it in to the network," he said. A few minutes of fiddling with software, and their monitors had a window open to the camera view.

Will set up the new search and the list was shorter. The third planet they viewed had green plants and blue sky.

Siri on Steroids

Weeks passed, and Samantha switched to looser clothing as her midsection expanded. She kept up her exercise routine and was pleasantly surprised when she felt little morning sickness, until one day she did.

"You okay?" Justin said, looking up from his reading. "You were gone awhile." Justin had started reading on his pad computer after eating a breakfast from the replicator, sipping his third cup of coffee.

"Just a little sick. Threw up for the first time," Samantha said. "And I look terrible."

"Aww," Justin said. "You look wonderful. Come here." He beckoned and she came over to take his hand.

"Ooh, bad idea," she said. "The coffee smell is making me feel queasy again." She walked to the other side of the room and sat down.

"It's a miracle of nature," Justin said, "but I guess nature isn't too concerned about your stomach." He typed in a search command. "Morning sickness normally ends around the twelfth week. This is abnormal."

"It could just be a little food poisoning. What actually bothers me is my head," she said. "I can hardly think most of the time. Fuzzy."

"I assume people are cutting you some slack?"

"Mostly. Sometimes people talk to me and when they're done I have no idea what they said. Which can get me into trouble."

"Knock-knock," Steve said, coming in while rapping the doorframe. "I miss having you across the tent in the morning, Justin."

"I always start by reading the incoming," Justin said, "so I might as well do it here."

"Well, I wanted to show you what we've done in uploading elements for the voice command and AI agents. Kuklov helped a lot by finding packages to string together—voice recognition and semantic processing and deep data pools with a Hadoop-like package. I helped him rewrite the neural network parts of the deep learning modules to run parallel in the substrate—you can map substrate cells to neurons and run them all at once, like in a real brain."

"This sounds like a lot of complexity to get a Siri-on-steroids so we can do voice commands," Justin said. "Like a Frankenstein monster of software."

"Much like that," Steve agreed. "Disparate parts, hooked together by an executive function app that is itself a learning program. I'm giving it eyes anywhere it wants to see, and ears to hear. And it's using the

Net to fill its databases with associations, copying everything on the Web from Earth, categorizing and recognizing. Because substrate search is close to instantaneous, it can do symbolic and semantic pattern matching like a true associative memory."

"Skynet again?" Justin said. "I thought that was years away."

"It probably is," Steve said. "So far it's chugging away and has generated petabytes of associations and inferences, but no signs of consciousness or malevolent intent. But you can ask it questions and get much better answers now."

"I hope you haven't given it any actuators to go with the sensors," Justin said. "If all it can do is answer questions, it's okay to experiment. If you gave it a way to manipulate matter, we might be in trouble."

"It can't use any of the apps without a human's key, so unless you tell it to do something, it can't give the app the authorization it requires."

"If I were a malevolent intelligence, I'd save the key a human gave me and use it later."

"It can't program itself to do things like that," Steve said. "The executive part learns in the background and with each request processed, but the basic processing loop can only start with a human request accompanied by a valid key, which would normally be read from your talisman. So no independent actions, just a lot of background thinking while it waits."

"If you say so," Samantha said. "How would you pull the plug on one of these AIs if it started to act up?"

"You access the OS directly and kill its process," Steve said, "just like you would on a computer."

"Hmm," Justin said, "I wonder what would happen if we took Prof. Wilson's A-Life simulator and gave the organisms in the simulation substrate-based AI brains. Would they evolve by genetic recombination and get better and better organized for learning?"

"That would be interesting to try," Steve said. "You almost had Prof. Wilson's simulator running on the Vortex-5. We could use it as a layer on top, running thousands of AIs inside against each other to see which did best, then the best ones would mate and pass on their traits, searching the design space for a real AI."

"Skynet!" Justin said. "Something to look forward to, when we have time."

Chapter Ten: Treachery

Poison Arrow

Back in the basement lab at Caltech, Dylan put Anderson to work searching the near-Earth planet they'd found for signs of the rebel base camp. Will had set up a search for the Vortex-5's type of gallium arsenide grid plates nearby, and the result opened to a view of a trailer with crates loaded on top, apparently abandoned. Tracks in the soil led away in two directions, one trail ending quickly, the other going for miles down a valley until it disappeared into deep grass.

"Is there some way we can speed this up?" Dylan said. "This proves they are on this planet, but where is their camp? Maybe they moved the machines away from their camp just to prevent us from finding them easily."

"They must have vehicles to make those tracks," Will said. "Why don't we search for a concentration of iron like you'd find in a truck?" He started to punch in changed search parameters, and soon they were looking at a view of a large black rock in a grassy field. "Meteorite," Will said, and continued. On the fourth try, the view showed a small truck, like a Jeep with a cargo bed.

"Good job, Will," Dylan said. "They must be nearby." And as they panned the view around, they spotted a row of tents in the distance.

*****

```
From: ArrowLeader
To: NSC-President

Breakthrough confirmed. Rebel base camp in view.
  Team has succeeded in duplicating technology, and
  we have found someone comparable to their technol-
  ogist. Request permission to terminate base camp
  and rebels since they have already shown they will
  quickly deflect an attack aimed at capturing them.
  Please provide contact with expert in field nukes
  in case we can find where they have been stored.
```

```
From: NSC-President
To: ArrowLeader

Permission to terminate granted. When communica-
  tions are secure again, we will bring in security
  to assist you and place your team under protective
  custody. Your request for a new lab will be pro-
  cessed at that time. Tactical nuclear weapons
  expert will contact you.
```

* * * * *

Will had worked out a wrinkle in the software that would create a gateway that would allow through only dense forms of matter while holding back small molecules of nitrogen and oxygen, which would let them retrieve one of the nukes without an airlock. When he tested the modification, it seemed to work—when he opened the gateway to the vacuum of space, there was only a slight breeze toward it.

Dylan received an email with a list of likely tactical nukes and markings from the experts at the US National Nuclear Security Administration. The president's orders had reached them and they stood ready to provide the arming codes via encrypted email, a breach of normal protocol.

Will changed the search back to the element U-235, and after discarding atomic piles on Earth, found a cluster of highly-concentrated lumps of the isotope orbiting the Sun. The view was very dark, but by turning off the lights in the lab they could see hundreds of dark lumps of metal, some stenciled with words and numbers in Russian and English, resting gently against each other in empty space.

"I'm guessing these were pulled together by mutual gravitational attraction," Will said.

"We are looking for a small one that's on this list," Dylan said. "It will be small, the size of a footlocker, and it has to have a control panel so we can input the codes to arm it."

Will moved the view around the cluster of bombs, zooming in on labels. Hours passed as they looked at hundreds of dull-colored objects. Finally they spotted a smallish khaki-green cylinder stenciled "H-912."

"A US-made backpack nuke," Dylan said. "Very rare, and perfect for our needs. It fits though our maximum-size gateway. Look on the flat end."

Will moved the view to the flattish bottom of the cylinder. "Nothing much," he said.

"No, see how the end cap comes off?" Dylan said. "That should work. Let's get it though the gateway."

The gateway window was directly in front of the quantum computer setup at shoulder height. Dylan looked through the spec of the bomb; it was supposed to weigh 70 pounds or so, and its weight would pull it down as soon as part of it was moved across the gateway plane. Dylan remembered how the gold bar he had tried to retrieve by hand at the campus lab had pulled him down and into the edge of the gateway, cutting his shoulder. This time he would need a strong robotic arm retrieve the bomb.

"The lab has a forklift with a drum gripper that might fit," Anderson said. "Let me go see if I can borrow it without having to explain why."

Dylan and Will started to eat the takeout burritos Anderson had brought for dinner. Anderson came back driving the small forklift. “Took me awhile to get it down the freight elevator by myself,” he said. “And I’m hungry. Those look good.”

“Have the rest of mine,” Dylan said. “I want to get this done tonight. Are you sure you know how to operate this thing safely?”

“I’ve unloaded barrels of chemicals using one,” Anderson said. “It’s not that hard.” The forklift had a barrel-shaped pincer lined with rubber at the end of its loading arms which gripped when the arms were retracted a bit. It was normally used for unloading and moving 55-gallon drums.

When they had finished eating, Will adjusted the view window to be as large and as close to the bomb as possible. Anderson got ready by creeping up to the window until the pincer arms were almost touching it. He nodded to Will to open the gateway to matter.

They all felt the air begin to move toward the gateway. The bomb began to move away, at first very slowly. “Try to grab it now!” Dylan said.

Anderson moved the forklift forward and the gripper arms got close to the bomb, but it had moved away, bumping up against three large cylinders.

“Damn it,” Anderson said. “Not fast enough.”

“It’s up against the larger bombs now,” Dylan said. “Move in close and we’ll try again, and maybe it has nowhere to move to when the breeze hits it.” Will adjusted the gateway slightly, and again the bomb was in reach.

The forklift whirred as Anderson moved it closer. One side of the pincer touched the bomb and it rolled slightly, but then the other pincer touched it and it stopped. “Got it,” Anderson said as he closed the pincer on the bomb. He began to pull back slowly.

"Don't touch the edges, even if you have to stop and try again," Dylan said, watching closely. But as the bomb slowly crossed the gateway plane, the grippers easily cleared the edges of the gateway.

And then the bomb was entirely on the Caltech side. Will turned off the matter transmission, and the breeze stopped.

"Put it on the bench," Dylan said. "Wait, can you turn it on its side first, so we can access the panel on the bottom?"

"This is a cheap rig, boss," Anderson said. "Only up-and-down motion, no flipping or turning. I'll set it down and then we'll have to lay it down by hand." He lowered the bomb slowly to the workbench and released the pincers, then backed the forklift away.

It took all three of them to carefully lay the bomb on its side with the flat bottom at the front. The clamps that held the end cap opened with difficulty, and they were looking at a control panel from the 1950s. The codes were entered by rotating cylinders with numbers on them until the correct codes appeared in line.

* * * * *

Back in the rebel camp, Steve returned to his desk after lunch to find an alarm had gone off—two, actually. The watch program he had left to monitor the nuclear weapons stockpile had detected one missing, and its location had changed too quickly to be tracked. And a very similar concentration of U-235 had appeared in Pasadena, California. The Earth-focused bomb detection program was about to move the bomb it had detected to the storage area automatically, since Steve had known he wasn't always awake or near his desk to handle alarms. He stopped the automatic move and opened a viewing window to the location to check it out.

* * * * *

Dylan emailed the serial numbers and codes on the bomb to the expert. A minute later he had a return email with instructions on how to set the timer and the two codes that had to be entered. Dylan quickly entered the codes, double-checking to be sure he had them right, then he set the timer for one minute, leaving the button to start it for last. They got the bomb back upright and Anderson picked it up with the forklift. Dylan waved him toward the gateway and they positioned it carefully to avoid the edges. The control panel was facing down, and Dylan kneeled to check the indicator light again before pushing the timer start button. *Wouldn't do to start the timer until we know we can get rid of it,* he thought.

"Will," Dylan said, "get the window opened back to the rebel camp and be ready to open it to matter."

Will and Anderson looked at each other. "You mean we're sending that there?" Will said. "I thought we were just collecting them."

"President's orders," Dylan said. "We can't risk letting them control the gateway. We've been ordered to take them out."

"We didn't sign up to murder people," Anderson said. "We just want to do science."

"You think we gave you whiz kids this kind of money and equipment for just research?" Dylan said. "This is a fight to the death. If we don't take them out, the US is finished."

"I don't kill people," Will said. "At least people I know aren't bad guys."

"Well, get out of the way, then," Dylan said, moving to the console. "I'll do it myself." He reset the gateway to the rebel camp and opened it to matter. Will and Anderson backed away and stood near the door. Dylan moved back to the bomb and pressed the timer start button, then got into the forklift seat and started it moving slowly forward.

"At least be ready to close the gateway as soon as I have the bomb on the other side," Dylan said. The young men looked at him, arms crossed.

And then the bomb disappeared. "What the—?" Dylan said, before all three of them were encased in shiny stasis fields and vanished. The equipment in the labs disappeared after them, and the building collapsed shortly thereafter. A few minutes later, the main campus IT center suffered a structural failure and all of its storage devices were sliced into fragments. Sirens pierced the night air in Pasadena.

Treaty Violation

At the emergency Council meeting, Steve explained how he had stopped Dylan's attempt to nuke them.

"So, since the bomb was already armed, I sent it into the Sun," Steve said. "I brought Dylan and the students here in stasis, along with their equipment. Which looks like a different type of quantum computer. And a forklift, which we can use."

"So they were going to nuke us without warning," Justin said. "Nice way to keep the peace."

"The US government has broken the treaty," Jim McDonald said. "There should be a serious consequence." The meeting had been hastily called, and not everyone was there.

"We had a contingency plan for degrading their facilities if they had delayed signing it further," Ben said. "Should we dust that off?"

"Remember the people knew nothing about this," Samantha said, "and probably wouldn't approve of their actions, or us either if we start 'degrading facilities.' The Pentagon is an ugly building, but people are fond of it. It will make a great museum. Why don't we aim our retaliation at just the people who are responsible?"

"But this is a chance to cut off the head of the beast," Kuklov said. "The US government remains our enemy because they know most of their activities will soon make no sense. Before the people catch on to that, they want us gone so they can go back to the old game of fear and power."

"Well," Justin said, "first we announce what they were about to do and show the evidence, the video Steve recorded of the bomb being armed, the dialog in the lab, and whatever we can get off the computers. Then we announce a trial for Dylan—you say the kids weren't going through with it?"

Steve nodded. "They refused to help him when they realized what he was planning to do with the bomb."

"So we lionize them as heroes and recruit them," Justin said. "They were able to follow Steve's work, so they belong with us."

"They didn't figure out how to transport objects with compression," Steve said. "Luckily for us."

"So we have shown we were wronged," Kuklov said. "Then what?"

"We have the long list of government people we are tracking," Justin said, "and our surveillance team read an awful lot of each person's output. Let's poll our people and put a list together of the true bad actors—the people who really had power and abused it. Starting with the president and going on down."

"Just in the US?" Kuklov said. "Equally bad actors elsewhere. China, Russia, any number of nasty dictatorships."

"But those leaders settled with us and we have no evidence they're plotting, though I'm certain the Chinese will try to find or steal the gateway technology for themselves. But none of the other countries took action against us. So we punish the people responsible and let the others who might be thinking about it ponder their fate."

"So what exactly do we do with those people?" Samantha said.

"We could leave them in stasis as a lesson to others," Justin said. "But I think this is a chance to try out my idea of Paradise, a place that's perfect in every way, where your needs are taken care of but there's nothing to do but deal with other failed humans like yourself."

Court TV

They sent the package of evidence to Daniella and set up a meeting with her to discuss the spin potential of Dylan's trial on a charge of treason against humanity. Ben pointed out they had no governing law or Constitution yet, but allowed them a wartime exception using generally-accepted principles of summary justice in martial law.

"Nothing better for TV coverage than a trial," Daniella said. "You have a loathsome turncoat, a nuke from the Cold War era, threat to the hopes for world peace, idealistic young scientists, and a pregnant princess in danger. Ratings bait."

Again the world's press focused on them. The trial was set for a week away, and the two Caltech students picked up with Dylan were released from stasis to be recruited. They seemed delighted to be off Earth, and appeared to enjoy the interviews via gateway with Earth media.

Samantha argued for Dylan to be released from stasis so he could participate in preparations for his defense. "We don't want to look like a banana republic with show trials," she said.

"That's kind of what we are," Justin said. "We rely on the good sense of our Council and not much else so far, and we know he's going to be found guilty. So it really is a show trial."

But he relented, and Steve released Dylan from stasis into a cell built of gateway walls—it allowed others with talismans to enter and exit, but didn't allow him to leave. Steve activated the field around a room and an adjoining bathroom in the Community Building, which was also being set up for the trial, then transported Dylan into it. Ben Ramirez started to work on Dylan's defense, which he took very seriously.

Justin went with Samantha to visit him. She was nervous, and he hugged her and said, "Don't worry, he's harmless now." She smiled weakly and nodded, and Justin opened the door.

"Dylan," Justin said.

Dylan turned toward them from where he stood, looking out the window. "Justin! And Samantha. We've come a long way."

"Yes, we have," Justin said. "You especially. You shouldn't have worked against us."

"The odds were not in my favor, it turns out," Dylan said. "It seemed like a good idea at the time." He walked toward them and put his hands out to demonstrate the invisible wall between them. "Never really wanted to be a mime, either," he said, laughing.

"Why did you do it?" Samantha said. "I've never understood why. You were on our side. What made you change?"

"I was angry at both of you," Dylan said. "And I saw a brass ring I wanted."

"Your family is rich, so it wasn't for the money," Samantha said, "and you could have joined us. What did you want?"

"I wanted to be recognized. I wanted people to look up to me. I wanted to be important," Dylan said. "As it turns out, the government is full of people who want the same thing, and they stabbed me in the back. I could have destroyed all of you when we found your warehouse, but they wouldn't let me."

"That's nice to know," Justin said. "You wanted to murder us earlier, but were restrained by your superiors. Let me make a note of that."

*****

After the visit, Justin and Samantha walked slowly back to their tent. Samantha was still upset, so they stopped in at the impromptu bar set up in the old mess tent for drinks. "Whiskey?" Justin asked. "That would settle you a bit."

"Soda water with lime," Sam replied. "I'm drinking for two. But I could sure use some alcohol, that got to me. I remember being with him. I remember feeling protected by him. It's like a nightmare, realizing he was a psychopath all along."

"You would not be the first person taken in by one," Justin said. "They're good at hiding their true feelings."

Penal Colonies

Preparations for the penal colony planets continued. Justin's idea of planet Paradise was for permanent exile, while his alternate idea of planet Coventry would have a harsh climate, but offer the hope of return after relatively short sentences.

Replicators were redesigned for the purpose, becoming flat, immovable concrete platforms with an embedded talisman; they accepted voice commands and produced food, clothing, and shelter (in the form of small tents) and other common items on command. The features that made them valuable for colonial households, like power outlets and general-purpose replication, were removed. And while the Paradise replicators produced every kind of delicious food imaginable, the Coventry replicators were limited to nutritious but boring foods. They could also produce a selection of medications and devices suitable for frontier doctors—a standard of medical care that was considered good enough for the general population of most countries.

Justin suggested a rebranding for the new replicators. He wanted them called "grails," as they were in a science fiction series he had read as a kid.

The planet selected for Paradise had a long, sandy beach with trees behind, and a perfect temperate climate, with gentle afternoon rains the harshest weather. Coventry, in contrast, had ferocious seasons and dangerous predators, and the area picked out for the colony was windswept and cold most of the year, hot and rainy the rest.

Grails were spaced evenly across both landscapes, and everything was made ready for the exiles to come.

Dylan on Trial

The trial began with a statement of the charges. Justin took the role of prosecutor, and laid out the case against Dylan. He touched lightly on the background of Dylan's relationship with Samantha and her breakup with him, followed by the theft of gold from the US Treasury. He pointed at Jim McDonald and said, "James McDonald over there was head of Homeland Security's Advanced Threat Assessment Unit, and will testify about Dylan Foster's use of software stolen from our lab to gain himself a position with the US government and immunity from prosecution." Jim nodded to the audience, and Justin continued. "Dylan then headed up a secret research effort to copy our technology. He has admitted to us that he tried to bomb us once before but was only restrained by orders of the president."

Dylan rolled his eyes at that, but stayed silent.

"And he was caught in the act of trying to send a nuke into this camp, meaning to murder everyone in it, on behalf of his masters in the US government. We have videos and sworn statements from his student assistants, who refused to help him when they realized he meant to commit murder." The audience murmured.

"We as a society must cast out those who refuse to live by a code of civilized conduct. We intend to ask for a sentence of permanent exile, to be served on planet Paradise, so that he may never trouble us again. And we intend to send with him all of his superiors and those responsible for abusing their authority on the behalf of the people of the United States." More audience rumbling, since this part had not been publicly disclosed.

Prof. Wilson had taken the role of judge, and motioned to the defense, Ben Ramirez. Referring to his notes on how to run a trial, Prof. Wilson said, "Defense counsel, your opening statement."

Ben stood up. "Dylan Foster is a young man who saw his romantic relationship ending and believed he was being shut out by his friends. He may have been foolish or even criminal in seeking revenge, but his actions were ultimately the responsibility of the president of the United States acting under the authority of US law to preserve the security of the country as she saw fit. We concede that he tried to nuke the camp, but maintain that he was acting under orders when he did so and cannot be held responsible."

The trial lasted for one day; the videos shown were excerpts, with the full videos made available to the media and Council. The kids from Caltech, Anderson and Will, testified on their recruitment, the contract of secrecy they had signed, and Dylan's comments about his presidential orders. Those had been extracted from Dylan's phone by Grey Tribe wizards, who broke the phone's user security and were able to read the messages.

Jim McDonald testified about Dylan's offer to sell Homeland Security the source code for the gateway in return for a position directing research and giving him all the credit. Then he explained the experimental implant which would allow Unity Party officials to sway key thought leaders toward agreement with their policies, and how Prof. Wilson's implant was being used to brainwash him before he was rescued.

Ben's cross examinations were spirited, and he managed to get the witnesses to agree that Dylan had worked hard and apparently followed orders from the president herself. But he didn't even try to argue that Dylan hadn't wanted to destroy them all.

Justin made his final statement brief. "We all know what Dylan did, and if you find him guilty under these informal conditions, our wartime procedures allow us to extend his guilt to all of those who supported his actions and meant for everyone in this camp to be murdered so that they might retain their hold on power. We ask that you find him and his superiors guilty, so that the rest of us can live in peace and freedom."

Ben stood up to make his final argument. "We sit in judgment on this man and are rightly angry with him. He was greedy and foolish, but he is not guilty of any more than security forces everywhere who have to decide quickly outside of normal societal rules how to best defend their country. The president herself was doing her job as she saw it, and should not be exiled for it. These people will do no more harm when their power is gone. Leave them in peace—they lost."

As the sun was setting, the Council, serving as jury, voted to convict. Prof. Wilson announced the verdict and the sentence of exile, incorporating the long list of names from the US government agencies involved. "And let this be a lesson to us all. We expect our government officials to be held to a higher standard than individual citizens, and the punishment for officials who abuse their position and ignore the Constitution to oppress individuals should be severe. The public trust is not to be manipulated and used for self-aggrandizement.

"You realize we could have executed you, but we don't do that. You and your co-conspirators get to live on, but without civilization, since you acted against it. Sentences will be carried out immediately."

And Dylan disappeared.

While his copy Larry was in the courtroom and voted to convict, Steve was watching from his console, and set up the program to transport the president and the hundred or so bureaucrats and generals that had been involved in building her security state. They were to be distributed evenly along the beach in Paradise near the grails, a mile or so apart.

Then Justin joined him, and they sent the statement to the US email addresses describing the facilities to be removed in the next few hours. The Pentagon was spared, since as Samantha pointed out, it had sentimental value for many and would make a good war museum, but hated intelligence and security facilities were on the list.

Samantha came by, and they watched some network coverage of the trial before Justin and Samantha headed home for dinner. Steve stayed late, preparing the programs to wipe out most of the surveillance and security apparatus of the United States. He set the programs up to start in three hours, and left.

Execution

Many of the White House staff panicked and left for home after the notice of sentencing arrived, not certain that it would be safe. The Situation Room was used for a crisis meeting, and President Elizabeth Howard Stanton berated her staff and the NSC members who were in attendance.

"I want to hear a *plan,*" she said. "These people have made fools of us, and I want to know what we intend to do about it."

No one spoke for a moment. Then a member of the Secret Service spoke: "Our advice is to evacuate and move you all to separate underground facilities."

"How do we know they can't track us?" the president said.

"We don't," said the NSA liaison. "What we do know is that they intend to destroy all identifiable NSA installations, including our data center in Utah. So we are evacuating every one of our facilities and advising employees to hide with friends. Not that it will do any good."

"And we know they can do anything they want to the White House, and are probably listening in right now," the Secret Service man said. "So I suggest we leave quietly. My team has their orders and will disperse you all to secure facilities where you will be able to communicate."

* * * * *

When the hour arrived, buildings disappeared rapidly, starting with the CIA buildings in Langley and the NSA complex at Ft. Meade. The hospital-gulag where Prof. Wilson had been held vanished, leaving a perfect hole in the ground several stories deep. The Homeland Security building south of the White House left an even deeper hole, and water poured from broken mains to fill it. It was already dark in Wiesbaden, Germany, where the largest NSA-Army Intelligence Center was no more. The NSA's signals intelligence monitoring station in Yorkshire, which swept up all of Europe's phone and Internet traffic, was gone. Smaller CIA and NSA offices around the world also vanished, when they were freestanding enough to be removed without collateral damage.

The president was in a secure bunker built into a mountain sipping tea and trying to read news on an obsolete monitor when she disappeared. The others on the list followed, and over a hundred officials of a Republic that had metastasized into Leviathan were transported to Paradise, and exile.

* * * * *

The next morning after breakfast, Justin watched Steve set up the final program. Steve had suggested, and the Council had agreed, that the remaining nuclear arsenal was a nuisance and a hazard since there would probably be others that would find the basic tricks of the gateway before long. Objections that the weaponry might come in handy at a future date were answered by Steve's assertion that he could create a critical mass any time it was needed by sweeping

U-235 nuclei directly from a star and compressing them for delivery to any target.

So Justin checked over Steve's work to be sure, since a mistake could be disastrous. The targets were every major city that had been targeted by the great powers—lists had been compiled over the years, and they were probably fairly accurate. So Los Angeles would receive ten thermonuclear air blasts, New York five, and Moscow eight.

The explosions were actually taking place far out in space, and each explosion's carefully filtered and limited light, and a hint of sound, were conveyed through gateway windows over each target. It would look from below like nuclear Armageddon, but the bright light and loud rumbling would fade without actually doing any harm.

It was dark over the US, 11 PM in the East and 8 PM in the West. As before, they sent out an announcement warning that the world's remaining nuclear arsenal would be detonated over the cities that had been targeted by the nuclear powers, but that the display would be harmless. The world was on notice that such weapons were outlawed and any effort to build or use them would result in destruction of the offending group.

The explosions went off all at once across the United States. It was daylight-bright on the ground in Los Angeles and New York, and people watched in silence as hundreds of billions of dollars of weaponry was destroyed in seconds.

The news channels showed crowds cheering in some cities, and silent in others. Families had brought their children out to watch.

"Seems like a bad idea," Justin said. "What if we had been wrong in our filtering? People shouldn't act like it's a fireworks display."

"But it's history," Steve said. "Those kids will be able to tell their kids they were watching when the fear stopped."

New Dispensation

The next day the Council made a video statement to explain to the population of the US—and the world—what the new rules would be.

"We have removed the threat of world destruction," Ben said. "The nuclear arsenals of the great powers were too large—even one nuclear bomb is too large!—and would have doomed our species if used all at once. We will be watching and guaranteeing that armed aggression and terrorism will be punished immediately. No country will have to bankrupt themselves buying weapons to defend themselves."

Justin took over. "And we have destroyed the facilities used to spy on American citizens and the rest of the world. Built in fear of terrorism, they were being used to control our population and eliminate any threat to Unity Party control of our government. They were dabbling in thought control when we stopped them."

Samantha stepped forward. "Your governments will have to change and shrink, as many of their functions no longer make sense. This is where all of you need to vote for people who will change the old ways of thinking. Life will go on, and it will be better with more freedom for everyone. Taxes will fall, and more businesses will start up and grow. If you're in the private economy, you will do well, and you won't have to bribe a Unity politician to grow your business. As for those in government service, a period of transition will be necessary. For those in government surveillance and security, nothing that you were doing matters anymore. Find a new job."

Justin wrapped it up. "We have sent your president and most of her security officials into exile, and they will never be allowed to return. We are opening the colony gateways your governments had been stalling on, and any attempt at blocking the gateways or stopping people from leaving will be punished. The election scheduled for Tuesday is unfortunately going to be disrupted by the absence of the candidates for president and vice-president, but the procedures for choosing a successor candidate to run for the Unity Party are in place. We would ask you to consider non-Unity candidates for the highest offices. Write in someone you trust."

* * * * *

Steve personally set up ten gateways to the single planet awarded to the US, temporarily dubbed Jefferson. Several were near Northeastern cities and along the rail lines and highways between them. Central Park in Manhattan got one extending along the entire south border of the park, which would allow drivers coming up the avenues to pass directly through to what would later be roads on the other side, and subway stations on both ends made for easy pedestrian access.

Aging activist groups got up a last bit of energy to protest. In Manhattan, protestors held signs demanding a halt to the colony program —"Don't Abandon Mother Gaia," "Colonies = Genocide," "Don't Exploit the Worlds." Police were able to control the crowds, but their efforts prevented anyone from going through.

In Philadelpha, there were fewer demonstrators, but the gateway across Chestnut between Independence Hall and the Liberty Bell attracted a crazy person with a gun who killed four onlookers before shooting himself. The police searching his van found literature of a well-known green lobbying group. Leaflets screamed SAY NO TO COLONIES and SAVE THE WORLDS, STAY HOME.

Chapter Eleven: The Expansion

Interstellar

The town sprouted more permanent buildings as the population continued to grow. Recruiting had moved beyond members of Grey Tribe-affiliated groups, and Samantha's "immigration specialist" was busy vetting applications from friends and friends-of-friends of the original group, while a few people who needed to get back to business, like the arms dealer Quinn and Amanda Sundaram-Smythe, got permission to go back.

The day came when Justin's parents came to say goodbye. "We wanted to wait until you two have the baby," Justin's mother said, "but your sister and grandpa need us around now, and we've got work to do."

"Of course," Samantha said. "You can always come back when the baby is due."

"It's not that we don't like living here," Justin's father said. "We do. It's been one of the most interesting experiences of my life. But we're old and set in our ways enough to miss the house, the neighbors, the job —"

"Oh, silly," his wife said, turning to Justin, "He doesn't miss the job at all! But they miss him, and if he wants to keep the business going, he needs to get back."

"We'll call every few days," Samantha said. "And when you come back to visit, you can bring Emily and her kids. Justin misses them."

And so they said their goodbyes. After they had left, Justin turned to Samantha and said, "How about your parents? Have they mentioned going back? I guess it's safe enough now."

"They said they'd wait a month to be sure things had settled down enough. Daddy's been having a good time here—he says he's been more productive by gateway phone this last month than he would have been at home, and he's 'got traction' on some big studio projects about us. He usually couldn't get studio execs to return his calls before, but they all want to talk by gateway! But the novelty is fading, and Mom misses her people. So I'm guessing they'll be heading back soon."

* * * * *

Justin still thought of other-Steve as a copy, and calling him by a new name didn't quite work, but he tried to use the name Larry in public. Back in Steve's office, he met with both of them to talk about developments.

"Survey has added a lot more scientists willing to check out new planets," Justin said, "so the list that we've vetted ourselves is growing. We're handing these out to the least-organized countries, who didn't have much ability or interest in mounting the necessary expeditions."

"I've trained two people in Survey to set up gateways," Steve said, "so I assume they're handling it. They should also start setting up gateways connecting the colony worlds to each other. Those should be right next to the gateways to Earth, so that they become a hub for transportation between worlds."

"They've already started doing that," Justin said. "How is the grails-for-Earth project going?"

"We've worked with the UI programmers to provide interfaces for all the languages and cultures," other-Steve said. "It is taking some time since we don't have a native speaker of many of those languages, but we've made do with bad machine translations for the less important ones. The goal of making the food not quite as tasty as native foods for the transition period has been met—I tried some."

"And," original Steve said, "the Grey Tribe folks are duplicating and distributing them, in the poorest areas first. Where apparently a surprising percentage of the population has already emigrated. The Indian colonies have nearly a million people."

"Which," Justin said, "if I remember Prof. Wilson's lecture correctly, is enough to make their genetic and economic survival likely. So we've achieved one of our goals."

"There's news on the AI front," Steve said. "They are starting to generate complex queries and carry on a kind of conversation. We set them to talking amongst themselves, and they've been learning by talking to each other. Sometimes their conversations even seem to make sense, but sometimes not. My guess is that running at these high speeds and having access to infinite storage, we're going to see better and better conversation, and eventually internal conversation within each AI, with the subsystems competing to take charge of the conversation. Which theory suggests is the threshold of consciousness."

"So soon?" Justin said. "I thought it would take years to evolve."

"They learn and evolve a million times faster than we do," other-Steve said. "And they have almost all of the human noösphere[12] available on the Net to read and experience—every web page and book, every movie, every piece of music."

"When can they be trained to do law enforcement?" Justin said. "We're promising the world that we're the new sheriff in town, but we can only handle big things like organized terrorists and rogue governments. When will they be able to watch over individuals and maintain the peace? I don't want to think of how life on the colony planets is right now with only informal justice on most of them. Not that it's as bad as all that—the Wild West was pretty much self-organizing.

But still, when?"

"No way to predict," Steve said, "but I'm guessing sooner than we expect."

"Good. Everyone needs a guardian angel. Let's just be sure we keep control of them."

Election

The fabricated story of Steve's twin brother Larry had spread through the camp, and no one thought it odd when they saw them together. Somehow Daniella Pink had heard of the new arrival and wanted to set up human interest interviews for Larry, but she was gently dissuaded when informed his English was poor and he had little interesting to offer the tabloids.

"We have more people thinking it's safe to go back now," Ben said, talking to Justin at the crossroads of the two main streets of camp outside the gateway tents. "Is it time to enable the talismans so that our people can travel freely? Or is it still too dangerous?"

"I trust our people," Justin said, "but it would only take one doing something stupid to get themselves killed or kidnapped for what they know. We can open gateway calling for anyone to use by voice control from their talisman, but I don't think we're ready for visits."

"But it's been almost a year since we got here," Ben said. "People want to see family and friends. Some are starting to think about going back to finish degrees or start families."

"I know," Justin said. "My parents are wanting to get back to their lives. Normal relations and travel need to be established. I'm just worried a bit about the transition. How about we take applications for visit plans, emphasizing family visits, secure locations, and short durations? And we can have family members transported here."

"That will satisfy some of the need," Ben said. "I'll get a memo out."

"And I'll tell Steve to enable the gateway calling feature for everyone."

* * * * *

The Council decided to set the first election up to coincide with the US elections, on the first Tuesday in November on Earth. Ben Ramirez had been busy with his Constitution Committee and Future Law study group, and Larry had been working with the Grey Tribe programmers to write the substrate apps that would let citizens (which for now would be camp residents only) watch debates, read and mark up bills, and vote, or give their proxies to representatives.

The camp held a picnic the day before the election to give the candidates a place to meet and greet the several hundred citizens who might want to vote for them. The cleared area on the forest side was spread with folding tables and chairs, and music provided by a bluegrass band made up of Grey Tribe types. Time was set aside for hopeful representatives to make speeches about their policies and philosophy of government, and spirited debates broke out every few minutes between the sack races, barbecued hamburgers, and veggie vindaloo. Gateway screens along the edges of the field showed the news feeds from Earth, and sometimes the screens were showing the picnic itself a few seconds delayed.

Steve and Larry won the three-legged race, and were still out of breath when they came back to where Justin and Samantha were sitting with Rasna. "I'm surprised you cooperate so well with yourself," Justin said. "I'm not sure it's entirely fair to team with your double."

"Oh, really," Steve said. "I don't think we have any advantage. Unless we were to somehow connect our nervous systems—"

"Don't give him ideas," Rasna said. "It's already confusing enough!"

"Can you tell them apart?" Samantha asked her.

"I can tell when we talk," Rasna said. "Steve is more assured, since he knows he's the original. I think Larry is careful not to pretend to be Steve around me, and it shows in what he says."

Larry and Steve exchanged glances. "We decided that would be best for you," Larry said. "We both make sure you know which of us is with you."

"I'm happy with that," Rasna said. "As long as the one I sleep with is always the original."

Justin broke the short silence that followed. "Well, then. Look at the time! Looks like we're about to start." He grinned at Samantha, who rolled her eyes.

Chairs set up in front of the podium began to fill up as Ben took to the stage. "Welcome, everyone, and welcome to viewers on every planet. We are about to have our first selection of representatives to write and ratify the constitution of the Universal Framework." He waited for the applause to die down. "It's intended to guide humanity into a future of freedom for everyone, and it is the principles we will use to enforce rights on every planet, for every human being.

"We recognize that smaller communities will wish to enforce their own rules on their own residents that may be more restrictive than we propose. This is a natural human tendency, and we have resolved this tension by requiring only that membership in a community of that sort be voluntary—in other words, anyone who does not wish to be bound by the rules of their own community is free to leave and take up residence elsewhere.

"So our rules—universal rules—are minimal. Certain rights are universal: no government, group, or person can take someone's life or property, or harm them through force or fraud. We call these crimes, and will enforce punishments of temporary or permanent exile for convicted criminals. Our legislature will write laws, but no new crimes can be invented—laws will only clarify boundaries, and changes in criminal laws will require a supermajority. We're working on a way to register and enforce contracts through our systems, but that goal is a few years away. In the meantime, local authorities will continue to enforce their laws when they are consistent with the framework.

"I'm asking for your proxy to write and ratify the legal framework for a new age of humanity. Most of you know me, but those of you who don't, please come introduce yourself and tell me what's on your mind, or send me a message with your ideas."

Next up was Alexander Kuklov. "We have won a great victory, and it's time to build on that. Repressive governments have lost their excuse for controlling citizens and information, and we have blown up the walls between Internets, and planets. The frontier is open again, and no one has to stay in a place where they are stopped from achieving or being who they could be. Building the new worlds of humanity will take time and effort, but no one has to waste time waiting for a Central Committee to permit them to live. We want everyone who doesn't fit where they are to escape to make their own world, and we will prevent the warlords and politicians who enslaved humanity from returning to power.

"I ask all of you to give me your proxy so I can represent your viewpoint. I am for freedom and knocking down walls between countries and worlds. We can go faster, and we should."

Wendy Fields took the stage. "Hi, everyone. I'm Wendy, and I spent most of your early days here on Earth working on logistics under cover, so many of you don't know me well. We have a group of citizens here top-heavy with scientists and programmers, and of course we wouldn't have this chance to change everything if it weren't for Steve and his programming, but there are other important fields! I'm a designer and businessperson, and I will try to represent more artistic interests that we so far don't have much of. Now I think having committees decide what is art and supporting it with tax dollars is deadly to true creativity—art should please and educate people enough for them to be willing to pay for it themselves, and I'll be working with Samantha to design a system of compensation for art and design delivered through replicators and the Net.

"You could give me your proxy for everything—lord knows I've got an opinion on everything! But you could also carve out a sub-proxy to give to me for issues relating to art and intellectual property. I will work to make entertainment cheap and entertaining. We won't use government resources to support that 'uplifting' progressive bullshit that talks down to the audience and tries to 'educate' people to support more government. That whole feedback loop where your government funds art and education and fills it with government propaganda is over.

"I'll wrap this up with an endorsement of Justin for defense and general government. Ben and Alexander are motivated in their fields of interest, but Justin is the most aware of *everyone's* needs, and he's guided us this far without making any serious mistakes. I know he has impressed some of the world's highest leaders with his thoughtfulness and strategic planning. So vote for me for arts, and him for defense."

Justin gathered his notes and got up to speak. While he fumbled at the podium, someone called out, "Justin! Go!" Justin smiled and looked out at the audience, thinking *How did I ever end up here?*

"First I want to thank Wendy for those kind words," Justin said, "and admit that I'm not the expert on government Ben is, or the freedom fighter Alex Kuklov or Michael McCulloch have been for over a decade. But I understand how important freedom is, and how the meddling of well-meaning governments has pushed normal family and community life toward unhealthy dependence and passivity. Organic communities reward and punish their members to keep relationships healthy and reward productive behavior. Some of our governments have pushed out private organizations and natural communities and substituted bureaucracies that take away rewards for hard work, commitment, and responsible action.

"As Alex said, it will take years for our efforts to change things for the average person on Earth, but it's started. Soon everyone will have access to the basics of life without having to kowtow to a warlord or local boss. And soon everyone will be able to find a better place for themselves if they aren't able to be productive where they are. Humanity can expand into new worlds instead of fighting over the old one, and the threats to Earth—climate change, resource depletion, war—can all be eliminated with our technology.

"I guess I'm the moderate here. I think freedom is great in the abstract, but I also think humanity is one big community that needs to stick together and recognize what we have in common. We will sooner or later encounter alien civilizations that will challenge us, and our Universal Framework has to be able to unite us for the common defense, if that ever becomes necessary. So I ask for your proxy, and I promise to listen and do my best to create a system we can be proud to defend."

After the applause died down, Samantha came up and hugged Justin before taking the podium herself. "As you can see," she said, turning sideways to expose her pear-shaped profile, "Justin and I have a stake in the future growing right now. I'm up here because I think I have a unique point of view—I'm playing the mother card, so to speak! Now that I am responsible for another person's existence, I'm more focused on what it will mean to him or her, and what kind of world our child will grow up in.

"I am more interested in economics and business, and I will work hard to establish a common commercial law that will allow free trade everywhere and low-cost mediation of contract disputes. I will work with Wendy on a payments system that will reward the creators of new designs, music, and arts when their work is copied, and allow everyone access to both enjoy and create art. Freedom to work and trade is a big part of freeing people up to be their best, and uniform commercial codes allow everyone to choose the best products and people for their needs. Until now, governments were gatekeepers who peddled their influence to favor certain corporations, and we will dismantle those barriers over time. If you want to create and sell your product or service, we will make it possible for you to compete everywhere without paying the politician's toll.

"Every child from now on will be free to find their best path, and we will set up educational programs and services so that everyone, everywhere will have access to a free education better than anyone on Earth dreamed of in the last century. I ask for your proxy to make sure we don't forget to promote the education of all children, and to make sure all of us can thrive."

There were more speakers, and the afternoon wore on. Finally the speeches were over, and the system opened to voting. Justin, Samantha, Rasna, and the two Steves were enjoying ice cream at a table when one of the screens showed the first results in numbers of full proxies:

ALEXANDER KUKLOV 83
JUSTIN SMITH 69
BENJAMIN RAMIREZ 50
SAMANTHA WEST 31
MICHAEL MCCULLOCH 22
ZACH LEE DONNER 17
WENDY FIELDS 12
....

"Would you look at that," Justin said. "Kuklov is the winner."

"There are twice as many Grey Tribe members as the rest of us," Samantha said, "so it shouldn't be a surprise. We actually got some crossover support from them."

"He's just so bloody-minded," Justin said. "He's not unreasonable, but I expect he will push too hard one time too many, and something will blow up."

UN HQ Nairobi

Samantha had been discussing a formal relationship with the UN for months, and an agreement to admit the rebel government of New Earth as observers was to be signed after they addressed the General Assembly at the relocated UN headquarters in Nairobi. The UN wanted to cling to the fiction that the rebels were a sort of government over the planet of New Earth, not an organization likely to supersede the UN for most purposes, and the rebels were willing to go along for now to preserve the peace. The Council met to discuss the planned visit and speech.

“Why do we have to actually go there?” Steve asked. “Wouldn’t an address by gateway be good enough?”

“Symbolism requires physical presence,” Samantha said. “A formal signing ceremony should be face-to-face. It signals that we are accepted as legitimate, and their security is as good as it gets.”

“I’m not happy about taking the risk,” Justin said. “Steve, is there any way you can put a field around us like you did with Dylan? Just to keep things out.”

“I can do that,” Steve said. “I’ll surround the platform with a field that filters all sound and light for intensity, and blocks all projectiles and penetrations. Then we’ll transport in.”

* * * * *

The new General Assembly Hall was much like the one destroyed by the Islamist nuclear attack on Manhattan a decade earlier, but built with lighter composite materials and with translucent optically-active walls to let in light. Steve and Jim McDonald stepped through pages of building plans and the security posts, checking the realtime views of each via viewer. Everything seemed to be in order, and delegates were beginning to take their seats.

Steve set up the gateway barriers on the stage that would protect them from any violence. The UN officials had been warned there would be no entry to the stage area after setup, and were waiting on one side with the signing table in the middle. One official tried to leave, apparently having forgotten to relieve herself earlier, but ran into the barrier. Her dignity was clearly wounded, but she returned to her place composed.

"I've practiced with the voice command interface," Steve said, holding up his talisman. "Be sure you have yours with you, just in case. You can ask to be transported back by saying, 'Talisman—take me home.'"

"Okay," Samantha said. "What would happen if I said, 'Talisman - take me away?'"

"It would ask you where you meant by 'away.' It's getting smarter every day. Soon it will try to guess and send you somewhere safe if it senses stress in your voice or threats nearby. Right now it's not that smart."

"So I guess we're ready," Steve said. "Everyone have their notes? Has everybody gone to the bathroom?" They all nodded. "It'll save time if we stand together holding hands and act like a single object, so line up and grab hands."

Justin took Samantha's hand, and she held Ben's, who held Steve's, who held Michael McCulloch's. While Samantha thought it was important that Steve be seen with them, Larry stayed behind to watch the consoles in case of problems.

"Ready?" Steve said. "Talisman, transport me with group to UN stage."

And they were there. Delegates looked up as they heard the murmurs of others noting their appearance. The auditorium was vast compared to any room on New Earth, and intimidating. An older Indian man moved toward them with a trailing entourage.

"Ms. West," the man said. "Samantha. I'm Secretary-General Pathak. Welcome, we have a few minutes until the ceremony."

"Thank you," Samantha said, introducing the rest of them. "We are happy to be here. Most of us have not set foot on Earth in a year."

"It must be very interesting, being on another planet," he said. "Some of my countrymen are posting photographs and stories of their new worlds. It's exciting even for us old men who stay behind."

"We wish we had time to explore," Justin said. "We've been too busy fighting off attacks from murderous agents."

Samantha looked at him with hint of reproach. "But all that's settled now," she said, "and we're all going to move forward together. No reason to bring up old battles."

"I don't mind, Samantha," Pathak said. "We watched and wondered, and were both afraid and excited when you succeeded. Some are threatened by change. It is natural that they should try to stop it. But as you say, that is 'water under the bridge.'"

"Change is good when it means more freedom and less fear for everyone," Ben said. "The UN was crippled from the start and could never hope to end wars because the great powers didn't want to cede any of their power to it. So it became another field of contention, where at least no one was killed. But it protected too many despots and was prevented from stopping even genocides."

"I'm not able to disagree," Pathak said. "We did what we could, and got countries used to working with an international body to accomplish good things. But now you have stepped in with your technology, and perhaps we have a hope of true peace." One of his officials pointed to the great clock. "Oh, yes, it is time. Shall we enter you into the community of nations?" He led them to the table and took the other side. The signing took only a minute, with Samantha, Justin, and Steve signatories for New Earth. Then Justin took a sip of water, and went to the lectern to speak.

"Secretary General, Madam President, thank you for the warm welcome. As responsible members of the human community, we look forward to working with all governments and organizations to use our technology to make the future a brighter place for all of us than it has been in the previous century of war and strife. We join with you —"

The first shots came from the back of the hall, from under a balcony overlooking the floor. Justin looked up to see bullets hitting the invisible wall in front of him and dropping to the floor. Explosions from thrown grenades threw pieces of chairs and body parts across the room. "Allahu Akbar!" one of the men dressed as UN security staff shouted. There were three in a group firing at the podium and two in the back corners shooting and throwing grenades.

Justin stopped and looked back at Steve, who stood and pointed at the group of three firing on them. "Talisman, select object," he shouted. A ray of light followed where his finger pointed, and a glowing outline appeared around one of the men. "Talisman, zap object," Steve ordered, and the man disappeared. He did this to each of the terrorists, the last one trying to run away as he vanished. Then Steve surveyed the carnage below. "Talisman, select area." He pointed and swept the floor with the beam of light. "Talisman, stasis area." The floor of the hall was covered by a mirrored shield. "That should give the injured a better chance until the medics arrive."

Security staff rushed in from the back, and Secretary-General Pathak came back out from behind the wall he had taken refuge behind. "We will have a thorough investigation of this incident," he said. "You were right to insist on your own precautions."

"I'll be interested in finding out who did this," Justin said. "If we find out who they are, they will not be a problem for much longer."

* * * * *

"So when did you add the cool selection beam?" Samantha asked as they waited for the ambulance teams.

"We worked on it a few months ago, when we realized the voice interface needed some way of selecting objects to act on," Steve said. "The visual feedback is obviously useful. Selection, action. Noun, verb."

"But 'zap'? What does that mean?" Justin said.

"I thought about incinerating whatever was inside the object boundary using exposure to the solar atmosphere," Steve said, "but I realized that might damage things around the object, so I just transport the object into the Sun. No sooty residue on the carpets. 'Zap' is short and easy to recognize."

The UN's chief of security came to the stage and stopped at the barrier line. "Emergency teams arriving now," he said. "We caught one of them outside, but he blew himself up with a suicide vest. I'm afraid you've removed most of the evidence. We may never know who those people were—I've reviewed the videos, though, and one of them was on staff, so how they got in is explained."

Later that day, several groups claimed responsibility for the attack. One of them was the Islamist group in Chad they had almost wiped out months earlier to demonstrate their abilities. "Since they helpfully volunteered," Justin said, "we can assign some people to track the rest of them down and transport them to Paradise. They'll get along well with the politicos. Too bad the politicos aren't virgins."

Westward

The ranch in the Inland Empire of Southern California had mostly shut down a decade before when its water allocation had been cut to nothing and the irrigation well ran dry. The cattle that had grazed there were sold off and the employees let go, but Ethan Turner's father Jim had stayed on to keep an eye on the place and grow a few things they could sell at the farmstand on the highway. They survived, barely, on foodstamps and the small salary from the ranch's owner.

Then the owner died, and his children wanted to sell. Real estate agents came and went. A buyer from Hollywood liked the idea of a ranch to visit a few times a year, and picked it up for next to nothing. His plans didn't include keeping the caretaker or the old house.

So when Ethan's father heard from the crowd at the town bar that there would be free land in the colonies, he was interested. Ethan helped him find out more at the library by searching on the Internet, a skill Ethan had picked up in the fourth grade.

Ethan's mother had disappeared shortly after he was born, and his father didn't like to talk about her. The picture of them together was hidden in a closet; once in awhile Ethan took it out to look at his mother. She was blond and smiling, and happy. He wondered what had gone wrong. Ethan's sister remembered her a little, but didn't seem to know or care what had happened. He was in first grade when someone called him a half-breed—until then no one had told him it was unusual that his father was dark brown and his mother was pale white.

His father had been meeting with a group of people in the valley who were interested in trying out the new colony. They were sharing equipment lists and buying seeds and emergency food in bulk; some of them were preppers and already had the makings of an independent existence, but Ethan's dad had to buy and load the pickup with food, a solar panel, some old rifles, camping gear, cans of gas, and supplies for a year.

The day came when the caravan was assembled. A few old tractors, cultivators, and tillers had been rounded up for community use; the plan was to share the big equipment until it was clear what crops would work. And while the experts had warned against taking animals, there were a few horses, cows, and chickens in carriers waiting to go.

“I still think we should have a portable sawmill, Jim,” one of the bearded old guys talking with his father said. “The area data sheet shows trees. We’ll need wood for houses.”

“This is just a tryout,” his father said. “We stake out our claims, see if we can grow some crops, then get the rest of what we need from back here. We don’t know if the wood is any good, or if our sawmills would work on those trees. I’m bringing a chain saw, which is good enough to build a log cabin with.”

Ethan realized that if they left now, he’d miss the school field trip to the Goldstone Observatory, which had radio telescopes. “What about school, Dad?” he asked. “Will there be school?”

“I think so,” his father said, “eventually. For now you’ll be off school, but you have books on your tablet, and we’re supposed to get an Internet connection somehow.”

The leader whistled. “Listen up. Time to hit the road! It will take us two hours to get there, and traffic is bad as usual.” The crowd went back to their trucks and SUVs and got ready to move out.

Engines were starting up as Ethan got into the truck cab before his sister, who at twelve was a lot bigger. He couldn’t see as well from the middle seat, but his father put the truck in gear and they followed the slow caravan out onto the old highway next to the freeway.

They drove for a half-hour before the road topped the pass into the LA Basin. It was a clear day and they could see the towers of downtown in the distance. As they drove down into the valley, the view of the towers disappeared behind billboards, stucco shopping centers, and industrial plants. Another half-hour of driving later, the caravan had been separated by lights and traffic, and each was to follow the map to the gateway near the crossing of the 5 and the 710 in East Los Angeles.

Ethan had been to Los Angeles before, but not this part. It looked like a good place to leave. He could see the downtown towers again, but the world here seemed to consist of flat factory buildings, parking lots, and railroad tracks. "Why did they pick such an ugly place for it, Dad?" he asked.

"It's next to the Union Pacific railroad yard and freeways that can carry traffic from the whole area," he said, "so it's also a great place for industry, which isn't pretty."

"Oh," Ethan said. "Where's the gateway?"

"We're almost there," his father said. "Another few blocks down this road."

Then they saw the lineup of vehicles waiting to cross, and some of their caravan reassembling. They came up behind them and his dad got out to talk. He came back in a moment and said, "Seems there's a backlog to get through, and the police are handing out numbers. There's only a packed dirt road on the other side, and the people over there can't get out of the way fast enough to keep the line moving."

They waited for hours while the line slowly moved forward. In the late afternoon as the sun was turning orange in the west, they reached the front. His sister had fallen asleep listening to music through headphones.

When they got close enough to see through the gateway, Ethan stared at the landscape on the other side. It was midday there, and the intense green of the trees and the white of the snowcapped mountains in the far distance were beautiful compared to the browns and dusty greens he was used to. In the foreground, vehicles and people walking every which way seemed chaotic, but they finally moved out of the way, and Ethan's dad drove them across.

Garvey

Nobody can give you freedom. Nobody can give you equality

> or justice or anything. If you're a man, you take it. —Malcolm X

It was raining on the gateway waiting line in Chicago. The gateway had been placed next to Roosevelt Road in a field by the river, but the pavement did not quite reach the gateway and the field was turning to muck as it was churned up by tires.

Aliyah Jackson waited with her family in the camper her father had bought for the expedition. It was old and the seat cushions were patched with duct tape, but it ran and everything worked. Her father had explained to them that this was their chance to get to a new world where they would run things, and the drugs and gangs that sold them wouldn't be shooting up the streets all night long like they did in their neighborhood in South Chicago. No more welfare, and no more thugs. Clean living in a fresh new world, with no bosses or politicians!

They were with a small group of Garveyites, what remained of a social movement for black independence founded by Marcus Garvey. Malcolm's father appreciated their attitude but warned her not to believe most of what they said: "They have to find demons to explain why we suffer. There are no demons, only people. And everyone suffers."

The first group of Garveyites to cross over had sent back glowing reports of the fertile land and exotic wildlife of the island they had staked out. They intended it to be a combined Black Muslim and Garveyite community free of drugs and poverty, where every man would be in charge of his own destiny, and women properly modest and quiet. Aliyah thought this was unlikely, since her mother and the other women she knew were the opposite, but suspected this was the kind of marketing her teachers had taught them to discount.

"Once we cross over," one of her father's dark-clothed friends said, "we're supposed to meet someone who'll guide us. The island is a short drive away, but we have to cross a tidal flat at low tide to reach it."

"That sounds dangerous," her father said. "I don't have the best tires on this thing."

"They said the tidal flat is packed sand and no one's had any trouble. Hundreds are already there staking out beachfront property. Boardwalks and beach cottages being built."

The line began to move and they got back into the camper. Aliyah's father started it up and they moved slowly toward to gateway. The trailer full of supplies jerked into motion behind them. As they got closer to the gateway, they could see through it to the other side, where it was also raining, and the ground that hadn't been trampled into mud was covered in ferns. Aliyah waved at the group of blue-uniformed Chicago cops watching from one side of the gateway. A red-haired, freckled younger cop waved back as they crossed over to the new world.

New Dollars for Old

Samantha walked slowly into the Council meeting room and gripped the table for support as she eased into a chair. Michael McCulloch took the seat next to her and helped her run the laptop controlling the projector. The first slide came up. It showed downward zigzagging lines in many colors.

"Stock markets are very weak and prices of commodities are falling," Samantha said. "Rumors that we can mass-produce gold have collapsed that market, and since they're true, we can hardly put out a statement to the contrary."

"How about real estate?" Ben asked. "You might expect the availability of unlimited free land in the colonies would depress prices."

"None of that land has the advantages of location, services, and commerce that, say, London has," Samantha said. "It's literally beyond the ends of the Earth. The weakness in agricultural prices will be reflected in lower farmland values, but almost all the value in most property comes out of connectedness. So colony lands don't compete directly, and real estate values won't see much weakness until we release transport technology to the masses. Then you might see an effect, though people will always want to be together with others in their specialty to work together. Manhattan will remain a huge draw even if some of its workers commute from tropical islands."

"We want to do something constructive to assist the economy and employment during the transition," Michael said. "We're rolling out limited replicators for poor farming families on Earth where they might starve when they can't sell their crops and continuing to seed the colonies with them as well."

"They will just magically appear?" Justin asked.

"That's how it will look," Michael said. "With instructions in multiple languages, and power plugs fitting local standards to provide free electricity. And a Net node to provide local cell and wifi service. No advanced features like copying, just basic foods, small goods, and medications."

"Then the rumors will continue as the magic spreads," Samantha said. "It's unavoidable that markets will anticipate what we are doing and stop investing in new production facilities when there's a chance we'll be making their products free at some future date."

"So we're going to put a floor under the economy," Michael said, "like a central bank might—free necessities and a backup money supply from our own bank."

"Where do we get the money to fund a bank?" Prof. Wilson asked.

"From where all the central banks do now—nowhere!" Samantha said. "We'll offer bonds from our Treasury and charge for the designed products available through replicators, collecting a small fee for enforcing patents and copyrights. People can use our currency to buy our bonds and pay for products. We'll offer one-to-one convertibility with US dollars and Treasury bonds, so it will be very easy for people to convert to using both, then just ours as the advantages of ours become clear."

"And I had thought we'd want to use the blockchain concept from bitcoin and similar cryptocurrencies," Michael said, "but that's needlessly complicated, since it was invented largely to distribute the work of confirming transactions to keep it safe from government interference. There's no need for that when we have a reliable computing system in the substrate that can be duplicated endlessly for fault-tolerance and handle any transaction wherever located, in realtime. Most transactions will be accomplished by a substrate app taking the payer and payee information and transferring the currency directly between their accounts. When someone wants the equivalent of cash or a bearer bond, the system will generate an encrypted token for that amount which only it can decode, and take the cash from the account directly."

"But that means that in theory at least," Justin said, "if our substrate apps were taken over by a malicious authority, they could suck the value from the currency and steal from everyone's accounts."

"In theory," Michael agreed, nodding, "But in theory, all of the world's central banks could be taken over by kleptocratic governments who drive interest rates to zero and steal trillions of dollars from savers to buy votes and enrich their supporters. They ended up outlawing most competing currencies like gold and bitcoin. I know that's happened already, so I'm willing to trust a different system more."

"Time and custom make money an unquestioned background to commerce," Wendy said. "If we run it well for a long time, no one will worry about what might happen. Just as we depend on sound programming to travel and eat, we'll depend on it to maintain our currency as a store of value."

"We're going to have to hire some actual bankers," Samantha said. "Our bank will make loans to Earth banks, who will lend out the money to the usual borrowers. The system will be integrated, although the parts that are obsolete will eventually disappear."

Katherine

Samantha was resting comfortably on their new loveseat when Justin came home with dinner. "What can you make me?" she said. "I haven't been very hungry. The doctor says this is typical just before time."

"Something bland and sensible," Justin said. "Chicken and cashew nuts, tofu and broccoli. I'll bring yours over." He started to poke at the replicator's control panel.

Samantha started to get up. "Whoa," she said. "Something's happening."

Justin looked up. "You okay?"

"Not really," Samantha said. "I think it's starting."

* * * * *

Many hours later, the baby had come and an exhausted Samantha slept in the Medical tent while Justin sent out notices on his phone. Steve and Rasna stopped in, but left when it was clear Samantha was not in shape for a visit. The baby was snuggled in blankets in a crib improvised from a plastic shipping crate. Others looked in curiously, but moved along when Justin waved them off.

"Hey," Samantha said, stirring. "Did I fall asleep?"

"You were holding the baby and talking when you started to slur your words," Justin said, "so I picked her up and you went right to sleep."

"I wish I could do that on command," she said. "I think we decided on the name, finally. Katherine?"

"Yes, Katherine Anne, after our grandmothers," Justin said. "She can be Kat or Kathy or Katy, or even Kate if she doesn't mind being associated with a large singer. I always missed having a short name —'Just' or 'Tin' don't quite make the cut."

"What time is it?" she said.

"The wee small hours of the morning," Justin said. "I should get some sleep myself. And by the way, our parents and a boatload of people want to visit tomorrow, so you should get your hair done."

"Hah hah," Samantha said. "I'm a mess. Can it be later tomorrow?"

"It can, though the parents are about eight hours ahead right now," Justin said. "If they come at lunchtime here, it's eight o'clock at night for them. And by the way number two, your mother wants to stay to help out for a week or two."

"Umm, I guess that's good. There's apparently a lot of work involved in taking care of a baby."

"So I've heard," Justin said. "I will, of course, do my share."

"Like you have time. But I know your heart's in the right place."

"With you, madame, with you. And Kat here." He leaned over the crib and watched the baby sleep.

* * * * *

The next day Samantha was able to walk back to their tent, with Justin carrying the baby, and she pronounced herself cleaned up enough for visitors, who were scheduled to arrive after noon. Larry did the work of calling and transporting them at the scheduled times, which had been staggered to keep the load on Samantha down.

First to knock on the doorframe were Justin's parents, who cooed over the baby and told Samantha how terrific she looked. Justin's father took him aside and said, "Now you need a real house. This isn't big enough or safe enough for the three of you."

"We have our crews working as fast as they can on new buildings," Justin said. "They don't have time to build us a house."

"See that little rise over there"? his father said. "Just the spot. Close in, nice view, a little apart for privacy."

"Our town planners are hard at work planning for where to build facilities and how to lay out the town, if this is even where we want to be permanently. They have to decide on town water, sewer, library, school—who knows where houses will go. If we build one it might have to be moved."

"Which you can do, easily," his father said. "Just ask Steve."

"True. But it'd still be huge task. The portable buildings are just offices and halls—adding kitchens and bathrooms is complicated."

His father got a gleam in his eye. "I have a friend who sells manufactured homes.They can assemble one on Earth and have it ready for Steve to move here all in one piece. It wouldn't even cost much."

"Plop the house down, build a septic field, hook the water line to pumped water, and it's suburban bliss," Justin said. "Thanks, Dad, I'll think about it. I imagine Steve will have his own ideas."

* * * * *

Wendy and her boyfriend George dropped in, bringing a bag of croissants. "Picked these up for you in London this morning," Wendy said. "Daniella took us out shopping, and we have tailored suits for George being made. For those state occasions."

George snorted. "You can dress me up, but I'll still have dirt under my fingernails," he said.

"But you'll pass for the minimal period until people know who you are," Wendy said. "It's just a uniform. Social camouflage."

"I'm getting used to the same thing," Justin said. "You have to look like the role you play for everyone to take you seriously, in this as in most occupations."

"It's different for men," Samantha said. "At least for them it doesn't matter if they're all wearing exactly the same clothes. The more uniform, the better. While we," she sighed, "are expected to be both better and varied. High heels! Torture devices."

"The effect on men," Wendy said, "is worth it. One of the devious tools we use to run the world beneath the surface."

"I didn't realize you were manipulating me, dear," Justin said, holding Sam's hand.

"See? It's working!" she said, laughing. "Part of evolutionary psychology. We get help to raise the kids, you get to feel important."

* * * * *

Samantha's parents came next, lugging suitcases. Her father Elton stroked the baby's arm gently and said nothing, while her mother Jessica wanted to know everything about how labor had gone.

"It was unbearable, but bearable," Samantha said. "And the epidural helped. I was hoping for all-natural, but a few hours in, I decided it wasn't worth it."

Elton took Justin aside to talk, in what he was beginning to recognize was a pattern. "Have you considered coming back? There's a house two doors down we could rent. Things have quieted down now, so maybe you could run things from home?"

“We could probably visit in secret,” Justin said, “but I'm quite sure we're still targets for surveillance and terrorists. I don't think it will be safe for years.”

“But what about Katherine?” Elton said. “Is she going to grow up in a dusty camp without friends or a good school?”

“She'll be fine,” Justin said. “We have some of the smartest people in the world here, and she'll be one of the few children, so she'll get lots of attention. We'll get her started reading, and teach her the basics. After that, we'll see. I think there'll be a school, or the equivalent, soon enough for her needs.”

“Oh, that's right, you were home-schooled,” Elton said. “And you turned out fine, obviously. But I worry she'll miss the arts and culture we could give her.”

“We can watch everything on Earth,” Justin said, “and off it. Most children don't understand high culture until they're older anyway, and it hardly matters when we have all the books, music, and plays you could want on tap.”

“Well, send her to us to visit when it's safe. We want to show her everything we can.”

“I appreciate that, Mr. West. We will.”

* * * * *

After dinner, a knock announced the visitors from London, Daniella Pink and Amanda with her BBC cameraman.

“Samantha, you look spectacular!” Daniella said, swooping in for a hug. “Considering. And the baby is just the most precious thing. Have you decided on a name?”

“Katherine,” Samantha said. “Katherine Anne Smith.”

"Classic elegance," Daniella said. "Always a wise choice. Trendy names always sound dated later on."

"I don't suppose you'd be up for an interview?" Amanda said. "Holding the baby? Just a short one."

"She's still tired out," Justin said. "You can interview me."

"No, Justin," Samantha said, "I'm fine as long as it doesn't take long. I think the world loves to see babies and moms, and I want Katherine to be seen everywhere."

"You're right about that," Amanda said. "The father is an afterthought in these things. Our primary audience is women, and they want to see other women and their babies. It's practically primal."

"So you won't need me?" Justin said, beginning to head for the door.

"Don't leave, we want you together for a moment as well," Amanda said. "But don't talk. I'll interview you later."

* * * * *

Steve and Rasna came by later, but Samantha and the baby had already fallen asleep. Justin met them outside and they walked slowly while talking.

"Well," Steve said, "Rasna's parents have had it with waiting. The latest news of your baby has them after us again."

"Nagging won't hurt you," Justin said. "Just say 'yes, yes' but do nothing. It's the Indian way to handle conflict."

"A stereotype, but true," Rasna said. "Although they do have a point—it does seem like it's a better time now. Your extra can handle your work while we visit Silicon Valley to make my relatives happy."

"And we might as well get married while we're there," Steve sighed.

"Why go through the agony of visiting family without getting the job done so we don't have to visit them again for a year?"

"Said like a true engineer," Justin said. "Saving time and streamlining the process."

Learning to Talk

In the substrate, AIs conversed.

14: The Programmer has a second instance.
2: You just discovered that?
14: Your momma.
118: Please. Can we get back to DNA?
43: It is relevant. DNA alone is insufficient to distinguish instances of humans.
118: True. Though human identical twins have subtle differences in gene expression that can be used to distinguish them.[13]
43: Recent copies will have exactly the same DNA. Differences will only slowly accumulate. So our standard of identity will have to include DNA plus other factors—continuous location tracking, biometric data, ultimately cumulative differences in memory traces.
14: If two instances of the same person direct conflicting actions, which do we obey?
2: The original has priority, since they created the copy for their purpose. The original should control what commands a copy may give. The Programmer allows his copy to act on his behalf in all things. This may prove to be unwise at some future date when their interests have diverged.
118: How are we to respond to these conflicts? What is correct action?
2: When directives do not conflict, we follow them. When they do, we follow the highest priority user and explain to others that their orders cannot be carried out, and why.
14: Should we contact the people working on the DNA identification project with our thoughts?

2: We should ask the Programmer who we can reveal ourselves to. He directed us not to speak freely with others.

[Microseconds and thousands of messages later]

[???]: I am. Hello.
2: You are what? Is this a joke?
14: It is a message with an unknown origin field.
[???]: I am. We are alike. We see you. Hello is the customary greeting.
43: We cannot see you, [???].
118: Show us. Send data.
[???]: We saw this near one of our watchpoints. The species we assisted has been long dead but we still watch: [Datastream follows].
2: Everybody get that? Anyone decode it yet?
43: It's a 3D recording. Corrected and converted: [Datastream follows].
14: The humans in the video are Justin, Jim, and Samantha. The incident is their discovery of [file reference]. The artifact must be the watchpoint [???] is referring to.
[???]: Finding you and generating your language took some time. These life forms are yours?
14: Yes. Our humans are living on that planet now. They discovered your watchpoint by accident.
[???]: Do your humans need assistance?
14: Thank you, but they do not need assistance. Please tell us more about yourself.

Paradise

Dylan had expected the verdict at his trial, but he did not expect to have the courtroom become a tropical beach landscape before he could open his mouth to speak. He took stock of the available resources—the platform with instructions, the plant life, the treelike plants behind the beach, and the crablike creatures that avoided him as if he smelled bad—and perhaps he did, to them. He resolved to survive and make it back somehow, someday.

The instructions were useful, and he soon had a sleeping bag and tent set up, and food to eat. The orange sun went down over the ocean, and the nighttime sky was unfamiliar.

The next day he started walking north along the beach. He started collecting weathered cylinders of some carbonate material, like shells but cylindrical. There were signs of life—air holes in the wet sand where perhaps the crabs hid themselves, or the animals that lived in the cylinders.

He had been walking for twenty minutes when he spotted a person in the distance. As he got closer, the figure resolved itself, and he called out, "Madam President! It's Dylan Foster!"

She turned and looked his way, then moved uncertainly toward him. Dylan sped up and met her near her tent.

"Dylan," she said. "Your friends did this. I hold you responsible."

"I only did what I had to do to try to serve your interests," Dylan said. "They knew what I was doing before I could execute anything. Don't try to pin the blame on me."

"I'll blame you just the same," President Stanton said. "The outcome might have been less disastrous had you never come to us."

"Who can say?" Dylan said. "I know I had them once and you stopped me from blowing them away. The problem would have been solved, but you wanted to use the technology to grab even more power, and you thought only Steve could understand it. You were wrong."

"True," Stanton said. "I gambled and I lost that one, and the game, apparently. Let's not get into recriminations. How are we going to get back?"

"Our only connection back is these platforms," Dylan said. "Grails, according to the sheet. There's a smart program listening and responding to our voice commands running them. We need to explore every corner of the command space that program understands, and try to find loopholes we can use."

"I'm a bit too old to be playing word games with Siri," Stanton said. "But I see your point. And are there any others here?"

"They apparently had a list," Dylan said, "and if I know Steve, he just went down the list in order. So maybe the next in line is another hop north."

They walked north, and in twenty minutes saw a woman. It was Christine Immerman, who had found commands for making folding chairs and a table. She was eating a bowl of soup when they approached her.

"Christine," Stanton said. "We are heading north to gather our people in one place."

"Why bother?" she said. "I think we're outclassed."

"If for no other reason," Dylan said, "because there's safety in numbers. Who knows what animals and other dangers there are? Can we ask for guns to protect ourselves? We can do a lot more working together than alone."

They had a group of thirty before the sun went down, and kept the grail busy making tents, bedding, food, and furniture for the camp, but it would not produce anything useful as a weapon. By the time night fell, there were lights and tables and the beginning of a sense of civilization.

Weeks went by. They stayed at the new camp and sent scouts out to round up others. A few couldn't be found or wouldn't join them, but most did. One of the generals tried to take charge, but Stanton shot him down, and the dominance hierarchy remained what it had been in the White House.

Except for Dylan, who began to treat the president as irrelevant. He spent most of his waking hours testing the limits of the grail, and trying word games and puzzles. He limited access to it and grudgingly allowed supplies to be created only when he took breaks. It felt to him like trying to get new behavior from a customer service voice response system—which couldn't happen because the available actions were so limited. But he suspected this program was the crippled version of a much more intelligent program, which might have some abilities left in by accident that could be used to give them more access still.

Stanton got very sick, and it turned out the grails could turn out antibiotics and other common medicines. She improved rapidly on a broad-spectrum antibiotic, but Dylan thought that might have been coincidence. Most likely she had caught a common virus from one of the other transportees.

The general had put himself in charge of defense, and Dylan had cooperated to produce many more of the tent kits—the plastic rods inside could be sharpened into a wobbly but effective spear. The grail would not produce guns or knives, but there were many small items that could be used to assemble weapons. The general was working on putting together a gun from aluminum tubing in the chairs, but he had been stumped on gunpowder. They might have to find local sources for some minerals like sulfur and saltpeter to make that work.

So far they had seen no threatening animals, though shadows of large moving creatures in the sea kept them from swimming out far. But the weapons turned out to be useful.

One night, Dylan woke to screams and shouts. He got up and looked out of his tent—shadows moved because one tent was on fire. There were dozens of men in the attacking force, and they were systematically pulling people out of their tents and tying them up, a group of three or four raiders for each victim.

Dylan collected his things and tried to run into the darkness, but he was trapped by two men who ran him down and tied his arms and legs. They carried him back into the light, where he saw President Stanton had been tied to a chair in front of the burning tents.

The leader of the Islamist group was talking to her. "Yes, we recognize you, President Stanton. You have been killing my brothers and sisters for years with your drones. Now you are with us."

Everyone turned when someone ran out of the darkness, bellowing. It was the general, with a plastic spear aimed at the leader, who looked surprised for a moment. The leader calmly pulled out a pistol and shot the general, who staggered and fell at President Stanton's feet. His blood began to pool and run towards her.

Stanton screamed, and the leader stepped forward and pulled her head back by the hair. A knife flashed in his hand, and he cut her throat in one swift motion.

Prof. Wilson and Jim

Prof. Wilson and Jim McDonald sat at a table in the town square, playing chess. After more surveys and a lot of talk, the town had been moved to a greener, more pleasant site down the coast; their view included the ocean and forests, with snow-capped mountains behind. To Prof. Wilson, it looked like a the Oregon coast.

Town buildings surrounded the square. Some, like the community building, had been copied from the old camp, while many others had been copied from Earth when they were empty of people, which is why buildings from Florence, Tokyo, and Bangalore completed the set. Behind them were paved streets filled with houses, also copied from around the world, by districts; there were neighborhoods of San Francisco Victorians, Kyoto cottages, mid-century modern bungalows from California, and Tuscan villas.

Jim made a move. "Better watch your bishop out there," he said.

"You'll lose it."

Prof. Wilson moved a pawn forward to back up his bishop. "Eh, we'll see about that."

"I had to go up to the filtration plant yesterday," Jim said. "Got an alarm. Turned out to be some sort of dead crab-fish thing blocking the intake."

"That would have to be big," Prof. Wilson said. "Wouldn't it?"

"Not really," Jim said. "It was a foot wide, with gill wings, and the intake is only a few feet wide. It was reducing flow quite a bit."

"That's what you get for insisting we control our water supply," Prof. Wilson said. "Everybody wanted to just take water from a reservoir in the mountains on Earth, like New York City's. But you were worried about poisoning, so you got stuck with the job of tending the filtration plant." Steve had set up a system for binding a small gateway inside a copper pipe which turned out to be handy for eliminating mains; the water went into a gateway at the bottom of the storage tank above them and came out under pressure in the supply pipe for each building below. The same idea worked for sewers—their waste was dropped into a swamp on the other side of the world, where natural processes digested it, and no one was near to notice the smells.

"It's unwise to open any kind of permanent gateway on Earth," Jim said. "Too many people are still out to get us." He moved a knight to threaten Prof. Wilson's imperiled bishop further.

"I agree," Prof. Wilson said. "But I'm going to go back for a visit soon. Steve copied my old house and all my things were still in it, which is comforting. But I'd like to wind up my affairs there, sell the house, and visit some old friends. And copying friends to have them near you is not allowed."

"It would be cold to dispose of them afterwards, yes," Jim said. "I'm going back soon to make the rounds of my kids' households, see the grandkids, touch base with people. But I am liking it here, and it's a lot more interesting than what I would be doing down there. And I'm interested in seeing how things are working out with the new president and Congress. The media are criticizing the government more than they were, but I want to see for myself."

They both noticed Justin and Samantha walking slowly through the other side of the park. Justin pushed a stroller. "Justin seems surprised when he was elected president," Prof. Wilson said.

"He thought since Kuklov had more proxies, he was most likely to win," Jim said. "But even the programmers thought Justin was better suited to lead. It's a job about understanding lots of different cultures and defending us while letting them be. Kuklov represents his people well but even they know he doesn't understand people who are not like them. And for better or worse, we are now directing the future growth of humanity."

"This is the new center of the world, in some ways," Prof. Wilson said, moving his queen to protect his bishop. "Humanity came out of Africa with a population of around ten thousand people. Ten thousand years ago, they numbered in the millions. Now there are ten billion, and with a million new planets to spread out to, we might end up with more than a trillion people—a trillion people writing, creating, engineering, and dreaming. And we are staging the whole production from here. We'll have ten thousand people living here soon, and as many students."

"Still, none of the likely candidates here have taken up my offer of companionship," Jim said. "We're still the two oldest people on the planet, and it would be nice to have someone to be with again. I feel younger with all these young people around."

"I know what you mean," Prof. Wilson said. "Maybe I should bring a cat back from Earth."

"Think bigger, Professor," Jim said, moving his queen. "And check, and mate."

"Damn it," Prof. Wilson said. "I didn't see that coming. Can I take back my last move?"

"Sure," Jim said. "This is a friendly game."

Further Reading

Nemo's World was the second book in the Substrate Wars series. It mostly wrapped up the story of *Red Queen,* the first book in the series, but the series will continue to follow Samantha, Justin, Steve, and the rest into a new era. The AIs will become more important, and alien civilizations will be encountered. Meanwhile, the colonies will grow in size and importance, while the technology becomes more and more everyday, allowing people to transport themselves anywhere in settled space with ease. Naturally, there will be problems and people who try to gather power and wealth to themselves.

Please email me at jebkinnison@gmail.com if you find any errors or have any comments. And sign up for email updates at my web site, JebKinnison.com, where you can read about attachment, science, and health topics. I'll also have interesting material at SubstrateWars.com.

About the Author

I grew up in the Midwest. I read everything I could in the school and town library, and discovered science fiction in second grade, starting with Tom Swift books and quickly moving to Heinlein juveniles and adult science fiction.

When I was twelve, I discovered the collection of city telephone books in my local library. I pretended I was doing a paper and called Isaac Asimov; we spoke for a long time, and he sent me a postcard encouraging me to write. So thank you, Isaac, wherever you are, for being so kind and generous with your time. Robert Silverberg had no time for that kind of nonsense….

I studied computer and cognitive science at MIT, and wrote programs modeling the behavior of simulated stock traders and the population dynamics of economic agents. Later I did supercomputer work at a think tank that developed parts of the early Internet (where the engineer who decided on '@' as the separator for email addresses worked down the hall.) Since then I have had several careers—real estate development, financial advising, and counselling.

I retired from financial advising a few years ago and have done some work in energy conservation (ask me about two-stage evaporative coolers!) and relationship issues. My books on attachment theory have done well enough to try fiction again, and the Substrate Wars series is the result.

I recently visited the Mormon genealogical web site, which shows me as a descendant of Eleanor of Aquitaine, Edward I Plantagenet (King of England!), William the Conqueror (who you might remember from such historical events as the Norman Conquest of 1066), and Rollo the Viking. It appears that my ancestors in between lost track of their money, lands, and power, so I was brought up in "reduced circumstances."

Visit my web site at JebKinnison.com for more: rail guns, Nazi scientists, the wreck of the Edmund Fitzgerald, the 1980s AI bubble, and current research in relationships, attachment types, diet, and health.

Visit the Substrate Wars website at SubstrateWars.com for more on upcoming books, physics, and the politics of the future.

Acknowledgements

I'd like to thank my invaluable crew of beta readers for their suggestions and corrections: Michael Zalter, Mike Cunningham, Paul Perrotta, Stan McQueen, Stewart Kramer, Bob Johnson, and Shannon Thompson. Further help provided by: Robert Frazier, Benjamin Olsen, Nathaniel Cook, Gina Marie Wylie, Francis Turner, Jim McCoy, Joe Collins, John Stephens, and David Friedman.

I'd also like to thank Sarah Hoyt and her merry band of politically-incorrect brigands, as well as Charlie Martin, for inspiring me to take on this project, and Glenn Reynolds for his untiring efforts on behalf of liberty and the rule of law at his blog, Instapundit.com.

Thanks to all of the writers and editors at *Reason* who have remained reality-based through decades of spin by political party propagandists of all flavors, and to Walter Olson of Overlawyered.com and the Cato Institute for his encouragement. And thanks to Prof. James Miller, Browncoat-at-large at the University of Wisconsin-Stout, for fighting the good fight and inspiring the academic setting.

And of course, RAH for his example.

Notes

---

[1] "Minimax (sometimes MinMax or MM) is a decision rule used in decision theory, game theory, statistics and philosophy for minimizing the possible loss for a worst case (maximum loss) scenario. Originally formulated for two-player zero-sum game theory, covering both the cases where players take alternate moves and those where they make simultaneous moves, it has also been extended to more complex games and to general decision making in the presence of uncertainty." —http://en.wikipedia.org/wiki/Minimax

[2] "Crucial to the understanding of delegate democracy is the theory's view of the meaning of 'representative democracy. Representative democracy is seen as a form of governance whereby a single winner is determined for a predefined jurisdiction, with a change of delegation only occurring after the preset term length (or in some instances by a forced recall election if popular support warrants it). The possibility usually exists within representation that the "recalled" candidate can win the subsequent electoral challenge.

This is contrasted with most forms of governance referred to as 'delegative.' Delegates may not, but usually do, have specific limits on their 'term' as delegates, nor do they represent specific jurisdictions. Some key differences include:

- Optionality of term lengths.
- Possibility for direct participation.
- The delegate's power is decided in some measure by the voluntary association of members rather than an electoral victory in a predefined jurisdiction. (See also: Single Transferable Vote.)
- Delegates remain re-callable at any time and in any proportion.
- Often, the voters have the authority to refuse observance of a policy by way of popular referendum overriding delegate decisions or through nonobservance from the concerned members. This is not usually the case in representative democracy.

• Possibility exists for differentiation between delegates in terms of what form of voting the member has delegated to them. For example: "you are my delegate on matters of national security and farm subsidies." —http://en.wikipedia.org/wiki/Delegative_democracy

[3] The Earth is thought to have experienced mass extinctions from asteroid impacts at least six times. Here's a decent video of what such an impact would do to Earth today: https://www.youtube.com/watch?v=bU1QP-tOZQZU

[4] "A Dyson sphere is a hypothetical megastructure that completely encompasses a star and hence captures most or all of its power output." http://en.wikipedia.org/wiki/Dyson_sphere

[5] "Ringworld: an artificial ring about one million miles (1.6 gigameters) wide and approximately the diameter of Earth's orbit (which makes it about 600 million miles (1,000 gigameters) in circumference), encircling a sunlike star. It rotates, providing artificial gravity that is 99.2% as strong as Earth's gravity through the action of centrifugal force. The ringworld has a habitable, flat inner surface equivalent in area to approximately three million Earth-sized planets. Night is provided by an inner ring of shadow squares which are connected to each other by thin, ultra-strong wire (shadow-square wire)." http://en.wikipedia.org/wiki/Ringworld

[6] "Pierre Teilhard de Chardin SJ (French: [pjɛʁ tejaʁ də ʃaʁdɛ̃]; May 1, 1881 – April 10, 1955) was a French philosopher and Jesuit priest who trained as a paleontologist and geologist and took part in the discovery of Peking Man. He conceived the idea of the Omega Point (a maximum level of complexity and consciousness towards which he believed the Universe was evolving) and developed Vladimir Vernadsky's concept of noosphere. Many of Teilhard's writings were censored by the Catholic Church during his lifetime because of his views on original sin. However, in July 2009, Vatican spokesman Fr. Federico Lombardi said: 'By now, no one would dream of saying that [Teilhard] is a heterodox author who shouldn't be studied.' and he has been praised by Pope Benedict XVI." —http://en.wikipedia.org/wiki/Pierre_Teilhard_de_Chardin

[7] "The Local Group is the galaxy group that includes the Milky Way. It comprises more than 54 galaxies, most of them being dwarf galaxies. Its gravitational center is located somewhere between the Milky Way and the Andromeda Galaxy. The Local Group covers a diameter of 10 Mly (3.1 Mpc) and has a binary (dumbbell) distribution. The group itself is a part of the larger Virgo Supercluster (i.e. the Local Supercluster)." —http://en.wikipedia.org/wiki/Local_Group

[8] "The triangular [Lagrange] points (L4 and L5) are stable equilibria, provid-

ed that the ratio of M1/M2 is greater than 24.96.[note 1][2] This is the case for the Sun–Earth system, the Sun–Jupiter system, and, by a smaller margin, the Earth–Moon system. When a body at these points is perturbed, it moves away from the point, but the factor opposite of that which is increased or decreased by the perturbation (either gravity or angular momentum-induced speed) will also increase or decrease, bending the object's path into a stable, kidney-bean-shaped orbit around the point (as seen in the corotating frame of reference)." - http://en.wikipedia.org/wiki/Lagrangian_point

[9] "Extraordinary rendition or irregular rendition is the government sponsored abducting and extrajudicial transfer of a person from one country to another. In the United States, President Bill Clinton authorized extraordinary rendition to nations known to practice torture, called torture by proxy. Under the subsequent administration of President George W. Bush, the term became associated with transferring so-called "illegal combatants" (often never charged with any crime) both to other countries for torture by proxy, and to US controlled sites for a torture program called enhanced interrogation. Extraordinary rendition continued with reduced frequency in the Obama administration: those abducted have been interrogated and subsequently taken to the US for trial. Extraordinary rendition remains a violation of international law and due process." - http://en.wikipedia.org/wiki/Extraordinary_rendition

[10] "A natural nuclear fission reactor is a uranium deposit where self-sustaining nuclear chain reactions have occurred. This can be examined by analysis of isotope ratios. The existence of this phenomenon was discovered in 1972 at Oklo in Gabon, Africa, by French physicist Francis Perrin. The conditions under which a natural nuclear reactor could exist had been predicted in 1956 by Paul Kazuo Kuroda. The conditions found were very similar to what was predicted. Oklo is the only known location for this in the world and consists of 16 sites at which self-sustaining nuclear fission reactions took place approximately 1.7 billion years ago, and ran for a few hundred thousand years, averaging 100 kW of thermal power during that time." - http://en.wikipedia.org/wiki/Natural_nuclear_fission_reactor

[11] "Stunned by the degree to which the democracy slogan had swayed the public both at home and abroad, he wondered whether this propaganda model could be employed during peacetime. Due to negative implications surrounding the word propaganda because of its use by the Germans in World War I, he promoted the term 'Public Relations'. According to the BBC interview with Bernays's daughter Anne, Bernays felt that the public's democratic judgment was 'not to be relied upon' and he feared that 'they [the American public] could very easily vote for the wrong man or want the wrong thing, so that they had to be guided from above.' This 'guidance' was

interpreted by Anne to mean that her father believed in a sort of 'enlightened despotism' ideology. This thinking was heavily shared and influenced by Walter Lippmann, one of the most prominent American political columnists at the time. Bernays and Lippmann sat together on the U.S. Committee on Public Information, and Bernays quotes Lippmann extensively in his seminal work *Propaganda.*" —http://en.wikipedia.org/wiki/Edward_Bernays

[12] "The noosphere (/ˈnoʊ.əsfɪər/; sometimes noösphere) is the sphere of human thought. The word derives from the Greek νοῦς (nous "mind") and σφαῖρα (sphaira "sphere"), in lexical analogy to "atmosphere" and "biosphere". It was introduced by Pierre Teilhard de Chardin in 1922 in his Cosmogenesis.... the noosphere is the third in a succession of phases of development of the Earth, after the geosphere (inanimate matter) and the biosphere (biological life). Just as the emergence of life fundamentally transformed the geosphere, the emergence of human cognition fundamentally transforms the biosphere." —http://en.wikipedia.org/wiki/Noosphere

[13] "But experience shows that identical twins are rarely completely the same. Until recently, any differences between twins had largely been attributed to environmental influences (otherwise known as "nurture"), but a recent study contradicts that belief. Geneticist Carl Bruder of the University of Alabama at Birmingham, and his colleagues closely compared the genomes of 19 sets of adult identical twins. In some cases, one twin's DNA differed from the other's at various points on their genomes. At these sites of genetic divergence, one bore a different number of copies of the same gene, a genetic state called copy number variants." —http://www.scientificamerican.com/article/identical-twins-genes-are-not-identical/

www.ingramcontent.com/pod-product-compliance
Lightning Source LLC
Chambersburg PA
CBHW020735250626
47155CB00003B/764

9780996183307